Kissing Cousins

BY

FENELLA CUTLER

Hutton Electronic Publishing
Westport

ISBN   978-09888775-6-6

Cover & interior design by Katie Johnson

Published by
Huttonelectronicpublishing.com
160 North Compo Road, Westport, CT 06880-2102
Manufactured in the United States of America

Kissing Cousins

Table of Contents

Chapter One

Maine Summer

It was a hot and sultry day in Maine. Under a sky of cerulean blue the harbor lay dreaming in the sunlight, causing chips of gold to sparkle atop the ripples. The village sprawled along the curve of the water in narrow streets with bird and Indian names: Heron, Kingfisher, Penobscot. Substantial houses hugged the shoreline with more modest cottages spilling behind up into the pine forests that embraced the town with spicy fragrance all the year long.

The Parsons' house had stood sentinel at the top of the harbor for two hundred years. White clapboard, like so many New England houses, with shutters of the darkest green to seem almost black, its front faced the headland marking the harbor entrance, with its back pointing to a stand of ancient maples shading the spacious backyard. It was surrounded by a picket fence, hemmed in by a border garden of old-fashioned flowers: snapdragons, sunflowers, bachelor buttons. Tall hollyhocks in shades of pink crowded around the front and back doors, and it was the visiting grandchildren's job to keep these beds free of weeds.

This August afternoon the grandchild from New York was making her annual visit to her Alden grandparents. Jessica Alden was nine that summer, her summer friend, George Parsons, whose family lived over the back wall, just coming up for eleven at his September birthday. They had spent the morning down at the pier, watching the boats come and go, both fishing vessels and the many pleasure craft kept by the summer residents. The native Mainers had no time for foolish

1

pleasure on the waters; their time was spent hauling lobsters and catching fish for the commercial plant down the point.

Jessica and George were dressed pretty much alike, in cotton shorts and striped tee shirts, sneakers on their bare feet. Both had bug bites and scratches from the summer, and Jessica was trying to alliterate a small patch of poison ivy on her right hand, gotten when she had carelessly pulled some weeds by the picket fence of the Alden house without first looking carefully for the tell tale trio of sharp, shiny leaves. The hand was plastered with calamine lotion, and she was doing her best not to scratch the offending pustules, thus causing the rash to spread.

The Congregational Church, with its four sided clock, was just chiming the noon hour as they pushed open the front gate to the Aldens and ran up the short brick walk to the front door. They entered the spacious front hall which ran the length of the house, from front to back.

"Grandmere," called Jessica, "I'm back. Can George stay for lunch?"

The grandmother did not appear but called from the back of the house, where she was helping the summer hired girl with lunch, "entertain yourselves for another half hour. I'll call you when the meal is ready. Tell George to run next door and tell his mother."

After George complied, the two children trailed out through the porch, which ran around three sides of the house and went down the steps to the back yard. They left their shoes on the top step, and ran through the soft grass of the lawn. There was always weeding to do but somehow, on this very hot morning, it did not seem to be a very pleasant prospect.

Under a clump of lilac bushes, dark purple in the early summer when the blossoms came out and perfumed the whole yard, was the Jessica's tent, pitched there at the start of each summer by Grandpop. It afforded a place for her to read her books and play with her dolls. George rarely entered the smallish structure, but today followed Jessica in under the flap and threw himself down on the canvas floor spread over the grass.

"I'm bored," he announced.

"Do you want me to read to you?" Jessica asked, rummaging through her pile of fairy tales and Nancy Drews.

"No, not now." George sighed.

"Then what do you want to do?"

"Dunno."

"We could play house. You be the father and go outside then come home for lunch. I'll pretend to get lunch ready and serve it when you get here."

"Boring."

"Then what do you want to do."

Again, "Dunnno. George considered his options for a moment, while Jessica remained silent.

"I know," George announced. "Let's play Doctor."

"Okay," Jessica agreed. "How do we start?"

"Well," George thought for a moment. "I'll be the doctor and examine you, like Dr. Sims did when you sprained your ankle."

Jessica obligingly stuck out the ankle she had sprained earlier in the summer when she was following George – illegally – over the top of the stone wall that separated the property from the Parsons next door. He had earned a reprimand from his father and a few swats on the rear end for leading his younger friend astray. Corporal punishment did exist for the friends during their summers, as opposed to their real lives in Boston and New York, but the spankings with Grandmere's heavy hand usually administered through Jessica's clothes, didn't really hurt very much and were soon forgotten. It was worth it to have so much of the golden summer in Maine on the water, away from the constraints, and school, which filled up the other three quarters of their year. On the other hand, George's father believed in plenty of hard spankings, sometimes with his hand, others, with his belt, which hurt plenty but which George bore with stoic indifference most of the time.

George pushed the ankle away. "No not that, silly. Let's have a full examination, like we do each year for school."

Jessica, used to following her older friend's lead, obligingly stripped off her striped tee shirt and tossed it into the corner. "Like this?"

"Sure. I'll thump your chest and back and listen to your heart." He put one hand over the other and, doctor fashion, thumped Jessica's back and front, and ran his hands over her flat chest. "Now take off your shorts so I can look down there."

Without hesitation, Jessica peeled off her shorts and threw them atop the tee shirt.

"And your underpants."

The little white cotton briefs joined the small pile of Jessica's other clothes.

George leaned in, the better to peer at the cracks, both front and aft. He ran his hand down her cheeks and came up between her legs, causing Jessica to wince slightly. Somehow what they were doing did not seem right, though Jessica did not voice her concerns. George always took the lead.

"Everything seems in order," he announced with what jollity he could muster, though his voice shook a little. "Now you be the doctor and I'll be the patient."

He shucked out of his own tee shirt and shorts, then knelt up and rolled his underwear down his thighs, sitting up and kicking the last garment into the pile. Both children were now completely naked. Jessica had turned away slightly as her friend undressed, but her curiosity got the better of her and she faced him now, eyes wide.

Of course she knew boys were built differently from girls; they had a male dachshund at home so she knew what a penis was, though she had never seen her father – or any other male – totally nude before today.

Unlike the dachshund, whose penis was contained within a sheath, George's was topped by a knob, with a minute hole which held one glistening drop of liquid. It was swinging free and had even stiffened a little, causing it to stand out at a slight angle from his body. It reminded

4

Jessica of the tiny toadstools they found sometimes in the woods and, almost, she giggled. Beneath it, much like the dog's, swung two little sacks, resembling ripe figs to Jessica's eyes.

"Examine it. See it everything's okay." George's voice shook a little as he took his friend's hand and guided it toward his growing tumenesence.

Neither child heard the footsteps approaching across the lawn; the lush grass deadened any sound, but, a moment before Jessica touched George's growing erection, a hand pulled back the tent flap, exposing the children in all their nakedness.

Grandmere let out a screech, so loud it brought Grandpop running from the shed, where he had been tinkering with the lawn mower.

"Roland," she exclaimed, 'look what the children are doing. Dirty, dirty, dirty." She grabbed Jessica by the arm and hauled her forcibly into the house, followed by her husband, who had George firmly by the ear.

"You know what to do," she announced to her husband, in a terrible whisper. "Turn George over to his father and I will punish Jessica."

She marched the little girl up the stairs to the large sunny bedroom at the front of the house she shared with Roland. George was unceremoniously handed over to his father dragged away to the Parson's barn which – like so many Maine dwellings – was attached by a short arcade to the house.

"You will never, EVER again expose yourself to a member of the opposite sex. It is disgusting and lewd and I cannot believe what I just saw in the yard," Grandmere told Jessica in a voice so icy Jessica could almost feel an arctic wind blowing through the room. She just hung her head, knowing better than to talk back to her grandmother.

The grandmother opened her top drawer and took out something Jessica had not known she kept there: a large wooden spoon. Bending the child over the edge of the old-fashioned double bed she took

5

up her position and applied the spoon, with deadly accuracy, to the tender, shrinking, little buttocks.

The first blow caused Jessica almost to lose her breath, so painful was the meeting of the flat, wooden bowl with her skin, and the subsequent ones, raining swiftly, one immediately after the other, set up such pain that Jessica was wailing loudly, tears streaming down her cheeks to drip onto the antique quilt on the bed. She thought the beating would never end; Grandmere had never punished her with this much force or anger before, but, finally, the blows stopped.

In the same icy voice the grandmother commanded her: "Go to your room. Put on your clothes and stay there until dinner, Think of what you have done."

Jessica turned and as swiftly as possible, fled down the hall, buttocks on fire and her whole body in pain, to the sanctuary of her room, where she flung herself face down on her bed and wept for what seemed like hours.

Meanwhile, out in the barn, George was facing his own punishment.

Daddy seemed agitated, unsure of what to say to his son. He marched George into the tack room and removed a stirrup leather from one of the saddles, putting together the buckle and the other end, and swinging it through the air as if for practice, where it made a sharp snapping sound as it landed on the leather of one of the saddles. George winced.

"You have to understand there are certain things you simply *do not do* and one of them is to molest girl, in this way. Your private parts are just that: private, and they are not to be exposed to a member of the opposite sex. **Do you understand?**"

George, figuring out what was in store for him, hung his head and nodded briefly.

"I want to hear you say it. **Do you understand what I am saying to you?**"

"Un huh,"

6

"Try again." Clearly Daddy was furious.

"Yes, Sir," George managed to stammer.

"That's better. Now bend over that form," he said, indicating one of the racks that held a gleaming saddle. Trembling, George complied.

The stirrup leather descended, making a loud thwack on George's naked behind, causing such pain as to make him gasp, though he did not cry out. Subsequent thwacks forced his mouth open and screams of pain out of him, so loud that the hired girl in the kitchen dropped a cup and Jessica, up in her room next door, bawled louder, both for her own pain and for George's.

Parsons counted as he continued the beating, "one, two, three..."

George counted silently along with him, though he had no idea the total number his father had in mind.

Finally, at twelve strokes, it ended. George's backside was a mass of welts and bruises from the stirrup leather; it was a long time before he could sit down again with any comfort and he bore a few scars from the beating for the rest of his life.

His father was red in the face and breathing heavily as he threw George a horse blanket and ordered him to his room. "Cover yourself, you little cretin," he ordered. "I'll tell you when you can come out of your room again. And stop that ridiculous sobbing. Try to be a man."

George threw the blanket around his nakedness and slunk out of the barn. He never again referred to his father as Daddy, or even Dad. From that moment on it became Father.

From her window at the back of the Alden house, Jessica could see the big double doors to the Parsons' barn. She was kneeling on her window seat, since it was much too painful to try to sit down, and she observed George in his blanket cross the lawn to his house. He was sobbing uncontrollably and the little girl felt instant empathy for him. She still did not understand what they had done that was so repugnant to her grandmother and, apparently, to George's father. A few seconds later Mr. Parsons emerged onto the lawn. Jessica was surprised to see his red face – Grandmere had beaten her without breaking a sweat - and

the huge bulge in his pants. She waited to see if anything more would happen next door on this most terrible morning of her life.

Mr. Parsons stopped under a wide-spreading beach tree, and glanced around to see if anyone was looking. He was behind the tree, which shielded him from the windows of his own house, and did not see the girl in the window of the second story bedroom next door. What he did next both riveted and repulsed Jessica, peering down from behind the sheer curtains that hung over the window.

Parsons unzipped his fly, allowing a gigantic erection to spring forth from his trousers. His penis was an ugly red, grossly engorged, and there was the same knob on the top Jessica had almost touched on George so very shortly ago, with the same bead of moisture at the top. George, though, had been a tiny version of his father. She gazed unbelieving as Parsons took this ugly thing in his hand and started stroking and rubbing it, causing it to enlarge even further. She saw his head go back and his eyes almost close as he rubbed faster and faster, then the penis gave a couple of quick jerks and a fountain of pale yellow gushed forth in an arc that cascaded onto the ground. Another couple of quick jerks and it was all over. Parsons shook off the disgusting thing then stuffed it casually back inside his fly and did up the zipper. A happy grin was on his face as he strolled off across the lawn back into his house, leaving Jessica gaping from her window above him.

For the remainder of the summer, the grandparents of Jessica and the parents of George watched the two children like hawks, never leaving them alone together for even a moment. Jessica had to help her grandmother with chores around the house, and George was assigned to the man-of-all-trades the Parsons employed as he puttered around the garden and the barn. Jessica's parents, as usual, went up to Maine from their summer vacation, for the long Labor Day weekend, at the end of which they drove their daughter back to their winter home in New York, school and the various friends at home. Both sets of parents, however, were treated to a long lecture one evening after the children had been sent to bed, about the terrible thing they had done out in the tent (which had been dismantled immediately after the punishment) and admonished to explain firmly to their respective children just how evil they had been that hot and sultry day in August.

Jessica never spent another summer at the grandparents' house in Maine. Grandpop had a stroke that coming winter, and Grandmere found it necessary to nurse him, first by herself, later with professional help, at their winter residence in Palm Beach. The house was closed up for a time, until Grandpop's death some three years later. Grandmere survived him by four more years, at which time the Maine property was jointly inherited by the two brothers, Jessica's father and his brother.

George was sent to camp the next summer, and, while the family did spend a month in Maine, relations with the older couple next door was frosty and there were no visits exchanged between the two families.

Though the two children never directly referred to the terrible punishment they had endured, they did share the 'sex talk' – with some hilarity amongst their respective school friends - each had received, Jessica from her mother, George, from his father.

Mr. Parsons waited until the family's return to Boston to have the talk about sex and love and desire...but mostly sex. Parsons was not a sentimental man; he had experienced a wide variety of different women in his youth and after he was married saw no reason to change his ways. If his wife was less than happy and drank a little too much on occasion, well that was the way it was. He was not a complicated man. His business, his golf, his male dinners for various organizations to which be belonged filled up much of his life. His family certainly suffered but he was a good provider, and his wife had not been trained in any field that would support her. So she pretty much closed her eyes to her husband's infidelities and filled her own life with her son, George, bridge and charity committees.

Jonathan Parsons was never one to mince words. When he called his only son into his study, he was all business.

"Sit," he ordered George, who wondered what it was he had done wrong now.

"You're not in trouble, Kid," his father told him. "I just thought it was time we had a little talk about – you know – girls."

"Girls?" George had no idea what his father meant.

"Yea, you know. Boys and girls together. Sex."

"Oh," said George, "sex."

Father had a large tumbler of his favorite unblended Scotch whiskey on his desk and took a long pull on the glass before continuing.

"Well, someday in the not too distant future you're going to want to do it with a girl so you better know how it works." He took another drink before continuing.

George had heard some of the older boys at school talking about what they did with their girlfriends on weekends, and now he was about to get the scoop from an expert. He perked up his ears. Maybe this 'talk' wouldn't be so bad after all.

"Well, you know there's a special opening between a girl's legs for us to shove our pricks, don't you?"

George had a vague idea of this event so he managed to murmur 'yes' while blushing bright red.

"Hey, it's the greatest feeling a guy can have, riding a woman and coming into that lovely moist cunt of hers. The more you do it the more you enjoy it. Believe you me, I know."

George blushed even more furiously. "But you have to take care. You don't want to knock someone up until you get married or get a STD – uh – sexually transmitted disease. But you can have an enormous amount of fun on the way." Mr. Parsons did not think it necessary to indoctrinate his son, at this young age, into the pleasures of extra marital sex. Besides, the boy would probably be dumb enough to tell his mother. "Always use a condom," the father advised, "and afterward always take a leak and wash your hands." He had emptied his glass by now and poured another one.

Cunts? Condoms? George had only heard these words in the locker rooms and only then accompanied by guffaws and winks as the older boys pooled their ignorance on such grave matters.

"Well, that about does it," Parsons concluded. "Anything you want to ask me?"

"I don't think so," George managed to stammer.

"Well, I'm here when you need me," father said. "I always get a huge charge about talking about sex. Doing it too." He actually winked at his son as George left the room wondering if his mother – so conservative and retiring – got the same huge charge out of sex as his father did. Naturally, he would never dare ask her.

Barbara Alden did not have the sex talk with Jessica with the same ease as Jonathan Parsons did with his son, but she carefully chose the time and place to try to explain the intricacies and joys of the sexual act. She had enjoyed a loving and a close relationship sexually with her own husband these seventeen years, the mother felt it was time to try to impart some of this to her daughter, who was just beginning to blossom into womanhood.

She chose a winter afternoon, when snow was swirling over Carl Schultz Park below the windows of the Aldens' Gracie Square apartment, when Jessica had just gotten back to school.

She called her daughter into the large, well appointed bedroom she shared with her husband, and seated Jessica on the chaise lounge positioned under a window, where she liked to do her reading, choosing the stool at her dressing table for herself. This way she could both talk to Jessica face to face or, when it became too embarrassing, swivel her stool toward the mirror and converse via the glass.

"You're growing up now, Jessica," she said tentatively, "and I guess boys are becoming part of your life."

"Oh, boys," Jessica scoffed. "Well, I can live with them or without them."

"There's that nice Johnnie Simpson at dancing school," her mother said, "and Harry Jenkins who asked you up to Rhode Island last summer."

"Oh, him," said Jessica, "well, all he tried to do at that weekend was get me in dark corners and feel me up. His parents were always around so he didn't get very far." And she laughed, remembering the clumsy fumbles of her weekend date.

Mrs. Alden jumped on this opening. "Yes, he may have been clumsy," she said cautiously, "but someday soon you will meet someone whose advances don't seem so clumsy, which you will welcome. And it can all start with something as simple as a kiss. Has anyone kissed you yet?" She cleared her throat and swiveled toward her mirror, the better to see her daughter in reverse. Somehow it made it easier to continue the conversation.

"Not really. I mean a couple of boys have tried but I've always turned away first." Jessica squirmed uncomfortably in her chair.

Her mother continued from her vantage point of seeing her daughter but only through the mirror. "You see, when you meet a man you like, someone you even come to *love* you are going to experience feelings that make you want to have a man – uh boy – feel you up, as you put it. Kiss you. Kiss you passionately. But it isn't clumsy, it's wonderful and it makes you want to go – well – further. I mean," she groped for the right word, "it's going to make you want to throw abandon to the wind and go to bed with him." There, she had said it!

"Go to bed with him?"

"Yes. Uh, have sexual intercourse with him. That's the most beautiful thing in the world when two people love each other. Uh, like your father and I do. You know how it works, of course," she added hastily. "But it's the feelings you don't know about which make it wonderful."

Mrs. Alden was blushing now; she could see, looking in her mirror, the color rise.

"You and Daddy? Ugh," Jessica told her mother.

"Not ugh, it's – well it's the most spectacular thing that can ever happen to you, if you really love and man and want to give yourself to him."

Jessica had a vague idea of what happened in bed; she had once walked in on her parents who had hastily drawn apart but not before Jessica had seen they were both naked under the twisted sheets.

"I can only hope someday you find a man who will make you as happy as your father has made me," he mother finished. "Oh, but you don't want to get pregnant, not before you are married. In fact, the most beautiful thing you can give your husband on your wedding night is your virginity." There. She had said it, done her duty and explained everything to her daughter. It was time to get on to other things.

"How's the history project coming along? Are you integrating Shakespeare into it?" She swiveled around on her stool and once again faced her daughter, relieved to have this oh-so-embarrassing discussion on love and sex and mating over and done with.

As soon as Jessica went off down the hall to her own room, however, Barbara Alden realized one of the biggest embarrassments of the 'talk' was that it had turned her on. She checked her face in the mirror, finding it red and shiny, and patted more powder over it. Her breath was coming quickly and she felt the familiar itch between her legs. She could hardly wait for her husband to get home from the office

Spencer Alden arrived home at his usual 5:45 p.m. time and was surprised with the ardor with which he was greeted by his wife in the front hall. Usually, they exchanged a chaste kiss and he hung up his coat before going through to the library where they shared a couple of drinks before dinner. Tonight, however, was an exception. There was Barbara, his wife of over fifteen years, clasping her to him with fervor, pressing the length of her still sexy body up against him, rubbing up and down like a cat in heat.

"Why, Barbara," he asked in surprise. "To what do I owe this unusual homecoming?" He pressed her to him, rubbing back.

"Can't a girl want a man when she has not seen him all day?" Barbara whispered into his ear, taking a practiced bite at its lobe as she did so.

"Sure, why not? Any special occasion? I know it's not our anniversary."

She took him, still dressed in his overcoat, by the hand and led him swiftly down to their bedroom, kicking the door shut after them. She flicked the lock, then pushed him onto his back on her chaise longue, coat and all. A few swift ministrations of her hands, and the coat was open and his fly pulled down. Barbara reached in and pulled out the willing prick, even now starting to stiffen.

"Hey, hold up," he exclaimed. "You're going to rupture me on my own zipper."

"Sorry, love," she said. "Guess I'm in a big hurry."

"You bet." Spencer Alden stood up for a moment, dropped his coat to the bed and his trousers to his ankles. "This do better?"

"Yes, oh yes," breathed Barbara. "Now lie down again and let me do my worst to you."

Laughing, he complied.

His wife knelt a moment at the side of her chaise, and lifted the thickening penis in her fingers, standing it to attention. She lowered her face over his groin, taking the head in her mouth and expertly flicking her tongue under the ridge, up and down the shaft, then closing her mouth over the whole and sucking gently.

Alden came to instant rigidity.

"God, Barbara, you're hotter than a two dollar pistol," he exclaimed. "Don't stop, I love it." He took her head in his hands and helped guide her in her ministrations. Happily, she obliged, becoming ever and ever more ready for him to thrust his manhood into her wet and willing vagina. She lifted her skirt and straddled him carefully on the somewhat narrow chaise. She wore no underwear and Alden quickly put up his hand and stroked her parted labia, fingering the tender clitoris. "Do you want it?" he queried softly, "is pussy galore – their special name for her vagina – ready for Tomcat to pay a visit?"

Barbara took her own hand and guided his quivering erection into her dark cavern, twisting and writhing to her own special rhythm

14

which always led to a quick explosion. Together they climbed, climbed, higher and higher, until they reached a mutual crescendo, crashing through a joint orgasm that left them both totally spent.

Five minutes later, she had smoothed her skirt over her nakedness, he had zipped his fly and, arm in arm, they went down the hall back to the library for their pre dinner drinks.

Chapter Two

Barn Party

The Harringtons had a large party barn adjacent to their Colonial house on a back lane in Darien. It was enormous, once the mainstay of a working farm which the property had been for over one hundred years, before a New York family had bought it for a gentleman's summer home in the late 19th century. They had added a columned portico and expanded the house itself, adding cupolas and servants' quarters, along with three extra bedrooms for their growing family, and had spent from Memorial Day to after Labor Day away from the hot city 40 miles down the road.

Having no use for the barn, they had let it slowly deteriorate, until the Harringtons bought the property in the 1990's intending to use it for their primary residence. Mr. Harrington had debated knocking down the barn entirely but his wife, who loved a challenge, had asked that she be given the job of finding someone to turn it into a wonderful party barn where they might entertain their friends. A decade and a half later it was the perfect place for teenage parties: the young guests could roister to their hearts' content and the house would remain pristine.

And so this Saturday night before Christmas, the teenage Harrington sons, Gerald and Mark, were throwing a large party for their friends and any of those friends of friends who happened to be visiting from boarding school. It promised to be a large crowd.

Jessica Alden, now 15, was staying for a few days with her school friend, Irina Cook, whose parents had a weekend house in Darien and who had received an invitation to the party at the barn. Naturally, as a house guest, Jessica was included in the invitation. She and Irina were upstairs in the Cook house, dressing for the Christmas party in the Harrington barn.

Irina had drawers pulled out with all manner of underwear and scarves and panty hose spilling out and had flung open the double door to her closet, the better to select what she wanted to wear to this party. Jessica, as a guest, had only her suitcase to peruse, and only one possibility of a dress to wear, which she had brought just for this occasion. But she joined with gusto in the romp through her friend's wardrobe, from which the two girls finally selected a bright green full skirt that would swirl around Irina's thighs when she danced. With it went a stretchy green top that showed off the beginnings of Irina's developing breasts. It was an outfit bound to tease the teenage boys who would be at the party, and the girl twirled before her full length mirror, pleased with what was reflected back at her.

Jessica took a fresh pair of cotton knit underpants from her suitcase, paired with a matching white cotton brassiere, devoid of any ornament, save for a tiny white bow between the two globes of her own developing bust. She pulled up a pair of panty hose, purloined from her mother's drawer, and dropped her dress over her head. Of red velvet, so cheerful in winter and especially at Christmas, it had a modest round neck that barely showed her collar bones, and a slightly full skirt which came a couple of inches above her knee. Both girls had black suede pumps, with sturdy low heels and rounded toes. Not yet for them the three inch spikes and pointed toes so dear to their older sisters and friends. Time enough in a few years to ruin their feet in such beautiful shoes.

Each had a small pair of pearl button earrings, which they inserted into their ear lobes, and a modest string of pearls. They checked themselves together in the mirror, and Irina produced one of her treasures: a small bottle of Miss Dior, which was all they were allowed to wear at their age. They self-consciously sprinkled a few drops here and there, then descended the wide staircase to the first floor, to be inspected by Irina's parents.

Mr. and Mrs. Cook were sitting in their living room, martini glasses in hand, and exclaimed with pleasure when they saw the girls appear.

"Look, David," said Mrs. Cook, "aren't they charming? And what a pretty dress, Jessica."

"You bet," echoed Mr. Cook. "Can't wait to see them blossom in a few years time, eh?" He gave his wife a wink which she pretended not to see.

"The Johnsons will be here in just a few minutes to pick you up," said Mrs. Cook. "Why don't you get your coats and stand by the front door so you don't keep them waiting. And have a wonderful evening! I'm sure you will."

Obediently, the girls got their coats and stood by the door, peering out through the side fan lights until they saw a car approaching down the drive. They called goodnight and went out into the frigid air, glad to climb into the warmth of the Johnson car and be borne a mile or two away to the site of the party.

There was a line of cars pulling into the Harrington's long driveway, disengaging a small mob of laughing teenagers, all calling to each other as they spotted familiar faces in the crowd. Jessica hung back, waiting for Irina to get out of the car and introduce her to some of her friends. She did not know many people in this group, and felt somewhat out of place: a houseguest from New York just invited because she was staying with Irina.

She was swept along into the barn, where she and Irina left their coats on one of the racks by the huge entrance doors, and made their way into the main part of the barn where the party was taking place.

Mrs. Harrington had, as much as possible, kept the flavor of the old barn, with original graying siding and smallish windows high up in the wall. But she had laid a new floor, of gleaming polished oak, wide planked and perfect for dancing. Around the sides were little round tables and chairs, each table with a shaded candle and a small vase holding evergreen shoots and red carnations. Along one wall was a vast trestle table, possibly original to the house, holding a mammoth punch bowl and platters of deviled eggs, cold cuts, assorted breads and all manner of Christmas baking: cakes, pecan balls, cherry winks, iced sugar cookies and German stolen. The punch was strictly fruit; there was no alcohol served at these teenage parties, though more than one boy had, with forethought, managed to smuggle a flask into the party in the pocket of his well cut tweed jacket. Smoking was also prohibited, but the more rebellious kids here had a special place, out behind the attached cow barn, that had, historically, welcomed the smokers in the group, one of whom was always stationed a little way off to warn of any approaching grownups or – even worse - an older brother or sister of one of the party revelers who had been roped into duty patrolling the party for just such behavior.

Irina tried to introduce Jessica to a dozen of her friends, but all had other people to pursue and other agendas to attend to. So Jessica found herself standing alone, by the punch bowl, trying to look as if she was having a good time. Fortunately, many more boys than girls had been invited, and soon a youth strolled up to her, held out his somewhat grubby hand and asked Jessica to dance. She looked up in surprise, to see a tall, gangly boy, in the requisite tweed jacket and gray flannels, with messy brown hair and a fair amount of facial acne, standing with outstretched hand. Gulping, she took the hand and let him lead her out on to the dance floor.

"What's your name," the youth asked, "and where do you go to school?"

"I'm, uh, Jessica Alden and I go to Miss Fox's," she managed to stammer out. "Uh, you?"

"Bob Reardon," came the reply. "I'm at St. Pauls. I'm a junior."

Jessica, who was only a sophomore, was impressed. "Do you – uh – live in Darien?"

"Nope. I'm visiting."

19

"Oh, me, too," Jessica was thrilled to have a topic of common interest.

"I live in New York. Oh, I guess you know that; I already told you where I go to school." She blushed, embarrassed over her blunder.

"Yeah, you did say that."

Jessica couldn't think of anything to say and sensed Bob was losing interest. When the dance was over he steered her back to the punch bowl and took off, leaving Jessica to scan the room again, try to smile and pretend she was having a good time.

A couple of dances ensued before another, older, boy asked her out to the floor. This time it was a blonde boy with lazy, long green eyes, certainly an improvement over her first partner.

They exchanged the usual information about names, schools and places of residence, then he asked abruptly. "This party's pretty tame, don't you think? How about I get us both some punch and we might take a walk, explore the rest of the barn or something." Jessica could but agree. She waited obediently by a post while her new escort, Jack somebody, went over to the refreshments table. He seemed to be a long time, but finally he approached her, two overfull cups of punch in his hands. He handed her one and took her free hand in his. It was sweaty and somehow unpleasant, but Jessica did not want to be a poor sport. She let herself be led away into the depths of the barn, away from the noise and the lights and the party.

They seemed to come to part of the structure which had once been used for horses, with large box stalls lining a central walk. There were dim lights every ten or so yards, little fixtures between the stalls that gave enough light to see where they were going, but not to see each other's features clearly. From some of the stalls came soft voices and it was clear that this was some sort of lovers' lane, information on this special out of the way place in Harringtons' barn probably passed down from one generation of randy teen age boys to the next. Jack led the way into one of the empty stalls, where a pile of horse blankets was spread in one corner, and pulled Jessica down to sit by his side.

"Drink up," he commanded, "it's pretty good punch, I think."

Again, wanting to be agreeable, Jessica complied, though the punch had a strange, acid tang she had never tasted before. Perhaps it was a special punch recipe of Mrs. Harrington's?

Jack took the empty cup from her and put it aside, sliding his arm around her waist as he did so. It seemed pleasant being here at the side of such an attractive boy, and Jessica wondered if he was going to try to kiss her. She decided she would let him; many of her friends claimed to have crossed this bridge and some even claimed to have enjoyed it. So when his face came close to hers, so close she could smell that same acid smell on his breath, she did not pull back, but tilted her head up and closed her eyes. It was the same smell Daddy and Mummy had when they went into dinner after their evening drinks, but she did not immediately connect it with the events of tonight. She was feeling relaxed, actually a little woozy, and the dim stall and the scratchy jacket next to her arm were not unpleasant.

The kiss, when it came, was sloppy and wet, and she had no idea how to respond or *if* she was supposed to respond. Everything was fuzzy now, and she seemed to be operating in slow motion. Before she knew it, Jack kissed her again, this time forcing her lips apart and inserting his tongue into her mouth. She gagged and tried to pull away, but he only pushed her onto the blankets and fell on top of her body. She felt him fumble between his legs and heard the distinct scratching noise of a zipper going up – or down. Jack reached into his pocket and, a moment later, she heard something tear. Expertly, he rolled a condom over his waving prick, letting the slimy, cold thing come to rest against her thigh. She wanted to scream, but who would come and how would it look to the occupants of the other stalls? No one else seemed to be having a bad time; indeed, the noise of kisses and even soft moans were emanating from all around them. So she desperately tried to fight him off, but her limbs were as limp as a rag doll's and everything seemed muddled in her head.

His hand suddenly came up between her legs, causing her to gasp, and he expertly slid his fingers under the band of her cotton briefs. She had no idea what he wanted, but his breath was coming faster now, ragged and rasping. She fought harder which only seemed to amuse him.

"Quite the little tiger, aren't you? Guess it means you are enjoying it."

Jessica saw his teeth gleam in the dim light. Panic engulfed her and she twisted and turned desperately, anything to get away from this maniac.

Suddenly she felt a finger slide into the special place between her legs, the place that had never been touched before. She gasped and opened her mouth to shout, but Jack clamped his mouth over hers again, shutting off any sound. His fingers probed and prodded, giving Jessica an involuntary thrill that ran from her engorged clitoris right into her inner core, sending a wave of not unpleasant shivers throughout her sexual organs. She gasped again, this time almost with pleasure, not unmixed with pain. She was flopping like a fish now, wondering just what else this boy was going to do to her, when she heard a shout above them.

A large hand descended, seemingly from nowhere, plucking Jack up and off of her, throwing him out into the passage between the stalls. A male voice asked "Are you okay? This is not the first time Jack's gotten in trouble for taking a girl away from a party. You looked like you could use some help."

"Oh, I do," Jessica was crying now, trying to get her pants back over her exposed labia and straighten her dress. How much had this new boy seen? What would he think of her? She tried to stop, but only cried harder.

"Hey," said the new boy. "Let me get you out of here."

Jack, who had been partially stunned by the toss across the stall, was coming to now.

"Don't you dare try anything like that again," the new boy informed him. "You'll have me to deal with." He escorted Jessica out of the stall and down the walk between the boxes, talking all the while.

"I'm sorry you had to go through this. I bet he spiked your punch. Did it taste strange to you?"

Jessica managed to breathe a soft 'yes' between her tears.

"Yup, it's an old trick of his. He's gotten himself into lots of trouble, girls, too. I'm surprised anyone invites him anymore."

The new boy looked more carefully at the tearful girl and gave a start.

"Hey, don't I know you? You look so familiar but I can't remember where we met?

The light was dim and Jessica could barely see the face of her savior.

"I'm Jessica Alden," Jessica said primly. "And I'm visiting Irina Cook, who goes to school with me. "But," she added, "If I knew what kind of party she was taking me to, I think I would have stayed home." She stopped, realizing how unkind a thing it was to say to this nice boy who had rescued her.

"My God," exclaimed the boy. "Jessica Alden! No wonder you looked familiar. Remember those summers at your grandmother's house in Maine and the boy next door?" He waited, expectantly.

"The boy next door?" Jessica said slowly. "Oh, the one who...." she paused and hung her head. The one who had exposed himself to her when she was nine. The one for whom she had been smacked with a wooden spoon within an inch of her life by her furious grandmother. The boy who now rescued her from another similar situation. "George Parsons."

"At your service." George executed a small mock bow. "I'm sorry for what happened all those years ago and I only hope I made it up just a little tonight. I got the beating of my life, you know. Wish someone could do the same to Jack now, he certainly deserves it."

Jessica thought a minute. She rubbed the traces of tears off her cheeks and faced the boy, now almost a man, who had saved her. "I guess we may be even now," she said, and preceded George back into the barn and with the throng other teenagers. Immediately they were accosted by a cute blonde, in a very short skirt. She had blue eyes and bouncing curls and, clearly, she was angry.

"Oh, there you are," she said to George. "I had no idea where you had gone to." She eyed Jessica suspiciously.

"Sally, this is Jessica. Jessica, Sally, We knew each other as children..." George trailed off, miserably and Jessica got the picture. This was the girl friend, and she was brooking no cutting in. The girl took George by the hand and, without acknowledging the introduction, led him off. And that was the end of that, her encounter with her kissing cousin from all those years ago in Maine.

Chapter Three

End of a Marriage

Jessica tripped down Lexington Avenue, swinging her bag from Dean and DeLucca. It was her first anniversary and she had planned a special dinner for her and Trevor.

The trees were out fully in Central Park, and the few that marched down her block were in luxurious foliage. It was early June and soon the city would be baking in summer heat. For now, though, the weather was about perfect: warm but not too hot, with the sun shining and no humidity.

She had opted not to go out, but to have a romantic evening at home; perhaps the sight of her in the new hostess gown from Bergdorf, and the spectacular meal, the specially chosen wines finishing up with a bottle of Dom Perignon, would lend itself to an evening of sex with passion. Certainly such evenings were few and far between, which perplexed her somewhat. She and Trevor were young and healthy and, from what snippets she had picked up about the marriages of her friends, all of whom seemed to be making love four, five, even six times a week, their own sex life was certainly very different. Initially she had appreciated what she considered his careful treatment of her: no awkward positions, little foreplay, tons of oral sex, few kisses. Lately she had come to realize that making love with Trevor was anything but committed, passionate - or original. Maybe she could change things tonight. And a few of the things he wanted to do actually made her shudder, remembering the degradation she had felt, though she quickly put such thoughts from her mind. Men were, she felt, extremely vulgar,

especially in matters of sex, and some of their wants simply had to be endured.

She dropped into Gristede's supermarket on the corner of Lexington and 90th Street. Satisfied with her purchases, she hastened toward her apartment building on 88th Street and Madison.

She and Trevor had met one Christmas vacation when both were skiing in Stowe for the week between Boxing Day and New Year's, a week full of parties and flirting and beautiful powder snow, perfect ski conditions for this New England resort. Somehow, amid the crowd of Ivy Leaguers they had hit it off, and, by week's end were spending much of their time together. He was probably the handsomest guy at the ski lodge, long and lean with a narrow face framed by a shock of wheat colored hair and gray eyes, a most unusual combination. What Jessica immediately liked about him was that he did not start to make sexy suggestions and paw at her in dark corners, a nice change from the usual give and take of a man showing interest in her. Somehow he was – what was the old fashioned word? – *respectful.* It would be nice to get to know someone of this ilk better, and they promised to meet again, when their skiing vacation ended, in New York. He was originally from the west coast, which made him somehow different. Most of Jessica's circle came from and around New York, and, while some of her friends had gone off to college in such remote locales as Colorado and even Ithaca, most of them had chosen the more traditional – and closer to home – halls of higher learning: Yale, Princeton, Smith, Vassar. It did nothing to expand their horizons, but it was tradition continued down the generations of many a family who had always sent their sons – and daughters – to the same colleges. Trevor was a few years older, already an up and coming young lawyer, and to be wined and dined by such a sophisticated older man seemed the height of glamour and romance. And Trevor knew how to pour on the romance: flowers sent at unexpected times, invitations to the Le Circe and the Daniel's, rides in hansom cabs in Central Park, weekends at friend's beach houses from the Hamptons to Watch Hill. Some of these friends were married and the hostesses usually put unmarried friends of opposite sexes who were seeing each other in the same room. With Jessica and Trevor, this was not possible, often causing logistical problems.

After dating Trevor for over six months, the least Jessica expected was a soft knock on her bedroom door at one of these weekends away, at which point she would have gladly welcomed Trevor into her bed. But the knock never came and she was left writhing uncomfortably between the sheets of her lonely room.

When he proposed, on the first anniversary of their meeting – again, so romantically – she didn't have to think twice about her answer. She was out of college, in a not very interesting job in a minor publishing house, taken to fill the days between the end of an education and marriage – so she accepted, expecting finally they would consummate their love. But again she was disappointed. She managed to bring up the subject one lovely winter night, as she leaned over the balcony of Trevor's terrace on East 88th Street. It was dark. The only light filtered out dimly from the living room and barely reached the terrace.

"Trevor," she said, "do you really love me?"

"You know I do." He took her hand which bore his grandmother's star ruby and brought it up to his lips. "Of course I do, my darling," he breathed. "Why do you even ask?"

"You've never tried to get me in bed. I mean, we ARE getting married and it would be nice to know....well you know, that we fit in that department."

Trevor laughed. "Fit? Me inside of you? Of course we will fit. I have no doubt about that. I'll fill every corner or that beautiful hot cunt, believe you me. But I want it to be special, to wait until we really belong to each other. You know I can always satisfy you, even so."

Jessica winced slightly at the c word. Somehow it seemed to demean her, but she guessed Trevor meant to be dirty to show the depths of his desire. And, for some time now he actually had been satisfying her, but never by full penetration. Still...

"We can at least get our rocks off, if you want, save the main event for when we are married. I'll satisfy you, I promise," he told her, and Jessica knew this much was true. He flicked his tongue over Jessica's left ear and down her throat, sending waves of desire through her. Skillfully, he slipped his hand inside the neck of her dress and found one of her breasts, which he kneaded expertly, causing the nipple to tighten and stiffen. Jessica gasped with pleasure, and leaned into her fiancé, wondering if real sex would be wonderful with Trevor.

"Please," she begged. "Please let's do it now."

"Not now," he told her, "after we are married." He drew her through the French doors to the living room and pushed her down on the wide and comfortable sofa, where they had grappled like this many times before.

"Close your eyes," he ordered. "Lie back and let me service you."

Obligingly, Jessica fell back onto the cushions and prepared to be pleasured by this man who would soon be her husband. He had no need to undress her, but pulled her skirt up to expose her pantyhose. Expertly, he peeled these down to her ankles, leaving the black v of her bush and her exposed labia ready for his ministrations. Without further preliminaries, his thumb found the pulsing bulge of her clitoris, which he commenced to knead with gusto, bringing her to almost instant orgasm. Somehow this orgasm, this quick rush of pleasure, left Jessica edgy and jumpy, having come yet not been totally satisfied. Was this what making love was all about? Was it wrong to want more? She would never dare discuss this with her mother, God forbid, of even any of her friends, it was all too embarrassing to her and she had no one with whom to compare Trevor's sexual habits, which seemed odd to her but how could she be sure?

"Now my turn," he announced, lying back on the sofa. Clumsily Jessica unzipped his fly and undid his belt. He raised his buttocks slightly so she could pull down his trousers and his shorts, letting his prick spring free. He took her hand and curled it around his hard on, making a substitute vagina. He had showed her how to alternate rubbing with firm squeezings, and very soon gave a gasp, spurting the sperm into a wadded handkerchief he had at the ready.

Trevor gave one last jerk and subsided. "See," he announced, "we've both gotten our rocks off and we still have the main event for our wedding night." Jessica certainly hoped so.

The wedding day, when it finaly arrived, was one of perfect sunshine and temperatures hovering below eighty, a glorious, magnificent June day. Jessica was up early, peering out over Carl Schurtz Park from her parents' penthouse apartment on Gracie Square. It was the view she had loved all during her growing up years, now she would be leaving it for Trevor's bachelor apartment, purchased by his parents years ago and now furnished and equipped in readiness for the bride and groom's return from their honeymoon in Bermuda. It was the setting, Jessica hoped, for true and meaningful sexual love, a topic she had steered clear of thinking about too deeply these last several months. Trevor had continued to insist that the true consummation would come only when they were legally married, a strange view in Jessica's eyes. It was a situation she had not mentioned to anyone, not her mother or any of her friends who would soon crowd the room to carry her off to church. Two of the bridesmaids were already ensconced in the second floor guest rooms of the duplex; four more were put up at the Colonial Club, who would be on hand to help dress the bride. The whole day was laid out, hour by hour, almost minute by minute, for the wedding, the reception and – finally – the checking into the Plaza and the romantic and totally sexy evening Trevor surely was planning for her.

Reluctantly, Jessica turned from her view, bidding it a silent farewell, and went into her bathroom to take a long bath and get ready for the day.

The hairdresser arrived at nine and started with her mother, then the house guest bridesmaids, then the four who were ferried over from the Club by limousine. Saks bridal department had sent all the bridesmaids' dresses to the Alden apartment, where they had been carefully hung in Mrs. Alden's closet, pristine and ready to be donned for the trip to church; Jessica's wedding gown, too, was ensconced in the same closet, and had not been allowed out to be viewed since it had arrived, a week earlier, from Vera Wang. Nothing had been left to chance or overlooked on this special day.

The bride stood in her panty hose and strapless bra, hair beautifully swept up into a French braid at the back, ready to lift her arms for the magnificent gown, of white organdie with appliqués of daisies scattered - seemingly at random – over the wide skirt. Unlike so many dresses of the time, it was not strapless, but had short sleeves and a low, square neck; Mrs. Alden, even in the 21st century, did not hold with too much bareness at a church wedding. Jessica was actually glad her mother had insisted on this model: she would be original as she glided down the aisle on her father's arm to marry the man she truly loved. And everything would certainly fall into place once the ring was on her finger; she was convinced of this. If a shiver ran down her spine at this moment, she shrugged it off as pre wedding nerves; surely all brides had them?

The bridesmaids oohed and aahed as expected at the sight of the lovely blonde, eyes shining, twirling in front of them in the sunlight streaming in from the windows over the park. Surely all this light and beauty boded well for the forthcoming marriage.

The cars departed: the first one holding the bridesmaids and the bride's mother, the second carrying the bride and her father, who had gallantly helped his daughter in, scooping up the long tulle veil and tossing it into the limousine to his radiant daughter. The cross town trip took but a few minutes, and they arrived a few minutes before the ceremony at the steps of the venerable Episcopal Church where the Aldens had worshipped for generations. A few passersby stopped to view the wedding party disappearing up the steps and into the portal, and one elderly woman even called out 'good luck my dear, what a beautiful bride' to Jessica who blushed and smiled.

Inside, the well dressed, well heeled crowd of guests turned at the start of the wedding march, to watch the wedding party, then the bride and her father start down the long aisle.

Jessica floated, as if on a cloud, next to her father, eyes forward for her first glimpse of her groom. He was standing next to Sam Brinkerhoff, his best man and roommate throughout his four years at Yale. He looked heavenly in his cutaway, the boutonnière matching the stephanotis in her bouquet and Jessica's heart swelled at the sight of him.

The wedding ceremony passed in a daze for Jessica, until the moment when the minister allowed the groom to kiss the bride. She lifted her face to his, expecting a fervent kiss, but his lips barely brushed hers. Maybe, thought Jessica, he meant this was too public a moment to express his desire for her; maybe this was the way it was supposed to be. Or was it? He offered his arm to lead her back down the aisle to the waiting car that would drive them to the reception.

They had kept one of the limousines which transported them from the reception, at Mrs. Alden's club, to the Plaza where they had booked a suite for their wedding night. The bell boy had left, there were flowers and champagne on a side table in the sitting room and the stage seemed to be set for the consummation of their marriage. Jessica was in heaven. Surely she had married the most charming, sophisticated and sexy man on the planet and finally her desires would all be fulfilled in the bed, visible through the open door to the bedroom, to which Trevor would soon take her.

He seemed nervous tonight, pacing around the room adjusting the shades, inspecting the glasses laid out for the champagne. Jessica motioned for him to sit beside her on the sofa.

"Come open the champagne," she said, "and let's have a glass. Do you want to order anything from room service? I didn't have much to eat at the reception; too busy talking and dancing." She gave a short laugh, hoping it did not sound strained.

"Sure," Trevor slouched over to the sofa, unlike his usual catlike walk, and took up the bottle. Expertly, he loosened the wire over the cork, and then twisted it three or four times. It exited from the neck of the bottle with the slightest slithering noise. Not for Trevor the loud pop so many people expected from champagne bottles. He poured two overfull glasses, causing some of the foam to spill down the sides onto the table.

"Want to make it a French 75?" he inquired as he pulled a flask from the inner pocket of his suit.

"No, this is fine for me," Jessica said, sorry to see the cognac glug into the champagne glass. He had certainly had enough to drink at the reception, so why did he need such stimulation now? She said nothing, however, and let him enjoy his drink.

Somehow they never got to the room service menu and that chicken sandwich, but Trevor managed a few more French 75's, then unceremoniously staggered into the bedroom and fell, fully dressed, across the bed where he passed out.

Jessica found her wedding night gown and peignoir in her suitcase, took it into the bathroom and examined herself in the mirror that ran the full length of the wall over the sink. She saw a white, strained face looking back at her, with eyes far too dark and sad. Slowly, she put on the beautiful garments she had selected so carefully for this night, then sank down on the toilet lid, dropped her head into her hands, and let loose a flood of tears. In the next room Trevor snored on.

It was not until three nights later, in their room in Bermuda at Horizons, that the marriage was actually consummated. Jessica was once again in her wedding nightgown, lying on the bed, waiting for Trevor to come out of their bathroom so she could turn out the light. He had drunk a fair amount at dinner tonight, but was far from drunk. He emerged from the bathroom, naked, with his penis in his hand. Only at half mast, he was rubbing and fondling it with expert care, bringing it to full erection. Without so much as a kiss, he flipped up her nightgown, spread her legs roughly with one hand and, with the other, guided himself into her. With no foreplay, not even a kiss, she was dry and the engorged shaft penetrating her delicate vagina hurt like hell. Nothing daunted, Trevor pressed on, causing her one agonizing moment of pain which subsided into the raw rasping of flesh on flesh, like sandpaper against a rough wall. Tears ran down Jessica's face as she gave her virginity, saved so long for this occasion, to the man she had chosen to be her husband.

She stepped into the marble lobby of her building, greeted the doorman and crossed to the west bank of elevators. Their apartment, on the penthouse floor, had a small terrace and a view over the lower buildings to the west over the trees of Central Park. All in all a perfect setting for what should have been a perfect marriage – which obviously it was not.

Jessica stepped out at her floor which had two front doors facing each other. The miniature hall had been furnished by her, with a handsome gilt mirror hanging over a miniature mahogany chest. A small oriental rug covered most of the floor and neither door was ever locked. The good Co-op buildings in New York had such tight security that no one – unless it was an inside job – ever got past the front door and the doorman, or the manned back elevator, with the operator waiting at each floor for any delivery man to deposit his order, be it groceries, liquor or dry cleaning, before whisking said man back down to the basement exit again.

She pushed open the door to PHB, and entered the foyer of her apartment, which was painted a vibrant cranberry red, offset by a great deal of white molding and a high ceiling. A miniature secretary sat primly on a blue and red oriental runner, and an X-stretcher stool, upholstered in navy blue, sat under the desk's slant front, open to show many pigeon holes and a handsome desk set in blue leather, a wedding present from one of Trevor's uncles.

It was after four in the afternoon, and Jessica had planned on a long soak with her gardenia bath salts, then dressing and laying out the meal, which was all but ready. She had been to the hairdresser, an event in which Trevor had shown some interest that morning before leaving for work, querying her what time her appointment was and how long it would take. Luckily there had been a cancellation and she had gotten in – and out – an hour and a half before she had expected to, giving her more time to prepare at home for the evening. She wondered idly why he cared about the time of her appointment, and then put it down to his excessive orderliness – about his clothes, the state of the apartment and always being on time for everything.

She left her bags in the kitchen, and then went into the adjacent dining room to lay the table for dinner. The finest linen placemats came out of the drawer of the small Chippendale sideboard, the Robinson hand made silver from the top drawer. She put out napkins then went to the small pantry where they kept the glasses, selecting a balloon wine and a tulip champagne, both from Baccarat. The flowers she had done the day before, she changed the white candles to a delicate pinky beige, the better to cast a romantic glow over the table, then stepped back to inspect her handiwork. Perfect. If only she could get Trevor on the right track, Jessica was sure she could put their marriage on a happier footing. She was almost humming as she made her way back to the front hall and entered the short bedroom hallway. There were two bedrooms off this hall, each with its own bath.

She entered the bedroom she shared with Trevor. It was her favorite room in the house, the one she had decorated with the most care and love, hoping it would see the fulfillment of all her romantic desires. The bed, king size (she had wanted a Queen, but Trevor had insisted they would be more comfortable in the larger size) had a padded headboard, tufted in pale, sea foam green brocade, with a matching bedspread in satin, bordered by the headboard fabric. An 18th century English mahogany chest on chest stood across from the expanse of pale green, for Trevor's clothes, and her own bureau, one from Grandmere's house in Maine was in matching mahogany but with a broad expanse of top, which held the massive silver set that had also belonged to Grandmere. The spanking spoon from the top drawer had been banished to the fireplace, burned the day of Grandmere's funeral in hopes of wiping out forever the memory of that awful hot morning in Maine so many summers ago. How odd she had run into George Parsons at the barn party in Darien! Small world department or something. She had seen nothing of George over the years between adolescence and marriage, and had no idea what had happened to him.

The bed, which she had made so neatly this morning, was in wild disarray, with the spread half off the bed, dragging on the floor. The pillows, so carefully plumped, were spread at crazy angles all over the sheets, and the back of Trevor's head faced her as she stood, transfixed, in the doorway.

For one wild moment Jessica hoped Trevor had simply come home for a nap, for some weird reason, and was alone in what was, after all, their matrimonial bed. But now, there was clearly someone under him, but the someone seemed to be presenting the back of a head, too. Her husband's buttocks, under the covers, were rising and falling rapidly and grunts of pleasure emanated from his lips, sounds he made no effort to contain. And why would he? He assumed he was alone with his lover, and who might that be? Trevor had not seen his wife enter, and the thick carpet that led down the short hall and covered both bedrooms, had muffled her steps.

Silently, Jessica backed out of the doorway, and moved oh-so-slowly backward down the hall. What should she do? Get the camera? Get a knife? Her head spun wildly and she thought she might pass out. Without thinking what she was doing, Jessica marched back into the room, then put out her hand, and jerked the covers off Trevor's naked butt. He gasped and pulled away from his companion, his pecker withering almost immediately. From a pulsing read member, engorged with blood, it shrank to a smallish lipstick size. He rolled over on his back, a look of terror on his handsome face.

Also face down on the bed, the other occupant flipped over and Jessica gave a scream. For the person Trevor had been pounding away into on the linen sheets was not a woman, it was their best man, Sam

35

Brinkerhoff, whose own large penis was deflating until it, too, resembled nothing more than a mushroom in miniature, sad and unimportant.

"Christ, Jessica," snorted Trevor. "What the fuck are you doing home at this hour? I thought you were supposed to be at the hairdresser until six."

"I got an earlier appointment," she began, the stopped. What right did her husband have querying her early return, as if it was her fault he had been caught out...and with Sam.

The best man had slunk across the room and caught up his pile of clothes from the lavender satin chaise longue under the window. "God, I'm truly sorry, Jessica," he had the temerity to say. "I'm sorry. How inadequate. I'm devastated. I hoped you'd never find out...." he trailed off, turned and left the room with dignity he could muster, which dignity was marred by his naked body and the ridiculous remains of what had been a serious erection.

"I want you out of here as soon as you can get some stuff together for a few days," Jessica said as evenly as she could. "I can't begin to tell you what this has done to me...." Suddenly she felt the tears coursing down her cheeks, tears of rage and shame and disillusionment. She turned and ran from the room and locked herself in the bathroom of the second bedroom, only emerging out when she heard the front door close. The apartment had never seemed more lonely to her, as she inspected the six rooms, empty of love, empty of happiness, empty of hope.

Chapter Four

Divorce Court

They sat in the corner office overlooking Lexington Avenue, the expanse of the desk, finished in imitation mahogany veneer between them.

Mickey Gold sat back in his impressive swivel chair, whose metal frame did not match the desk, and viewed his new client with interest. He had been born Malacai David Gold and, prior to moving his office to New York the year before, had practiced on Queens Boulevard in the borough where he had been born, and coined the nickname 'Mickey'. Now he was in the big time in New York, perhaps he should call himself M. David Gold and drop Mickey. Somehow it sounded more posh in his ears, maybe what the clients, who had started to come to him for all sorts of divorces would expect. This one in front of him seemed no exception: probably adultery which she could not handle. The S.O.B should have been true only to her. But how few of them were. Mickey Gold focused on the woman sitting in front of him.

She perched primly in one of the client's chairs, her two feet together, hands neatly in her lap. He could tell her clothes were couture, even though the dove gray suit was simple to the point of plainness, but so well cut it draped perfectly around her sexy body almost like paint. A discreet ruffle of the snowiest georgette framed her face, accented by one single strand of large, perfect pearls, while a small leaf pin sparkled on her lapel. Even with his nearsighted vision, which he hated to correct with glasses, he could spot the quality of the diamonds winking there. She wore no wedding ring, though the fingers of her right hand continually stroked the empty finger, but her right hand sported a very large star ruby, with a diamond band on top, anchoring it safely. Mickey knew it was the wedding and engagement rings, changed from left to right, signifying that this woman was about to sue for divorce. And divorce as what M. David Gold did best. Indeed this woman, who surely came from Park Avenue or its environs was just the sort of client this attorney was seeking. A few referrals from someone like her would bolster his practice so he could become the divorce lawyer to the Social Register crowd. Maybe he would even be invited to join them at play: at dinner parties in the smartest buildings, charity events at the New York hotels and private clubs, perhaps even a weekend here and there at their summer places in the Hamptons and Fairfield County. Indeed, life was looking up for Mickey Gold that hot summer morning.

He leaned forward a little, the better to both peruse his client from a better vantage point, and seem to lend his sympathy to her tale of woe.

"I am sure I will be able to help you, Mrs. Jellingdorf," he almost purred. "I am very discreet and most sympathetic to women in your position. Believe you me you have my every trick of the trade at your disposal." It sounded like a pretty good speech in his ears, one he would edit and perfect to be used again and again with good looking woman who came to Mickey Gold for a divorce from some obnoxious Ivy-league type whom they had married, no doubt believing at the time in riding off into the sunset and love everlasting. "Please tell me what brings you here and what your husband has done to upset you so."

While he waited for her to speak, he ran over the possible settlement he might get during the divorce in New York State. He bet this woman had experienced the ultimate humiliation: adultery on behalf of her husband.

"This is so hard for me to tell you, Mr. Gold," Jessica Jellingdorf said, so low that Gold had to lean even closer to hear her. "You see, my husband and I were married when I was pretty young, not much over a year ago. I guess I didn't know him all that well but..." she paused to collect herself. "What I am trying to say," she paused again, obviously unclear how to continue. "Well, there was someone else," she managed to whisper. "And I walked in on them, and they were in my own bed...." She couldn't continue but pulled a pristine handkerchief from her alligator bag and covered her eyes with it.

Gold was practically salivating at this information. A lovely young bride and a case of adultery. As gently as he could he asked the $64,000 question. "And did you know the woman you found your husband in bed with?"

Jessica sat up straighter and looked her new attorney directly in the face. "Oh, but it wasn't a woman," she said. "It was our best man. From our wedding. He was in bed *with another man.*"

Gold sank back in his chair. He knew this happened, even in the best of families, but it was the first instance of such behavior in his law practice and, for a moment, he was rendered speechless. He cleared his throat before speaking.

"Well, Mrs. Jellingdorf, this is somewhat irregular. I mean, even in a not-fault divorce someone has to be at fault, if this makes any sense. And certainly there is no question in this marriage who was at fault. I know you could make a sensation out of this and get a great deal of money from the – uh," he almost said bastard, "other party."

Jessica's eyes turned to steel. "No, Mr. Gold, no scandal. Couldn't Trevor just admit to adultery – but let the judge think it is with a woman?"

"Sure, sure, if that's what you want." Gold was disappointed he would not be the attorney in such a scandal, but he saw Jessica's point. Obviously the husband had been hiding his sexual preference for years, possibly from everyone and he had even managed to keep up the pretence for a year of marriage. But how? Dare he pry?

"Uh, are you sure he was actually having sex with this other man?"

"Mr. Gold," said Jessica, "they were positively stuck together, and in my bed. No, there is no doubt at all about what happened.

39

Gold drew a pad toward him and uncapped his fountain pen, bought recently at Tiffany and one of his favorite accoutrements. "Well, let's get started on what you want out of this divorce," he said. "And, as it's nearly one o'clock, let me take you out to lunch. We can always continue this meeting over a decent meal." He scrambled in his head through the restaurants that were not too far away and – because this was a special client, he would throw cost to the winds! In any case, he'd just add the lunch check, disguised as something else, to her bill.

Gold knew his limitations as a man of sophistication and class, but he also knew that, somehow, he appealed to the opposite sex and this was one time he would turn on the charm, and his entertaining personality big time. This woman was his passport to the big time, he was sure, as he escorted her out of his building a half hour later and a taxi that would take them over to the west side.

"Driver," he announced after handing Jessica into a passing cab, "21 Club, please, West 52nd Street between 5th and 6th." He sat back for the short ride and almost wished he could take the hand of the exquisitely dressed woman beside him.

While the divorce proved reasonably easy, since Trevor would do just about anything not to have his sexual proclivities found out, Gold invented numerous occasions on which he 'needed' to see Jessica in his office for conferences. He always scheduled these appointments right before lunch time or, when they had established some sort of rapport, as the last meeting of the day. Either afforded him the opportunity to ask Jessica to join him for lunch, or cocktails or even dinner. Most of the time she accepted readily, especially as Gold told her they would continue the legal discussion out of the office. His intent was to use her to other rich and lonely women in need of a divorce lawyer, one who would listen with sympathy and pander to these women's needs, bereft as they would all be of male companionship. It did not take too long, however, for him to come to like her immensely and admire her for her courage in facing up to the fact she had married a homosexual, surely an ego crushing downer for any woman.

The money was proving no problem: Trevor, or at least his family, had plenty and were quite willing to buy him out of a marriage that clearly had not worked. How much they knew about his sexual orientation Mickey Gold did not know, but, as long as they were agreeing to the terms he laid down for his client's benefit, he really didn't care. Let the guy take himself and his prick to some Greenwich Village location where he could indulge himself as he wished. He wondered if word about the scene Jessica had viewed on her first anniversary was making the rounds of the young upper crust set around New York. Were people snickering behind their hands at cocktail parties and summer weekends at club dances? Had Trevor showed himself around town, pretending nothing was wrong? He knew Jessica was leading a monastic existence, seeing only her family and very close friends and not going out anywhere at all. He hoped to change this situation once the divorce was final. Mickey knew better than to get involved with any female client before her divorce came through; once the final decree was in hand, he was off the hook and no longer representing her. And he planned to make his move in as soon as that day came.

It was another hot day when they went to court to dissolve what had been a brief and very unhappy marriage. Again Jessica was impeccably dressed, this time all in navy blue with a classic Gucci bamboo-handled bag slung over her arm She wore the same pearls, this time with a gold bow pin, scattered with nice size diamonds, but the rings had been left behind. Both her hands were bare. She sat quietly by Mickey's side at the lawyer table across from Trevor and his attorney and neither looked at the each other. It was a sad ending to what was supposed to be a lifetime commitment, but it was all over now.

The opposing lawyers presented the facts: the marriage had irretrievably broken down, the husband had committed adultery, there was no hope for a reconciliation. Trevor took the stand briefly to describe a weekend in the Catskills with another woman and yes, he had slept with her. He exited the stand without glancing over at Jessica, who sat like a statue, twisting a handkerchief in her hands, out of sight under the table. It was only afterward that Mickey wondered who had chosen the place for this supposed adultery to take place? Surely people like the Jellingdorfs didn't exactly fit the profile of guests in the Catskills' resorts. Surely infidelity at the Waldorf or the Pierre would have been more in keeping?

The Judge was used to divorces such as this. He did not question any of the information presented, simply declared the marriage over, which took a few seconds. They all stood as the Judge left the bench. Mickey bent over to gather his papers together and looked for Jessica to escort her out of court and to some dark watering hole where he could begin his carefully planned suit. He was surprised to see her firmly planted in the middle of the aisle, confronting Trevor as he started out of the courtroom.

"I want to wish you good luck, Trevor," she said evenly, 'in your new life. I'm sorry things didn't work out between us."

'God,' thought Mickey, 'what class the woman had!'

Trevor paused, surprised. He had a hard time looking at the woman who had, until a few moments before, been his wife. "Thank you, Jessica," he said, then bent over slightly and gave her a small – a very small – peck on the cheek. He exited with his attorney and that was the last of him, at least in the life of Jessica Alden Jellingdorf.

Mickey Gold hugged his now former client. "Well, hon," he told her. "That's over. Let's go and get wasted. How about the King Cole Bar at the St. Regis?" He could feel the familiar tingle in his trousers, and hoped a large boner would not spring up and embarrass him. Somehow, he thought Jessica would like a little more finesse.

"Thanks, Mickey," said Jessica, "but I'm kind of done in. It's been a stressful day and I just want to go home and take a bath and watch some dumb detective on TV. Give me a rain check."

Somehow Malachai David Gold knew that rain check would never be redeemed. He put Jessica in the requested taxi, waved her off then reentered the Court House, heading to the men's room on the ground floor. At this hour it was usually pretty empty, and such was the case today. Shutting himself in the farthest stall, he locked the door, unzipped his fly and let free the swinging piece of meat he had hoped to ram home into the woman who had just gotten away. It would only have been a kindness to her, after all. But, what the hell, if she didn't want it, no need to waste such a spectacular hard on. Gritting his teeth, to make sure not a sound escaped, he commenced stroking and jerking until, even through clenched teeth, he let out a loud and involuntary groan as his sperm spurted forth, jetting onto the rear wall of the stall. He waited a moment to let the spasms subside, shook it off and jammed it back into his pants. When he strolled out of the men's' room, after carefully washing his hands, he was just another attorney who had won his case for his client. Maybe the next client would be more receptive.

Chapter Five

Marcia Ramer

It didn't take Jessica long to realize that her former social life with Trevor was over; dead as the proverbial dodo and was not likely to come back anytime soon. Being without a husband – or permanent boyfriend – pretty much excluded her from all the couples' activities she had experienced with Trevor: dinner parties and dances and even weekend invitations from old friends. True, a few couples who sympathized with her new state remained loyal and did everything they could to include her in their various activities. And many of the wives of these same couples made sure Jessica was invited to their lunches and charity events, but not to the boy/girl parties where she might come alone, or, worse, encounter Trevor. For no one knew why they had divorced; Trevor and Sam Brinkerhoff had been too discreet for that. The time would come when their love was out in the open, but, for the moment, both men chose to pass for straight, and were welcomed enthusiastically to most of the events which Trevor and Jessica had attended together. Some hostesses even invited the men – separately of course – to squire a still single friend to a dance or other event, leaving Jessica sitting home to twiddle her thumbs and watch endless English mysteries and costume dramas on television.

Enter Marcia Ramer. She was one of those strange, elusive women on the fringes of someone's social circle, certainly not firmly planted in the middle of the group, but wafting somewhere on the outer edges, always happy for a notice from someone well placed within the sacred perimeter. She managed to wangle a few invitation to various places: an extra ticket going for a performance at the Amateur Comedy Club, a last minute fill in for the bridge groups at the Yale or Harvard Clubs, a fourth for tennis some summer weekend when someone canceled at the last minute. She was fairly well versed in a number of accomplishments: she was an adequate partner at doubles, she could crew, fairly competently, on someone's boat, she played a decent hand of bridge and was au courant with politics and current events and the theater. But no one ever found out just where she came from, or what her background was. And she wasn't telling.

She had a nice, if small, apartment, in one of those converted tenement buildings now becoming fashionable on the East Side; perhaps a little too far east. It was furnished with a mish mash of pieces from different periods and schools of thoughts, but Marcia had a certain flair with fabrics and managed to pull the whole thing together so it looked like she meant it. There were a few good ornaments scattered here and there, and some fairly respectable looking studio portraits in silver frames, though who they were, Marcia never said. But she was always available to help out on a charity event, if it was only to address envelopes and keep lists of replies, and she was a regular attendant a fashionable church on the Upper East Side, though it was not clear if she had ever been either baptized or confirmed. She also was not adverse to sleeping with various husbands and single men too, as long as she thought they might further her social ambitions in some way.

All in all Marcia was an enigma, but as no one paid a great deal of attention to her, she managed to get by and was even beginning to make a little headway.

She had long admired Jessica, and even sat at her table for one large charity dance at the Plaza, noting an empty seat after the first course was served and gliding over to Jessica, explaining her escort was somewhat drunk and she was afraid he might cause a scene. Naturally, Jessica asked her to take the vacant place, and thought no more about it. But Marcia thought about it a lot and now that she heard Jessica was divorced, decided to make her move.

45

She waited until a long holiday weekend was approaching before going forward, deciding that, if Jessica had not been invited out of town, she might well be up for some fun and games, girl style, rather than be alone over the three days.

Marcia waited until ten o'clock of the Saturday morning to call, praying Jessica was home. And she was.

"Hi, Jessica," Marcia chirped brightly. "How are you? It's Marcia Ramer." She did not remind the other woman where they had met, trusting Jessica's innate politeness to not ask.

"Hello," Jessica sounded a bit perplexed but waited for Marcia to pick up the conversation.

"I didn't know if I'd find you in town this weekend. But since you are perhaps you'd like to come out and play with another single gal. We can always have fun while all our married friends are sunning in the Hamptons or Connecticut or the Vineyard." Jessica did not say anything, so Marcia rushed on. "Would you like to meet me for lunch? Somewhere outside, Orsay possibly?" She did not know the restaurant, but had heard it was a posh Upper East Side place to eat. And surely, on a holiday weekend, they would be nice even to two single women, washed up on a beach by divorce.

"That would be nice." Jessica still sounded tentative, but at least was willing to give the lunch a try. Probably better than staying home alone.

"Shall we make it one? I'll make a reservation. Ramer. R-A-M-E-R. Just in case you don't know how to spell it."

"Fine," Jessica said. "See you then."

Marcia hung up, a big smile on her face. Her plan to draw Jessica in as a friend seemed to be bearing fruit. Now what to wear? She had observed Jessica over the years: always smartly turned out, never anything outré or overboard. Okay, she'd wear the pale green skirt and matching sweater, with a plain white wife beater. She wouldn't even pull it down in the front to show her considerable cleavage, a ploy that always worked with the men. But she wanted to reel Jessica in, to make friends with her. Then she'd see where this new relationship would take her.

Marcia made sure she arrived ten minutes early, and took the table outside on the side street terrace she was offered. How nice, lunch outside on a relatively hot day. The small marble tables and Paris café chairs gave her a feeling of anticipation, as if the lunch she had arranged would go smoothly. She studied her face in her compact mirror, dropped the compact back into her oversize bag and sat back, contentedly, to wait for her lunch companion.

Forty minutes later the two women were into their second glass of chardonnay, and getting quite chatty. Marcia was drawing Jessica out, asking about her schools and travels and other interests, carefully neglecting to say anything about herself. It was a ploy that had worked well before, on both men and women. Her subjects were flattered to be the center of such rapt attention and sometimes let slip information they should not have, which was carefully filed away by their listener for future use.

The women could not have presented a more striking contrast. Jessica was pale of skin – indeed she burned easily and had to be very careful going out in the sun, while Marcia's complexion had an almost olive cast. She had very dark hair, which she wore long, swept over one side of her forehead to cascade down her back. One could almost imagine her in a gypsy camp, a gay bandanna bound over her locks. She would always stand out as someone exotic, different from the rest. Jessica, on the other hand, exuded East Coast WASP from every fiber of her being. She sat up very straight and looked her lunch companion straight in the eyes, as she had been taught was proper. But the wine had relaxed her a little and she was beginning to enjoy this somewhat different woman who had been kind enough to ask her out on this weekend, which had stretched so long and boringly into the future just this very morning.

The waiter, who had hovered over them for some time, stepped forward and presented the menu: a long, large card listing all manner of wonderful French bistro food.

"What do you want?" asked Marcia. She found it expedient to find out first what her guest liked, then order the same or something similar. She did not want her limited tastes to be found out, and had suffered through many a meal when she was not sure what she ordered, finding out only when it was put in front of her. Maybe with Jessica she could relax a little.

Jessica scanned the menu quickly. "A salade nicoise, I think. It's good in this weather and I never seem to have all the ingredients on hand at once to make it at home."

"Good idea," Marcia agreed. "One for me, too, waiter." That weighty subject being taken care of, Marcia realized she had an opener for another round of questioning. "You like to cook, I take it," she said. "When you said you never have the right ingredients for our..." she paused for a moment, afraid to mispronounce their lunch choice, "salad."

Jessica laughed, and took another sip of wine. "Oh, yes, I love to cook. It's one of my favorite pastimes. Can't you tell by looking at me?" She indicated her gentle curves, which in no way suggested any lavish eating in Jessica's past.

Marcia was thrilled that Jessica seemed to be opening up, even making this little joke.

"Sure, you'll have to be on the Biggest Loser soon," she said. "Like you have to worry."

Jessica actually giggled at what she perceived their amusing banter.

"Well, you asked, didn't you? I studied at the Cordon Bleu in Paris many years ago. I was actually a teenager but I needed something to do for a summer so Mother sent me over there. It was a wonderful experience and I've loved to cook ever since. I don't have anyone to cook for really anymore." Suddenly she looked sad.

"Well, you have me," Marcia told her firmly. "You love to cook and I love to eat. A match made in heaven." She raised her glass and Jessica did the same. "To us." Solemnly they clinked. "What the hell," Marcia added. We don't have anyone expecting us. "Let's have a third glass. Let's get drunk." She signaled to the waiter, just noticing a single man who had been seated at the table behind them, and was even now eyeing the pair with interest. Marcia eyed him right back. He was probably in his forties, well dressed, in a sharply cut blazer and an open neck shirt, perfect creases in his beige linen slacks. She gave him a quick wink before turning back to her lunch companion.

The two chatted some more over their tuna fish, vegetables and olives, then ordered coffee and called for the check. Jessica insisted on paying and Marcia did not argue. They pushed back their chairs somewhat unsteadily and made for the street, where Marcia put her hand in her bag and gave an exclamation.

"My glasses case! I must have left it on the table. I'll just run back in and get it. Oh, and don't wait. I think I'll go up to the ladies room, too. Call me. Let's do something soon." She saw Jessica out the door, made sure she would not turn down the side street on the way home, and made her way back through the restaurant to the terrace on the side. The man was still sitting at this table, alone and somehow expectant. Marcia slid into an empty chair opposite him and gave her most seductive smile. "Care for a cup of coffee with me?" she asked. "I've got all afternoon."

Her new companion gave her a lazy smile. "So do I," he said. "And I'm staying right around the corner at the Carlyle. Maybe you'd like to come up to my room for awhile and get out of the heat."

"Love to," Marcia replied. "And let's skip that coffee, shall we?"

Arm in arm they strolled out of the restaurant, over to Madison and turned north for a block or two. As the man had promised, he was at the Carlyle, but not in the regular hotel. They turned in on the side street that was the entrance to the Carlyle apartments, somewhere Marcia had never been. The lobby was cool and hushed on this Saturday

49

afternoon. They took the elevator to the fifth floor and proceeded down the corridor to the end, where the man took his key from his pocket and inserted it into the slot. The door swing soundlessly open to reveal a living room, with spacious bedroom beyond containing one huge bed, a table with a couple of chairs under the window and a large armoir, holding the television and mini bar.

"Would you like something?"

"Just you," Marcia murmured, and that was all it took. The man lifted her up and slung her down on the wide bed in the next room. "Let's open this baby up," Marcia said. "Oh, and what's your name, by the way. I'm Marcia." She threw back the spread and blankets, exposing pristine, crisp white sheets.

"Marcia, I'm Pedro. Let's see who can drop our clothes first." He grabbed at his belt buckle, pulled it apart, then ripped his shirt out of his trousers. Unbuttoning the top ones, he pulled it over his head and threw it toward one of the chairs, where it landed, crazily, spewed all over the place. His belt followed, then he sat down and pulled off beautiful Italian loafers. He wore no socks, so all he had left to go were trousers and undershorts.

"Hey, I'm way ahead of you. Let me help." He helped her out of her pale green sweater, then lifted the wife beater over her head, exposing a lacy brassiere and the magnificent cleavage she had hidden from Jessica. Expertly, he popped the hooks at the back and the breasts swung free. Pedro's quick intake of breath told Marcia her little babies had done their work, and she unzipped her own skirt and pushed it down as he buried his head between the two globes. She kicked off her sandals and they faced each other, both bare chested.

Pedro reached out and took the nipple of one breast between his thumb and forefinger, kneading it until it stood up, hard and brown, from the surrounding olive skin. She gasped with pleasure and reached out, indicating he should remove his own remaining clothing. He stood for a moment, pushing his trousers and undershorts off together, and kicked them off across the room. He was a magnificent specimen of manhood, long and lean, with a jet black bush from which sprang the beginnings of a serious erection. Once again he lay Marcia on the bed, and pushed the thong down over her thighs, her knees, down to her ankles, where she gave an impatient kick and forced the garment down and away. He leaned in over her, his rose in her crotch, his fingers insistent on her breast. Marcia lay back. This was going to be a most pleasant afternoon.

He gave her one quick round of pleasure, squeezing the breasts in tandem with a long middle finger inserted into her vagina, finding and massaging her oh-so-sensitive g-spot until she was squirming and writing with ecstasy, almost coming a couple of times, but each time he lessened his ministrations and pulled back, leaving her begging and pleading for more. He took one of her hands and put it on his pulsating, throbbing penis, totally erect now, thick and hot, ready to penetrate her and fill her up with his sperm.

Marcia heard herself pleading, "now, now, please. Come into me now. Make me come. NOW."

Pedro gave a low chortle in his throat and reached into the bedside table, drew out a condom package and ripped it open. Marcia thrilled at the familiar sound of latex being rolled out over a rampant prick. Pedro lifted himself on top of her and rammed himself into her without further preliminaries. The rough foreplay, which had lasted but a few moments, had readied her for him, and she was hot and slippery, taking the length of his engorged penis easily into her. He only had to thrust himself forward three, four, five times. She was moaning in earnest now, and he kissed her, for the first time, to stifle her cries. She wrapped her legs around his back and thrust upward. Six, seven, eight. She could feel the tremendous explosion about to happen, and squeezed her eyes shut. Nine....ten. At ten, her whole body erupted in huge spasms of the oh-so-familiar pain-pleasure-pain of a million fireworks, bursting and crashing until she thought she might pass out. She heard Pedro give a mighty cry, and felt him twitch and pulse inside her, once, twice thrice. He fell on top of her and was, finally, still.

Somehow they both fell into a fitful doze and lay, entwined in each other and the twisted sheets for a good half hour before either surfaced.

Marcia was the first to recover, and lay, staring into her lover's face, watching the slanting afternoon light play over his handsome features. He slowly opened his own eyes and gave her the return wink she had given him during lunch.

"That was pretty good," he said jokingly. "Care to try for another round."

"Yes, please," said Marcia. "Just let me up for a minute. I want to go into the bathroom.

"Be my guest." Pedro lifted the sheet off her, the better for her to climb from the bed and watched those amazing breasts jounce on their way to his bathroom. Smiling, he lay back and contemplated how best to segue into round two.

In the bathroom, Marcia peed, washed herself off with one of the pristine washcloths and patted herself dry. Round one completed so satisfactorily, she could not wait to get on to Round Two. A quick rummage through Pedro's dop kit, and a perusal of his medicine closet revealed that he did not have any obvious drugs with him, which was a big plus. She smoothed her hair as best she could with her fingers, examined herself in the many mirrors and returned to the bedroom. Arms across her chest, to still some of the bounce, she found Pedro still in the bed, on his back, waiting for her.

He reached up and removed her arms from her chest. "Don't ever cover those magnificent tits," he told her. "Not while I'm around."

She dropped a mock curtsey and rejoined him in the bed. "Your wish is my command, sir," she said lightly.

"I hope so," he said. "Now come here." He pulled her down beside him, then propped himself on one elbow, the better to examine the whole of her body that lay spread out beside him. "Ah, such beauty," he murmured, seemingly to himself. "I won't be so quick this time, I promise. I'm going to make you beg for it like you never have before."

Happily, Marcia lay back and submitted to his ministrations.

The sun crept lazily down into the western sky as Marcia and Pedro expanded their carnal knowledge of each other, leaving few tricks untried, few positions overlooked and incorporating years of shared sexual experience.

They came at each other ravenously, almost as if they had not already shared an extremely satisfying orgasm. It was as if each was starving for sexual recognition, groping and clawing at the each other as the afternoon hours went by and shadows began to steal over the city.

Pedro started his ministrations on Marcia's willing body in a fairly standard manner, beginning with the curve of her neck and the lobe of her ear. He nuzzled into her, just under the ear, stroking and licking her tender skin, making her arch her back and start giving small cries of pleasure. When he nibbled, then gently bit her ear lobe, the cries intensified and she grasped his upper arms, willing him to continue. With one last thrust of his pointed tongue into the cavity of her ear, he left the interesting landscape of her auricular region and pulled her fully into his arms, crushing those magnificent breasts against the black curly hair of his chest. Side by side, thrashing in the sheets, he took her lower lip gently in his teeth and gave a small nibble, causing her to open her mouth to fully receive his tongue. Together the tongues danced, one against the other, flicking in and out in perfect rhythm and harmony.

"I can't wait to get my prick in there," he murmured into Marcia's hair, and she could but nod in vigorous assent, as he thrust his tongue deeper into her mouth.

When she thought she could take no more, needing to come up for air, he briskly withdrew his tongue and started to lick her in maddeningly erotic strokes, starting with her neck and moving down her body. Neck, sternum, each breast lovingly tongued, leaving the nipples standing hard and proud, he moved even further down, and then stopped abruptly.

"I want to tie you up," he whispered. "I want to totally dominate you, make you beg for it."

Marcia was so far gone in the throes of desire she could but nod.

Sliding open the bedside table drawer, Pedro withdrew a couple of silk neckties and made her wrists fast to the ornate headboard, tying slip knots expertly, leaving Marcia's torso laid out for his pleasure.

Should she feel afraid? She had no idea, so in tune to the foreplay she was enjoying at that moment.

Mission accomplished, Pedro continued the downward path of his tongue, this time bringing his hands into play. Tethered as she was, Marcia could only thrash her legs in response, dying to get her hands on him, too, but unable to do so.

His fingers came up and stroked her inner thighs, with gentle, feathery strokes, causing the writhing to gear up a notch, inching nearer and nearer to the erect clitoris and the dripping wet cunt beyond.

Marcia thought she was going to pass out from desire. Her sounds had become almost animalistic, 'now, now, now,' she grunted.

"Oh, definitely not now," Pedro managed to gasp. "A long way from now."

Expertly he flipped himself around, so he was positioned above her, his enormous hard on hanging in her face. "Open your mouth."

She obliged, happily and he inserted his penis into her, at the same time forcing his head between her outspread legs. "Wider," he grunted, 'wider."

She could but comply, stretching out her legs in the widest 'v' she could manage, digging her heels into the softness of the mattress.

His tongue found her clitoris and commenced little spurts of licking and sucking, driving her nearer and nearer a huge orgasm. He began thrusting his engorged hard on in and out of her mouth, almost gagging her with its length and breadth until she managed to relax her throat and take more of him into her.

Marcia felt as if she would die if she did not climax and, at that instant, Pedro suddenly withdraw with a whoosh from between her slippery lips and hot interior, and flipped himself right side up again, taking her gently in his arms.

"Now for the interlude," my beauty, he breathed into her hair. "Now we calm down a little and wait for the next onslaught."

"No," murmured Marcia. "Now make me come, come, COME. Please, Please."

"Oh no," Pedro almost chortled into the long hair. "Later. It will be so much better later. You have no idea."

"But I'm dying for it, for you. Inside me," Marcia pleaded.

"As I said, later. Behave yourself.' He gave her backside a gentle swat. "Or I will be forced to punish you."

The slap brought additional pain/pleasure to Marcia's inner core, and she moaned, softly.

"Oh, it's that way? Well, then I will punish you." Pedro reached up and released the knots tying her hands to the headboard. She reached out to caress him, but he grabbed her hands, raising her arms above her, and sat up on the edge of the bed. Without any effort, he flipped her across his knees, pinning her back into his thighs with one well placed elbow. "This time the hand," he told her. "And if you continue to misbehave, perhaps I will use the belt."

Marcia moaned her assent, and Pedro rained a series of sharp slaps on her naked buttocks, starting fairly gently, though each blow stung, intensifying his blows until the smacks made a loud noise with each up and down of his hand. Tears started in her eyes as the punishment became more severe, but each blow sent her to a higher plane of desire, until she thought she could take no more. At a dozen spanks, Pedro suddenly released her, throwing himself on his back into the bed, pulling her on top of him. She kneeled over his heaving body, guiding herself over the largest erection she had ever experienced, then lowered herself down as far as she could bear.

It took but a few thrusts to – again – bring a huge orgasm, one that seemingly went on forever, swelling in intensity until she thought she was going to die. She heard pent up screams emanating from somewhere, then realized they were coming out of her own throat.

Pedro clamped his hand over her mouth. "Quiet, my darling," he said. "The hotel will think I am murdering you, even through these thick walls."

He thrust himself upward one more time, and she felt a jerking inside the walls of her vagina as Pedro claimed his own orgasm.

Afterward, they lay side by side, his arm and one leg thrown carelessly over her, waiting for their panting breaths to calm down. At length, Marcia could speak and she nuzzled into his neck, murmuring," that was amazing for me. Was it for you, too?" Immediately she felt foolish. Women simply did not ask this question of their lovers, for what was the expected answer? 'No, it was totally commonplace, or no good at all?' She wished she could take her words back but, unexpectedly, Pedro did not seem to mind.

"Yes, I do believe it was as good for me. But another time or two will tell. Now let's get some ice for your backside then take a shower so we will be clean for the third act."

Sore though she was from the past hour of lovemaking, Marcia could only nod her assent happily.

Pedro got a towel from the bathroom and ice from the mini bar and made a rudimentary ice back which he applied to Marcia's flaming behind as she lay, face down, on the now destroyed bed. Little by little the burning subsided, until only the slightest tingle remained. She turned over onto her back and smiled up at her lover.

"Next time maybe it's my turn," she purred.

"Perhaps," he agreed. "Now into the shower." He preceded her into the bathroom and, flipping up the toilet lid, prepared to take a leak. Though this was somewhat unexpected, Marcia made no comment, only admiring the length of his penis as it gushed forth into the water of the toilet bowl. Shaking himself off, he flushed, then leaned into the walk in shower to turn on the taps. Water gushed like a geyser, splattering all over the glass walls. He opened the door and Marcia stepped in. How wonderful the fountain felt; she turned and twisted to get all of herself wet, then felt Pedro step in behind her and put one arm around her waist. Expertly he cupped the curly black hair of her mons pubis, squeezing it hard while, at the same time, pushing her labia together with his fingers. He continued to knead, never parting the slippery lips to get his finger inside of her, and a strange, shuddering sensation started between her legs and traveled up through her body until she was experiencing spasm after spasm of pleasure. God, another orgasm and he wasn't even inside her! What else could this incredible Latin lover do to her, she wondered?

Quickly, without turning her around to face her, Pedro reached for his own burgeoning hard on, tugging and stroking, bringing himself also to almost instant orgasm. He groaned loudly into the back of her neck and released her.

They stood together for a few more moments under the strong jets of the shower, then stepped, side by side, onto the bath mat. He threw her one of the huge, fluffy towels, taking another for himself and proceeded to towel himself down.

"I'm hungry," he announced. "If you have no plans for dinner, why not have it with me? You could go home and get into something glamorous, then I can take you somewhere nice. Come back immediately and I'll be ready. I just have to make a couple of phone calls before I go out."

"Yes, that would be nice." Mentally Marcia scanned her not too large wardrobe, wondering what to wear on this so special night.

She got back into the skirt and sweater she had worn for lunch with Jessica, seemingly so very long ago. Everything was sadly wrinkled and crushed and it would be embarrassing to walk through the lobby of this posh residence, but she would hold her head high and manage it.

"Let me keep these as security you really will come back," Pedro said, holding aloft her lacy thong like a trophy.

Marcia giggled. Not only would she be walking through the lobby in disreputable clothes, she would be panty less. What a joke!

She gave him a quick kiss on the jaw and went out into the hall, hearing him on the phone as she shut the door. Idly she wondered if he was breaking a date with another woman for tonight, or if he really had business calls to make. Who cared? It was Marcia he was taking out tonight, Marcia who would get the attention and the fancy dinner. It would be Marcia – she would bet her bottom dollar on this – who would spend the night with him. She had better take a small bag with her when she returned with toothbrush and paste, a hairbrush and some makeup. Probably an extra thong wouldn't go amiss; he seemed to enjoy talking her underwear and why not? It would only serve to remind him of her.

Marcia made the fastest change ever and taxied back to the Carlyle Apartments, arriving less than an hour after she had left. She paid off the driver and sashayed into the lobby, now dressed in her sexiest dress: black, with a low neckline and a slim skirt, which showed off her long legs. She was stocking less and wore little black silk sandals on her feet. Thank goodness she had gotten a pedicure on Thursday; her toe nails were nothing to be ashamed of and were painted a bright, sexy red.

She entered the lobby and started for the elevators. A man, dressed in a somber gray suit accosted her and she stopped, confused.

"Miss Raymer?"

"Yes, I am Miss Raymer."

Mr. de la Hoya left this for you." He held out an envelope, monogrammed with the hotel logo. Marcia realized she had never asked Pedro's last name.

'Mr. de la Hoya apologized profusely for having to break your date," the man added most respectively. He was nothing if not discreet: what Mr. de la Hoya did as a guest of the hotel was no one's business, as long as it was done quietly. This young woman was probably a pro, certainly she looked like one with the tight dress and long, glossy hair, but that was Mr. de la Hoya's business.

Marcia took the envelope and slit the flap.

'Dear Marsha,' she read. *God, he spelled her name in the normal fashion, which fashion she had jettisoned years ago as being too common.*

'It is with the deepest regret I have to break our date. A family emergency called me home and I had to leave immediately for the airport but here is a number on which you can reach me. I am in New York at least every other month for a few days. Please do call so we can reschedule what promised to be a stellar evening. Believe me, yours, Pedro.'

Marcia's happiness evaporated like a wild flower at evening. She dragged herself out the door onto the hot street, waving away the doorman's offer of a taxi. She started down Madison Avenue, not noticing any of the windows she was passing, turned over to cross Park to Lexington and finally fished out her Metro Card and boarded a bus southbound. She had a bottle of rum in the apartment, and decided to get drunk that night. Tomorrow, with a hangover, perhaps she could shed the memory of one of the most wonderful afternoons of her life.

Chapter Six

Two Bridge Games

Having established contact with Jessica, Marcia was all ideas and plans for their future relationship, which she was going overboard to promote. She practically bombarded Jessica with invitations, from an outing to a new movie, or a Broadway musical, to lunches and dinners out at various places. She even offered invitations to meet some of the men Marcia had acquired over the years: those whom she had slept with and broken up with and those whom she didn't particularly fancy. To these latter invitations Jessica, so far, had said 'no' but Marcia was sure the time would come. And, with Jessica's interest in bridge, she was determined to arrange a game, perhaps with some sideline fun and games. To this end she contacted an old pal, who lived in a modern building in Murray Hill – not, perhaps, the most fashionable or exciting address – but good enough for her purposes. Said friend knew an older widow on a higher floor, who would make up the fourth. And, if things worked out as Jessica hoped, there would be an after party the likes of which Jessica had never experienced. Such would draw her into Marcia's snare.

The game was set for Thursday evening, and Jessica was taking a main dish for their dinner. Marcia would provide the salad, from her local Korean greengrocer, and the widow had promised dessert. The host, Marvin Gaylord, would make himself responsible for the drinks. So that morning, Marcia had invited herself over to Jessica's, ostensibly to help with the cooking, in reality to soften Jessica up for what could prove a most interesting evening.

The two women were in Jessica's kitchen, a spacious one overlooking the side street. Marcia was perched on a stool, while Jessica was at the long counter running along one wall, assembling the ingredients for the Chicken Marbella, a favorite dish from the Silver Palate which Jessica had served many times, always to acclaim. As she said, it was the perfect dish: almost everyone liked chicken and this particular chicken entrée could be served hot, cold, or room temperature, making it perfect to take out to a party. She had marinated the chicken pieces overnight with its plethora of added ingredients: dried apricots (which Jessica always substituted for the original prunes), capers, olives. She laid the pieces neatly out in a large Pyrex dish, then sprinkled generously with dark brown sugar. Into the oven, the timer set, and she was ready to go on to the next project: what to wear that evening?

The two women repaired to Jessica's bedroom to examine her wardrobe. She no longer slept in the room she had shared with Trevor, but in the second bedroom, at the back of the apartment, which overlooked nothing more than an alley. This alley though which, if one looked hard enough, gave a narrow view of the trees in Central Park, down at the far end of the block. In this room was an antique sleigh bed, single, made up as a daytime divan, with lots of throw pillows and a bolster against the wall. Jessica's desk and computer were in here as well, together with matching white wooden file cabinets, low enough to house plants and family photographs, with a couple of club chairs, flanking a tilt top table, under the double windows. All in all it was a comfortable and an attractive room, though with nothing to suggest that it was more than an office, with a spare bed for the occasional visiting guest. Jessica could no longer bear to sleep in the room where she had discovered Trevor in flagrante delecto with Sam; the memory was still too keen. She planned to sell or give away the furniture in that room and totally redo it for herself. But she was not yet ready; hence the decampment into the apartment's smaller bedroom.

'Wear something sexy tonight," Marcia urged. "Hey, you might even like Marvin. He's really cute."

"Cute," scoffed Jessica, though with a smile. "You know I'm not ready to meet anyone yet."

"You never know," he new friend told her. "He's pretty special, sex on wheels, you know. Or so I hear," she added hastily. "You two might really hit it off."

"Okay," Jessica said. "So I'll keep an open mind. Now how about this little liberty print?" She held up a plain dress, with a round neck and short sleeves, in a pastel print which Liberty was famous for.

"Too school girlish," Marcia pronounced. She rummaged through the hangers and pulled out a halter dress in slinky knit silk with a skinny skirt and no back.

Jessica almost recoiled. It was one of the numerous dresses Trevor had bought for her, and insisted she wear, probably trying to show off to his friends 'look what I have. Eat your hearts out, boys." Jessica had always felt like a tramp in the dress, but Marcia insisted this was the perfect costume for the dinner and bridge that night and, finally, Jessica agreed. She could always cover her arms with a little sweater or jacket and maybe no one would notice the bareness of the top.

"I'll find something equal to this, if I have it, and we'll both be knock outs," Marcia said as she took her departure. Pick you up at 6:15 in a taxi, you have the food to lug with you." She disappeared out the front door, leaving Jessica to take out the chicken and prepare for the evening ahead.

The two women arrived promptly at Marvin's building, and were directed to an apartment on the 9th floor. It was the kind of building with long corridors, with doors opening at either side, carpeted and dimly lit with sconces every ten yards. Marcia strode purposefully along the hall, however. It was not the first time she had been at Marvin's apartment, and probably would not be the last.

Ignoring the bell, Marcia rapped on the door: dah dah dah dah DAH, dah, dah, and it swung open to disclose a long, somewhat narrow living room, and the host himself, hand on the doorknob.

He was of medium build, but with broad shoulders and a tapered waist, dark haired with startling hazel eyes, with which he gave Jessica a definite once over. Apparently he liked what he saw. Drawing the two women into the apartment, he gave Marcia a small kiss on the lips, then a slight brush on the cheek for Jessica. Admittedly, it kindled the smallest of flames in her, for it had been awhile since she had come in such close proximity to an attractive man.

"Marcia, thank you for bringing such a lovely fourth for bridge." He took the canvas bag holding the chicken from Jessica and ushered the two women into the living room. An elderly gray haired woman, dressed in lavender, was already there, sitting on the broad couch that ran along one wall under a set of built in bookcases. "Lilly, this is Marcia and Jessica. Ladies, meet Lilly." They bowed in acknowledgement of the introduction, and Marvin went off to the kitchen to get drinks and put the dinner away.

Everyone got a glass of white wine, and polite conversation ensued for a few minutes before they got to bridge, on a round, white Formica table under the windows of the apartment. Even with the air conditioner on – which did not entirely dispel the heat – there were noises from the street below. Lexington Avenue was full of traffic, with various bars and restaurants along the thoroughfare, which attracted a noisy bunch of drinkers and diners, all of whom seemed to be shouting at each other. Sirens blared from time to time, as police cars and ambulances swept through the neighborhood. All in all, it was a noisy part of New York.

The foursome drew for partners, and the game was on. Initially Jessica played with Lilly, though after each rubber they changed partners, so for the third rubber Jessica played with Marvin. They seemed well matched and even though it was a first partnership, they seemed to understand each other's bidding and so made a small slam on the last bid.

"Well," said Marvin, "that was good fun. Jessica, we should play more often. We seem to have such a good fit."

Was he flirting with her? Jessica wasn't sure, but she gamely answered, "Yes, we sure do," then wished she hadn't played along with him.

"Can I have you in the kitchen to dish up the dinner?" Marvin asked. "If Jessica will help I can leave you other two to chat and have another glass of wine." He put the cards away and got out some ratty placemats and mismatched cutlery, which he piled on the table.

"I'll set the table," Marcia offered. "You two get dinner on." She gave an imperceptible wink to Marvin.

In the kitchen, Marvin insisted on helping Jessica out of the beige shrug she had thrown over her dress. "It's much too hot for that," he told her. "Sorry the air conditioning isn't doing its job, but I don't want you to expire."

Somewhat reluctantly, Jessica allowed him to divest her of the shrug, leaving her feeling extremely vulnerable. And did his hand accidentally brush against the contour of her breast, unprotected as it was by any sort of undergarment? Probably it was just a mistake. As she dished up the plates, dressed the salad and found some serving spoons in the back of a drawer, she was acutely aware of her host hovering just behind her in the small kitchen. Almost she asked him to leave, letting her get dinner ready on her own, but she did not want to appear rude. It was his apartment and his kitchen after all. He kept her wineglass full and she had at least an extra glass she had not planned on by the time all was ready. This time, when she turned to carry two of the plates to the living room, he managed, while pretending to wipe down one plate with a paper towel, to brush the back of his hand across the flimsy material covering her breast. Her nipple stood up at attention and she saw a small smile begin at the corner of his sensuous mouth. Almost, Jessica stumbled at the kitchen door, but Marvin's strong arm caught her around the waist, covering her naked back and allowing his hand to once more caress her.   A pleasurable tingling started between her legs and she stepped into the living room somewhat gingerly, balancing the two plates, which she set down on the table.   Marvin followed her with the other two plates, then went back for the salad, giving Jessica time to sit down and compose herself. She was placed between Marcia and Marvin, who pretty much carried the conversation during dinner, which allowed him to gesticulate with his hands from time to time, which somehow seemed to end up on her naked back or arm. And surely that was his foot, toying with her ankle? She pretended to drop her napkin, which allowed her to look under the table. Sure enough, his foot was bare, having slipped off one tasseled loafer, and he was caressing her bare skin with his long toes. What a meal!

A great deal of wine was poured, and they finished up with Lilly's dessert of strawberries and ice cream.   At the end of the meal the older woman excused herself, with many thanks. She was tired, it had been a long day and she wanted to let the young people enjoy themselves without her hanging around. Marvin saw her to the door, then returned to the living and threw himself down in the middle of the couch.

"Comes on," girls, he said. "Join me.   The cleaner's coming tomorrow and she can do the dishes. I'm lonely all by myself." He patted the cushions on each side of him. Marcia sprang to obey, and plopped herself down on Marvin's left side, leaning into him and giving his ear a gentle nip.

Relaxed by all the wine, Jessica gamely positioned herself on his other side, though a few inches away.

"No way, hon," Marvin told her. "Scoot over next to me." His long arm reached out and drew her close, then dropped to her waist. His fingers explored the edge of her halter, then crept to the nape of her neck, where he lifted her hair with fingers that brushed and caressed and titillated.   He turned his attention to the edge of the halter, running one finger down its edge, which sent shivers all through her. Jessica she knew she should halt his advances, but they were so pleasant, she decided to let well enough alone, at least for the moment.

The probing fingers returned to the back of her neck, and Marvin found the tie to the halter, a small satin bow that was all that held the dress together. Expertly, he tugged on one slender ribbon, and the top parted, falling away in an instant to Jessica's waist, leaving her entire chest exposed.

"Ah, what beauties," Marvin murmured, and, dropping his other arm from around Marcia, lunged. He pinned Jessica's arms on either side of her against the back of the sofa and bent in toward the enticing mounds of Jessica's breasts. Expertly, he took one nipple in his mouth, sucking and licking with expert intensity.

It took Jessica a moment to realize what he was doing. She writhed under him on the sofa, trying desperately to get away, but he had her arms pinned so securely she was no match against his strength and desire.

Letting one arm go, he took his hand and thrust it up under her skirt. She could hear the material rip as his middle finger probed insistently against the crotch of her knickers.

"Marcia, help me," she screamed, thrusting herself sideways and away from her attacker. Her cry must have momentarily distracted him, for Marvin paused for an instant, but that instant was enough for Jessica. She rolled onto the floor, causing a painful disengagement from her nipple, for he bit down hard, before letting her go. She staggered to her feet and ran for the door, managing to pick up her handbag, which had been left on the hall table, in her flight. Thank God the door was unlocked, and she jerked it open and almost fell into the corridor. She raced down the hall, hearing footsteps behind her.

"Wait, Jessica," she head Marcia call. "I'm right behind you." She got to the elevator where she frantically pushed the down button. Marcia ran up behind her, panting.

The door slid open and both women flew in. Fortunately, Marvin had not followed them and they made the lobby safely. If the doorman found them somewhat disheveled and the worse for wear, he gave no sign, but simply flagged down a taxi that was cruising Lexington Avenue.

Jessica tumbled in, then turned to wait for Marcia.

Her friend leaned in the open door. "I'm so het up I'm going to walk a few blocks," she said. "You go on. And Jessica, I had no idea Marvin was such a letch. I really apologize, you must believe me."

"Well," said Jessica slowly. "At least we got out of there on one piece. And we'll never set foot in that building again!"

"Absolutely never," Marcia agreed.

Jessica waved out the open taxi window as it pulled off. "Talk tomorrow?"

Marcia waved back. "Absolutely,' she called, then watched the taxi pull into the traffic on Lexington. Her phone pinged, indicating a text was coming in and she fished in her oversized bag for it, hitting the play button. A video of a man's rampant penis was displayed, and as she watched, a disembodied hand came onto the screen, holding a small tinfoil package. The fingers ripped it open, drew out the condom and expertly rolled it down the hard on that she knew, from much experience, belonged to Marvin. The accompanying text read: *'Ever ready, especially for you. Come back. Now'*

Marcia made sure Jessica's taxi was out of sight before she retraced her steps to Marvin's building. The doorman showed no surprise at her return as she crossed the lobby and got into the elevator. Marvin's door was, as she expected, unlocked.

She pushed open the apartment door and found Marvin, trousers down to his ankles, still seated on the living room couch.

"Well," she told him. "I did try. But I guess Jessica is just not up to you yet."

"Either that or she's one of the biggest prick teases I've ever met," Marvin told her. "You know Mickey Gold was dying to get into her pants, but she wasn't giving him the time of day. I was dying to fuck her so I could lord it over Mickey."

"Yea, I know you two compare babes you've slept with. Guess that's one you are never going to be able to dissect, are you?"

"Nope, but you score high with both of us," Marvin told her. "Now let's stop talking and get some fucking in."

He held out his hand and guided Marcia to kneel over him, spreading her knees further and ever further as she dropped her hot, wet pussy over his swinging meat.

Firmly in the saddle, Marcia squeezed expertly a couple of time, bringing a moan of pleasure from her partner.

"Marcia, you're the best," groaned Marvin, as he began thrusting deeper and deeper into her willing vagina. He positioned his finger firmly on her throbbing clitoris and they exploded together, going higher and higher up the scale of pleasure until – loudly – they crashed over the top.

Even though Jessica had vowed never again to enter Marvin's Murray Hill apartment building, the widow who had been their fourth at bridge that miserable night managed to change her mind.

Lilly Hanover was the widow of a Wall Street trader who had left her comfortably, if not extremely, well off. Lilly had a two bedroom apartment in the co-op building where Marvin rented his apartment, in which apartment she had lived for most of her married life. She and her late husband had produced no children during their 41 years of marriage, but she had many friends around New York, and some nieces and nephews scattered from Pennsylvania to Florida, whom she visited on holidays. She had an elderly poodle named Francoise, and was a member of one or two clubs. Bridge was her favorite pastime and she had regular games on Tuesday and Friday afternoons, and often got up one table in her apartment on Saturday evenings, early. She had enjoyed meeting Jessica, instantly recognizing her as a person of quality, and wanted to include her in the bridge circle, for Jessica was an expert player, totally up on most of the new conventions that had swept away the Goren system which Lilly had grown up on.

And so when one of her 'regulars dropped out two weeks from the game at Marvin's she called to see if Jessica would 'fill in'.

"It's only some old crocks like me,' she told Jessica on the phone, "but we have lunch first then play for a few hours. You'd be home in time for a date that evening."

"Like I have dates," Jessica told her with a laugh. "Yes, Lilly, thanks, I'd love to play."

Bridge, with all its complications and the possibility of billions of different hands at least kept her mind focused, and not on the disastrous marriage she was just free of, but which seemed to have robbed her of any enthusiasm or creativity. Jessica certainly hoped this situation would not continue for any length of time; she was usually a happy person with lots of good ideas to pass around. Trouble was, right now no one except Marvin had seemed to be interested in her, and she would not give him the time of day. So it was nice to while a way an otherwise dull afternoon with lunch and bridge. Actually, it sounded quite wonderfully old fashioned.

She arrived promptly at noon, and surprised the doorman by asking for Mrs. Hanover's apartment. He was used to the steady procession of women in and out of Marvin's and surely this was one of the women who had barreled out of the elevator a couple of weeks ago; this one clutching her ruined dress over her practically naked breasts? Well trained to ignore the foibles of the tenants of the building, he simply picked up the house phone and announced Jessica's arrival to Mrs. Hanover.

Lilly lived on the top floor, with a view over some lower buildings toward the river. Her apartment was charmingly furnished with some nice antiques, interspersed with old fashioned flowered chintz on the sofa and chairs. Though there was no dining room, a spacious alcove off the living room held a table that would easily seat six, set with dainty organdie placemats and sparkling silver. Jessica took a seat and relaxed. It looked like a nice afternoon.

Two other older women had been invited: Marjorie, who lived in the building, and Susan, who was a few blocks away. Both were avid players and, after a lunch of crab salad and raspberry ice, they settled comfortably at the card table set up under the picture window of the living room, spread with an ultra suede bridge cover, complete with Lilly's initials, and two new packs of cards with matching score cards. The women cut for partners, and Jessica drew Marjorie.

"We usually play for a tenth a point," Lilly announced while the cards were being shuffled and cut. "Is that alright with you, Jessica?"

"Absolutely," Jessica told her. "It's not much fun playing for nothing. No incentive to do our best."

The other ladies beamed at her. It seemed this new recruit of Lilly's was a woman after their own hearts. Both Marjorie and Susan vowed to add her to their bridge rosters without fail. Some young blood would infuse new spirit into their games and there might even be a possibility of producing a nephew or son to meet this charming new divorcee.

Jessica had a good run of cards, and ended the afternoon over two thousand points up, which netted her two dollars and forty cents for her efforts.

"I hate to take all your money," she joked. "But do come to my house for another game, soon." The women exchanged phone numbers and parted cordially. Jessica arrived home happier than she had been in some time. If it was bridge that would pull her out of the doldrums, all to the good. She actually found herself humming as she cut up chicken and shook up some dressing for a salad for her dinner. There even was a rerun of 'Inspector Lewis' on the television, so she settled in her bedroom in front of the television to eat her supper.

One game led to another, and players were swapped around among the various games that take place all over New York. Jessica was often asked to fill in when a regular player was away or sick, and met a new circle of friends, both men and women and of all ages. One man in particular seemed to stand out, a Don Maddenly, nephew of Susan's, who was a vice president of one of the major banks. Bridge was the initial mutual interest, but soon they were stopping for a drink enroute home after a game, and they began to get to know each other. There was no hint of romance, or sexual tension, which had so frightened Jessica, but there was developing a mutual rapport which made her realize there just might be another chance for her.

One stormy winter night, shortly before Christmas, they were leaving a game at Lilly's and had to walk a few blocks to find a cruising taxi. Jessica gave her address to the driver and they moved slowly up Madison Avenue.

At her canopy she turned to Don. "It's not that late. Would you like to come up and have a drink? Or some coffee?"

"That would be great." Don took out a credit card, inserted it in the slot and paid off the cab.

Together they crossed the lobby to the west bank of elevators and rode up to Jessica's floor in silence. Now they were actually alone together, going up to her empty apartment, both became tongue tied.

Jessica pushed open her door and ushered Don into the foyer. She had left a couple of lights on so the apartment was not totally dark and the living room beckoned invitingly. She hung up her coat and Don's in the hall closet and led the way.

A fire was laid in the fireplace, and she took a long match from a holder and lit the paper under the apple wood logs.

"I could have done that for you," Don said.

"Of course. I guess I am getting used to doing almost everything for myself," Jessica said lightly. "I don't do carpentry or wash windows, of course," she joked. "But almost everything else."

Don fell into the spirit of things. He leaned up against the mantel piece, gave Jessica a wicked look and burst into a spirited baritone:

"'Anything you can do I can do better,'" he sang,
"'I can do anything better than you'...."

Jessica took up the challenge. She had loved singing, in the madrigal society of her school, later in her church choir. Somehow, with Trevor, the singing had taken a back seat and she realized she had not sung a single note in over a year.

"*No you can't,*" she sang in her perfect soprano voice.

"*Yes I can,*" he answered, and they went back and forth in the words of the song from 'Annie Get Your Gun' which had played on Broadway in the mid 1940's

"*No you can't* "

"*Yes, I can. Yes, I can.*"

They both remembered all the words and sang the two parts back and forth, back and forth, finally finishing with Jessica/Annie trilling oh-so-sweetly

"*Yes, I can, can, can.*"

And Don replying: *"Yes, I can, No you can't!"*

They fell onto the couch in a heap together, laughing hysterically at their cleverness.

Don took one of her hands, and brought it to his lips. "I think, Jess Jellingdorf, that you and I are going to become great friends!"

"Jess," she said wonderingly. "No one has ever called me that before. I never had a nickname."

"Well, you do now," Don informed her. "But only I can use it."

"Yes," said Jessica. "Only you." She allowed his arm to come around her and snuggled up next to him, smelling his masculine odor of expensive soap, cleanliness and a whiff of bay rum. Just like James Bond, perhaps the sexiest man in the world, at least when Sean Connery was playing him.

Gently, he kissed the top of her head. "You know," he said, "it's getting late. I really should go."

"Must you?" asked Jessica. "But if you must you must."

"Don't worry, I'll be back. Soon."

She walked him to the hall and got his coat out. "Thank you for bringing me home," she said politely.

"My pleasure." He shrugged into his coat and bent down to brush her cheek, then brushed his lips over hers, eliciting a pleased sigh in response. Jessica had almost forgotten what a kiss felt like; certainly Trevor's had been as cold as the deadest fish on the marble slab, lips firmly together and no warmth. Even though this was the gentlest of kisses, somehow it boded better things to come, and as Jessica closed the door on her new friend, a happy smile spread over her face.

In spite of Mickey and various other men around town, all of whom were glad to service Marcia whenever the mood struck her – or struck one of them, she still mourned the one that got away. Often she thought back to the charming and sexy Pedro, of the Carlyle apartment, and that never forgotten afternoon of pure lust between his beautifully ironed sheets. She could not find the phone number he had given her, hard though she searched, and finally concluded that she must have dropped it in the street when she had rushed home to change for the romantic dinner he had promised her. It was a sad state of affairs.

One dull Sunday afternoon in late October, Marcia decided to do a task she had put off for far too long: cull some of the totally unnecessary clutter from her bulging closets. Association with Jessica and her friends made her realize that she needed to make her image more – well – conservative. She needed to jettison the heavy plastic bangles she had liked to wear with her summer clothes, get rid of the high heeled espadrilles with ankle-wrapping ribbons, throw away the daring two piece bathing suits and replace them with one piece garments, capable of stroking laps in the huge pools of the clubs to which many of these women belonged. They did not lounge on the beach, hoping to pick up some stray man, they did not lie in the sun, fearing wrinkles and skin cancer. And not a plastic bangle was to be seen anywhere; pity as they so cheered up many a simple linen shift, which these women wore with real white coral beads or the simple gold chains which cost a fortune at Cartier or Tiffany. Some of the large straw purses at the back of her top closet shelf joined the pile of discards on her bed, until she pulled forth a smallish leather handbag, a Ferragamo knockoff someone had brought her back from Korea. The friend had assured her no one would know it from the real thing, though Marcia was not sure of this. Impatiently, she pulled open the zipper and delved into the bottom of the bag, where she found a couple of discarded Kleenex. One pocket held a receipt for a restaurant, while the other one had a small piece of paper holding a single telephone number. Almost Marcia put it into the wastebasket, then, suddenly, stopped dead. And remembered. The small piece of paper held the magic number of one Pedro, given her as she left the Carlyle on that sill remembered afternoon.

She hesitated about calling him. It had been so long, and it was, after all, just an afternoon of mad passion with a man she had picked up, so casually, after lunch at Orsay with Jessica. But what the hell? It was either his number or it was not, and he could avoid her call, or give her the brush off.

She picked up her white phone, noting the receiver could use a thorough cleaning. She dialed the number.

On the third ring a man's voice answered, the same warm, somehow sleepy voice of that other afternoon, with the trace of a Spanish accent.

"Hello?"

Marcia found it hard to breathe. "Pedro?" she said, 'It's Marcia…." She didn't know how to continue, but it was not necessary.

"Why Marcia, how wonderful! Where have you been these many months? I was so sorry to let you down for that dinner, but I really did have an emergency at home. My mother had had a stroke and I had to get the next plane back. And I never got your number, and I thought, when you didn't call, you did not want to see me again…." he paused.

"Oh no," said Marcia. "I really did want to see you again. But I put away my bag with your number and only now found it again. Stupid me."

"Stupid you, indeed." But his voice was teasing. "When we could have had so much wonderful time together."

"Where are you now, back home in South America?" she didn't even know which country he called home, just that he had seemed so – well – Latin.

"Believe it or not, I'm here in New York, at the Carlyle. I don't suppose we could start over again. Let me invite you to dinner. This time I will be here for you. Would you like that?"

"Oh yes, "breathed Marcia. "Yes, I'd like that."

"Would you meet me at the Capital Grille, the one on West 51st Street, at seven thirty?"

"I'll be there," said Marcia, and hung up with a huge grin on her face. The Capital Grille, so expensive, so trendy. And he was buying her dinner...before even maybe resuming their love making. She ignored the pile of unwanted clothes on her bed and raced for the bathroom to take her second shower of the day, and slather herself with expensive bath oil Jessica had given her.

Exactly an hour and a half later Marcia passed through the two lions flanking the front door to The Capital Grille and pushed open the heavy door. Inside all was cool and silent, mahogany paneling shining and brass gleaming. A pretty girl at the reception desk took her name and handed her over to a captain who led her past the private wine cubbies of the more regular customers, past the really terrible portraits of not-so famous people, which were duplicated in each branch of the posh restaurant, to a quiet booth at the back. Pedro rose from the banquette, suave, beautifully dressed and sexy as ever. He kissed Marcia on both cheeks, then seated her on the inner curve of the large booth, sliding in beside her. His muscled thigh, in its flannel trousers, pressed up against her flank, hard. He took her hand and brought it to his lips, giving a light kiss between her knuckles that sent a wave of desire coursing through Marcia. God! And they hadn't even ordered a drink yet. She wondered how she would ever be able to keep her hands off him through dinner. Fortunately the table cloth draped a goodly way toward the floor, affording some privacy if they decided to indulge in any sexual play while here.

"It is so good to see you again," he told her, his long hazel eyes boring into hers.

"You, too," Marcia managed to answer. "It's been so long. I really thought I'd never see you again; my stupidity. I should have taken out your number and kept it safe."

"Well, perhaps absence makes the heart grow fonder. Certainly I was hoping for some months to hear from you, then gave up hope. Imagine my pleasure when you called this evening." He pressed the hand he had just kissed and returned it to her. "Now, what would you like to drink?"

He gave the drink order to the hovering waiter, and waved away the huge menus for the present.

"Tell me what you have been doing since I last saw you," he said.

"Oh, the usual. Working, going out to movies and plays, getting into trouble." She dropped the last phrase to see what he would say.

"Getting into trouble? But I do not understand."

She laughed. "I was just teasing. Actually I cried into my pillow every night missing you." The last was said with lowered eyes.

"I hope I never have to miss you again," he said sincerely.

"Really?" Marcia did not dare to hope.

"Yes," said Pedro firmly. "Sometimes two people are fated to meet, I think, to be together. I felt that about you the minute you sat down at my table last spring and asked if I wanted to have coffee with you."

"We certainly didn't have that coffee." Marcia grinned wickedly.

"Most certainly not. We realized we were perfect in bed together. You are the most perfect woman I have ever known."

Marcia was about to ask how many women that was, but desisted.

"It is rare when a man and a woman make such spectacular love and only want more. I want more. I hope you do, too."

"I sure do," Marcia told him. "But please, could eat first?"

Pedro laughed. "But of course." He signaled the waiter and took the menus. "Shall we split a chateaubriand? I like mine rare."

"Me, too," said Marcia. "And some creamed spinach would be nice."

"Creamed spinach for two," Pedro told the waiter. "And six oysters each to start. Yes?"

Marcia nodded her assent.

While they waited for the food they found it easy to chat; it seemed they liked the same music, had seen some of the same plays, loved Paris but not so much Munich, and Pedro adored Venice, where Marcia had never been. "I'd like to take you there someday," he said expansively, but his face clouded over a bit.

"What is wrong?" Marcia asked, concerned for his change in mood.

"You must have guessed I am married," Pedro said. "I can come to New York on business many times a year, but probably never go to Venice with you, much as I would love to.

Marcia was expecting this. All the good ones seemed to be taken. Why would this hunk from Colombia be any different?

"It was an arranged marriage," he said. "But we grew to love each other and we are Catholic. Even if I wanted a divorce, it would be impossible. Besides, Camilla has been an exemplary wife. She has raised the children and managed my home and kept me very well. She has my respect, but whatever physical love we felt for each other ended with the children. She lost all interest in me sexually and we have separate rooms now, have for some years. She is perfectly content for me to have other women, as long as I am discreet. She understands a man's needs."

"And I am just one of those other women," Marcia tried not to sound bitter."

"But that is just it," Pedro told her. "You are definitely not 'just one of those other women' as you put it. I realized that the instant I held you in my arms a couple of months ago. You are the one woman I want."

"But you live far away and I live here. I don't see how this would work."

"As I said, I travel here many times a year on legitimate business," Pedro said. "I am sure we could work out something between us."

He broke off then as the oysters arrived and, for the rest of the meal, conversation remained general. But Marcia wondered. Just what did he have in mind for her?

The oyster plates were removed, replaced by a huge helping of rare, sizzling steak. The waiter again withdrew, leaving Pedro and Marcia in their private corner of the restaurant.

"Much as I take pleasure in good food," he told her. "I cannot wait to take pleasure in you."

Marcia was stumped for a moment. She had her period which she had not wanted to mention to Pedro, though how she thought she could have avoided the subject was unclear. His hand had crept under the tablecloth, and was stroking the tender skin on the inside of her thigh, moving upward ever upward toward her tender core.

"Uh, Pedro. Now isn't a good time for that. I mean...she trailed off." Why, in God's name, should she be ashamed to tell him what a normal function of the female body was, after all?

"You are bleeding?" His abrupt knowledge of what she was not saying startled her.

"Yes, sorry. Maybe we shouldn't have met tonight...." She trailed off miserably. Had she spoiled everything? Should she have made some excuse not to meet for dinner, tried to put him off for a few days. She stared fixedly at her steak, the blood from the meat congealing on the white plate.

"It makes no difference to me, none at all," he assured her, and he did not remove his hand from its gentle ministrations. "We will go back to your place and I'll caress you and put you to bed. I have a very early morning tomorrow. But I hope you will bring a few things by tomorrow evening and spend the weekend with me. We'll get to know each other better."

Suddenly Marcia felt her heart sing. He didn't just want her for sex! Was it possible he might like her for herself?

They finished the steak in companionable silence, then ordered Tiramisu for dessert with small cups of espresso. If the thick, rich coffee kept her awake, so what? She could lie in bed fantasize about Pedro.

He paid the rather large check, left a generous tip, and ushered her out onto the street, where an empty taxi was passing.

Somewhat reluctantly she gave the driver her address. Would Pedro think the less of her because she lived in a walkup, albeit on a fairly good block but with no doorman. She wished she had a posh apartment like Jessica's to take him to. But why hide her somewhat impecunious state? He said he liked her for herself; let him prove it.

He paid the taxi off and they ascended the stairs to the second floor, where she put her key in the lock and swung open the door. The living room was tidy, with the throw cushions neatly arranged on the beige couch, but her bedroom! The bed was piled high with all the clothes she had discarded for the thrift shop. Uncertainly, she stood in the middle of the living room. What to do now?

Squaring her shoulders she led the way into the smallish bedroom.

"I've been cleaning out my closets to take things to the charity shop," she said somewhat defiantly. "And I didn't put anything away, just ran out to meet you."

Behind her Marcia heard Pedro laugh, a long, rich sound emanating from his throat.

"You are the generous one, Marcia," he said. "Now let's pile all this stuff on the floor. I just want to lie down for a bit and hold you close in my arms. Nothing more than that. There is plenty of time for anything else."

And so, pushing heaps of bright fabrics and many pairs of shoes to the floor between the bed and the window, Marcia and Pedro flopped

79

down on top of the covers and, for a half hour, lay contentedly in each other's arms. When he roused himself, wished her a good night and planted a kiss on her willing lips, Marcia felt closer to this man than anyone else in her life.

The weekend that followed was a revelation to Marcia. They ordered dinner in on Friday when Marcia arrived with a small suitcase for the weekend stay, then snuggled up on the couch to watch pay for view movies on the large television which was usually hidden behind doors in the library's huge bookcase. They both liked British costume dramas, and had fun with reruns of 'Downton Abbey', which they analyzed to death, especially the scene in which the Turkish diplomat died in Lady Mary's bed. Pedro was adamant that such a situation had never happened: no matter how randy the diplomat was that weekend, and however Lady Mary may have led him on, he would never have seduced the daughter of the house wherein he was a guest. Marcia, who had read an interview with Julien Fellowes, told him that actually, such an event had taken place; it was in a letter written by a great aunt many years ago which verified the diplomat and his seduction.   Pedro countered that okay, maybe, but surely with an older married lady guest? Not the earl's oldest daughter? They got to laughing about the scene and, before they went off to bed, played out what might have happened, with Marcia being Lady Mary, Pedro, the diplomat. They fell beneath the sheets, still laughing and again Marcia slept in Pedro's arms, with no lovemaking first.

Saturday, Marcia actually began to feel as if this was a real relationship, as Pedro marched her down Madison, where they browsed in many of the boutiques lining the broad avenue, to lunch at Le Chat Noir on 63rd Street, where they lingered over a good bottle of Pouilly Fume for hours, then strolled up to the Frick. Back on foot to the Carlyle, where Pedro actually drew a bath for Marcia, then sat with her while she luxuriated in the deep tub, amidst a swirl of bubbles. Saturday night they strolled out to Daniel's, where another great meal and bottle of wine sent them back, replete to the Carlyle for another night of snuggling in bed.

Marcia was almost beginning to feel like a wife, when they took off, Sunday morning, in a drive yourself car, for La Cremailliere in Banksville, that iconic restaurant started so many years ago by one of the country's great restaurateurs, now owned and run by his son.

The leaves were turning, the autcmn season seemed about half way to winter, and glimpses of fields showed sere grass among the greener swaths, as the car sped up the Hutchison Parkway, continuing on to the Merritt at the border as New York flowed into Connecticut. They turned off at North Street, continuing north for three or so miles, then crossing back into Westchester County with the Colonial building housing the restaurant immediately coming up on their right. From the moment they crossed the threshold of the Cremailliere, and climbed the short flight of stairs to the restaurant proper, Marcia felt as if she was in an enchanted land.

Waxed flagstones underfoot led past the bar into the first room of the restaurant, with its pink tablecloths and autumn flowers beautifully arranged on the tables, murals of the departements of France adorning the wall. Obviously Pedro was well known here, for the Proprietiere himself greeted them cordially and led them out to the outer room, full of light from the many windows ringing the walls. They were seated with a flourish side by side on a comfortable banquette, and a captain came over immediately to take their drink orders. A martini for Pedro, a Cosmopolitan for Marcia, and they were left to admire the warmth and beauty of the room, and eye the other diners, obviously all well heeled and used to gourmet dining. Marcia sighed with pleasure. This was the life! How sad Pedro would be leaving tonight and who knew if or when she would see him again. Giving herself a little shake, she decided to live in the moment and enjoy this special meal.

And special it was, from the oysters, perfectly chilled and served on a bed of shaved ice, though the wonderful rack of lamb with morels, something Marcia had never eaten before, to the perfect Grand Marnier soufflé, presented at the table, which literally melted in the mouth, and finished off with frothy cups of cappuccino, the meal was sublime. Marcia was practically purring as they left the restaurant, ushered out like royalty. Never had there been such a meal, and with such a guy!

The ride back was more silent than the one up to Banksville and La Cremailliere, both Marcia and Pedro seemingly lost in private thoughts, and they drew up at the Carlyle as the autumn afternoon was waning. If every city has its season, certainly New York's is autumn, when everyone is back from the summer and everything starts up again. Marcia could feel the beat of the city she called home, and ached to have Pedro share it with her on some sort of meaningful basis.

"Come up for a bit," Pedro said to her on the street outside the private entrance. "Keep me company until I have to go out to the airport." He was taking the last flight out of Kennedy and had to be there in a few hours; would it be the last hours they would spend together?

"Let me ride out with you," Marcia begged. "I'll wave you off."

"I'd love that," Pedro gave her an appreciative hug. "Now why don't you help me pack and we can order something up to eat before we go. Would you like some sandwiches? Maybe a nice light wine?"

'Heavenly," said Marcia, who would have agreed to tough kidneys and ice water, if it meant spending more time with this wonderful man.

The limousine ordered by the hotel sped them over the bridge to Queens, and they rode by the site of the 1964 World's Fair and on out the busy highway to Kennedy Airport. Their hands were loosely entwined and from time to time Pedro leaned over to give Marcia a gentle kiss. She luxuriated against the supple leather of the car, watching the lights pass by in the darkening night. Soon it would be winter and she fervently hoped this man would be back for her, no matter how infrequently, no matter how short a time he stayed. She realized she had fallen in love this weekend, something she thought she might never do again.

At Kennedy, he embraced her one more time, then swung out of the car, telling the driver to take Miss Ramer home, please. A final wave and he was through the doors and lost to view. She gazed out of the back window as the terminals receded behind her, only turning toward the front as they left the airport exit and headed back into Manhattan.

Somehow, during the next several weeks, Marcia did not feel like encountering any of her stable of randy men she usually saw, bedding several of them during a week. She instead sought out Jessica for her input.

The two women met that Thursday at Sel et Poivre, one of Jessica's favorite restaurants in New York, on Lexington in the sixties. Over a glass of Chardonnay, Marcia tried to tell about her new man.

"He's so handsome, so masculine, so suave," she began. "But there's something more, I don't know quite what it is."

"Maybe it's that he likes you," Jessica offered, though she was on unfamiliar ground. Certainly she had not experienced the feelings that Marcia was trying to describe or, if she had, they had been thrown back in her face.

"Maybe," Marcia said slowly, twirling her wineglass in her hand. "But Jessica, he's married. And he's not doing the usual 'my wife doesn't understand me' routine. He was strictly upfront with me on that. He's Catholic and they can't get a divorce. I'm not even sure he wants to."

"Does it matter to you? People seem to have little honor for marriage these days," Jessica said, thinking of the debacle of her own marriage.

"Well, I'd like it for him to be available. I mean there are those other men out there – you know – who supposedly are available but I really don't want to get seriously entangled with any of them." Marcia didn't specify exactly which men she meant, and Jessica didn't ask. It was, after all, Marcia's choice who she saw and with whom she slept. Jessica often envied her for her ability to hop from one bed to another, seemingly without any involvement with the men in those beds. No hang-ups, no regrets. It must be a nice way to live.

"But if he is not really available, if he never divorces his wife, would you rather be with him than anyone else?" Jessica asked.

"Yes, I would," said Marcia without even thinking. "He is so far above and better than those other – well, men I sleep with. He really seems to care for me, not just for a quick roll in the hay. You know, this weekend I had my period and it didn't matter to him at all. He just held me and wasn't even trying to get sexy. He seemed to enjoy me just for me, not for what I could do for him in bed."

"It sounds like you've got it bad," said Jessica. "But maybe he does, too. When are you going to see him again?"

"I don't know," said Marcia sadly. "He said he'd email, call. Maybe that was just b.s. I hope not."

I hope not, too," said Jessica. "Hey, I'm, starving. I've been looking forward all day to soupe au poisson. Maybe moules mareniere afterward. What appeals to you?"

Marcia who, by now, had learned something about French food, perused the menu carefully. "I think I'll just have the chicken fricassee," she said, and they turned to give their orders to the waiter. "Jessica," she asked as the waiter stepped away from their table. "Do you think the less of me for wanting a married man? I mean it is the 21st century, but what future is there in this kind of relationship?"

"A future that at least should make you happy until maybe someone else comes along who really *is* available. In the meantime, who are you hurting? His wife never comes to New York, does she? She doesn't know about you. And if they have stopped having sex she must realize a man like Pedro isn't just going to become celibate."

"Or spend a lot of time jerking off," said Marcia, and liberally buttered a piece of the baguette on the table, popping it into her mouth.

Marcia turned down all invitations from her various men friends...to go out to dinner, or a movie, with the unspoken implication that any activity would be followed by vigorous and often kinky sex back in someone's apartment. She didn't want to sleep with anyone else but

Pedro, which surprised her, but she was going to go with her gut feeling that he would come back to New York – at least for the present.

There was no word from him for a week after his departure, a week which kept Marcia almost biting her fingernails and sitting on her hands to email or call him. One evening late the bell pinged on her I-Pad and up popped the number 1 on her email icon.

Eagerly she opened the program.

To: MarciaK175@aol.com
From: PedrodelaH@hotmail.co.
Subj: Our next meeting

Chere Marcia:
Desolate without you and anticipating our next encounter in New York where I expect to be this coming Friday. Can you meet me at the Carlyle at six? We'll take it from there. Bring your toothbrush. Abrazos, Pedro

Almost Marcia thought to play hard to get, and answer it the next morning or even a couple of days hence. How stupid! Who was she fooling? She pushed the reply button:

To: PedrodelaH@prodigy.net
From: MarciaK175@aol.com
Subj: Friday.

She thought awhile before composing the body of the note, her very first to him. Finally she typed:

Until Friday. Have toothbrush and will travel. Don't think I need much more luggage, do I?

She thought awhile how to end it and at length typed:

Your Marcia

It could mean everything or nothing.

She pushed the send button and resolutely turned the I-Pad off, sliding the shut up button. She put it out in the living room and tucked herself into bed. But sleep was a long time in coming

The next morning another message popped up:

To: MarciaK175@aol.com
From: PedrodelaH@prodigy.net
Subj: Toothbrushes.

Probably a toothbrush is sufficient. If necessary, we can buy anything else you need. See you Friday at six. I wait to kiss your lips, and perhaps a bit further down as well. Abrazos Pedro

Marcia actually hugged herself, then picked up the phone to call Jessica.

"Oh Jessica!" she exclaimed. "He's coming in Friday. He wants to see me. I'll call after the weekend when I come up for air." She put down the phone and danced around her tiny living room. A toothbrush and nothing else. It should be quite a weekend!

Friday finally came and Marcia invented a late afternoon doctor's appointment to get out of work an hour or so early, the better to prepare for Pedro's arrival. She hurried home to soak in a long, hot bath, then carefully dressed herself in her very best, from the inside out, starting with a pair of knickers that had actually come from a La Perla sale, a lacy push up bra and an easy to shed jersey dress that was particularly flattering. She even had a garter belt, and old fashioned stockings clipped onto the garters, and left her apartment, carrying only a medium size tote bag with her toothbrush, makeup and clean underwear. He had, after all, told her to travel light

The doorman at the Carlyle Apartments actually bowed her into the lobby, greeting her by name.

"Good evening," Ms. Ramer. "Please go up. Mr. delaHoya is expecting you." He escorted her across the lobby to the elevator and handed her over to the elevator man. All the way up to Pedro's floor, Marcia thought she might keel over from excitement, but she managed to step from the car, thank the elevator man, and walk, though somewhat unsteadily, down the hall to ring the bell of Pedro's apartment.

He must have been standing behind the door, for it immediately swung open and he embraced her in a huge bear hug, leading her into his foyer where he kicked the door shut behind them.

She was in his arms, his mouth on hers, hot and lusty, then his tongue darted between her lips and explored the inside of her mouth, causing her to gasp with pleasure. Without losing his hold on her, he walked Marcia backward through the living room into the bedroom of the apartment, and on through into the bathroom. "What now?" she thought, but all her senses were so engaged Marcia only waited to see what was coming next.

Pedro seated her on the closed lid of the toilet, then knelt before her. Slowly he drew off one shoe, then the other. His fingers crept up her legs to the garters that held up the stockings, and, expertly, he unfastened these and drew the stockings carefully down and over her ankles, then her feet. He took a washcloth from the side of the bathtub and, after turning on the faucets, wet it and took up a new cake of soap, exquisitely scented with lavender, rubbing it into a foam on the wet cloth...

Gently, he proceeded to wash Marcia's feet, first the right, then the left, soaping between her toes, over her high arches, under the instep. He rinsed out the cloth, removed every trace of soap and proceeded to pat the feet dry with one of the hugely fluffy hotel towels. Marcia just sat there, mesmerized by his ministrations. She knew some men liked feet, but no one had ever washed hers for her, and with such tender care.

Feet dry, Pedro tossed the towel away and took the right foot in both his hands. His fingers began kneading here and there, especially at the apex of the arch and hot desire cascaded throughout Marcia's sexual organs, causing her to gasp with both pleasure and surprise. Pedro simply grinned up at her as he continued, thumbing and kneading, causing involuntary gasps of pleasure from Marcia.

"Oh, my God," she breathed. "Stop it I love it." He intensified his efforts, making Marcia want to jump from her seat and drag him into the large, comfortable bed she could see through the bedroom door. Finally, when she thought she could stand no more, Pedro stood up and offered her his hand.

"Come with me, my darling. Let me make such love to you as you have never experienced before."

'Make love, she thought ecstatically, 'make love to me.' Surely the Mickeys and Marvins of the world would have phrased it 'Let me fuck you, baby.' What a difference such a simple phrase meant. Willingly she let Pedro lead her over to the bed, where she lay down on her back, waiting to see what would happen next. She was bound to let this divine man take the lead tonight, to do with her as he would.

Pedro lifted her skirt and pulled the beautiful La Perla thong down and off her. He took it up to his nose, inhaling her essence, his head flung back, lips curling. "Ah, it is you, only you. I will always remember this special scent." He brought the garment to his lips and kissed the crotch once, twice, then almost reverently put the wisp of silk and lace on the bedside table.

He turned her over onto her face and drew down her zipper, then rolled the dress off her hips and over the thighs and so down over her feet. She lay on the bed, naked except for her brassiere, waiting for his next touch, his next caress. He undid the hooks at her back and pushed the straps down over her arms, then lay on top of her, fully clothed, and cupped her breasts from behind in both his hands.

"Ah, the beauty of your breasts," he murmured into the hair at the nape of her neck. "I can never get enough of these. At night I dream of them." He rolled off of her, pulling her along with him until she was on her side, he on his back.

"Please, I beg of you, undress me," he breathed, "but slowly, slowly. Let us enjoy this special night."

Special indeed, thought Marcia as she began to fulfill his request. First the silk socks, rolled off over the racehorse ankles, then dropped on the floor. Next the shirt buttons, tiny and difficult, with the shirt peeled off his muscled, hairy chest. Next the belt, unfastened, leaving the hook at his trouser waist band. She could see the flannel material straining over his groin as his erection grew and expanded, begging for release. She thrilled at the sight of it, big and hard and proud, as she slid down the zipper, exposing the silk shorts beneath, and, without removing his trousers, she bent down and took it in her oh-so-willing mouth. Carefully, lips folded around her teeth, she began to suck and lick, up and down, causing him to arch his back and thrust further into her.

"Slowly, my darling," he cautioned. "You do not want me to come just now. I am here for your pleasure, too."

"Your pleasure is my pleasure," Marcia managed to say, lifting her head for a moment from its joyful job.

"But we have all night," he protested, raising her head with both his hands and putting her down at his side for a moment. He lifted up his hips, shed his trousers and the silk shorts, and lay down next to her, as naked as she.

For a moment each examined, hungrily the beauty of the other body, then Pedro bent one of her legs under her, putting his head on her triangulated thigh, his nose but a few inches from the curly black bush that hid her vagina and clitoris. "Now lie still for a moment," he admonished, "and let me get my tongue and my fingers into you." He pushed his nose into the black triangle, then his tongue found her clitoris and she moaned, falling back, letting him do his work.

89

His tongue licked up one side of her vulva and down the other, pausing at each revolution to give a flick to her clitoris, sending her higher and higher into the stratosphere. She would come in a few seconds at this rate, leaving him behind, and she tried to stop the waves of pleasure washing over her, to keep the moment of release somewhere in the distance.

Abruptly he withdrew from his vantage point, lay on his back and flipped her over on top of him. She felt the pulsing penis groping between her thighs, and reached down to guide him into her oh so willing snatch. Ah, the feel of him, slipping into her hot and slippery insides. Oh the joy he was giving her.

"Lie back down, between my legs," he commanded. "And spread yourself out for me. Now."

Without thinking she obeyed. They now lay, heads far apart, each other's feet somewhere in the shoulder region of the other. He took both her hands in his and began a gently rocking motion that barely engaged their sexual organs, making a lingering connection of penis to vagina, slowing down the crescendo which, but a moment before, had threatened to overwhelm them.

The gentle movement of their bodies, hand fasted, was pleasurable, without making either Marcia or Pedro frenzied in the desire to achieve orgasm, soothingly singular yet still a build up for wanting more. Marcia was swept away by the sheer romance of this position, which she had never experienced before. Always, her sexual partners had seemed hell bent on getting their rocks off, hasty and direct. But this oh-so-experienced man had almost brought her off just through the reflexes of her feet, while in her present position, she knew they would be joined for a long time to come, before going on to higher planes of desire.

It was some time before Pedro pulled gently out of her, moving her again to a position on her side facing him. "I am going to go down on you again," he told her, "and I want you to put your head on my thigh – so – and do the same to me. I want my cock in your mouth, your tongue probing and licking me just as I am going to probe and lick you." He drew his heel up under one buttock, leaving a perfect pillow for Marcia's head on his thigh, and moved his own head down to be in contact with her willing labia and clitoris.

Together, in perfect synch, his fingers explored, parting her labia, thrusting two fingers deep inside of her, while she took his rampant cock in her two hands, thumbs beneath, fingers playing in staccato rhythm under the glans, around the head, up and down the shaft. They moved from fingers to mouths and tongues, Pedro sliding up and down her quivering labia, into her opened vagina, up and down the shaft of her enlarged clitoris. In turn, Marcia took the length and breadth of his erection into her mouth, sucking and twisting, while her hands cupped his scrotum ever so gently, drawing forth loud moans from him.

It seemed as if they would both explode with the wanting of each other until, a moment before orgasm Pedro pulled out of her mouth, flipped himself on top of her and finished off what they had started a couple of hours before, with both of them gushing together, as a volcano sending its enormous spume of fire and smoke upward to the heavens, shattering everything in its way.

Back in her own apartment Monday night, Marcia tried to figure out just what had been different about the weekend with Pedro, but she could not, for some hours, put her finger on it. Then it suddenly dawned on her: Pedro had treated her like a lady all the way. The other men she had slept with truly only fucked her. Pedro had actually spent time and thought and consideration doing what he called making love.

Chapter Seven

At Sylvan Glade

Don soon became a fixture in Jessica's life, albeit a somewhat uneasy one. He had heard around town that Jessica had just gone through a dreadful divorce, though no one actually knew the true facts and seemed to be scared of any man who made a move on her. So he vowed to take things extremely slowly, and be there when Jessica was ripe for the plucking. Certainly they enjoyed each other's company outside of any sex; they were both vital, educated people, who had read a lot and absorbed a lot and loved the theater, the opera, concerts and the more serious movies. It gave them much to talk about and if conversation did not immediately lead to bed, well, perhaps in time it would.

For her part Jessica was delighted to have a good looking, well dressed and heeled man to escort her around town. She had greatly missed out on the man/woman events she had enjoyed with Trevor, and having a S.O. gave her entrée back into some of the groups that had shunned her as a single woman. They joined a tennis group that played mixed doubles in Riverdale Saturday mornings, which usually led to lunch and a swim, then back to town where Don found ever new fun places to have dinner. They drove out to Katonah a couple of times for the music festival at Caramoor, taking along a picnic to enjoy before the concert, driving back to New York through the velvet blackness and almost deserted highways.

Friends even started inviting them for weekends again, though it became difficult the first few times when the hostess tried to put them in the same room. Once Don even ended up sleeping on the living room couch, which made for an awkward breakfast time, and they left early. Word went out that – for some absurd reason – Jessica and Don were not sleeping together, and hostesses only invited them when they had two free guestrooms, which was not often. Available rooms in the Hamptons and on the Gold Coast of Connecticut and the beaches in Rhode Island were always at a premium in summer, and hostesses found it easier to invite married couples, or unmarried couples who at least did not mind sharing a room. Two singles took up more space than they warranted.

Jessica did not mind. She was getting back into her former circle, however slowly and she hoped that soon she would be able to welcome Don into her bed. She liked him immensely as a friend, and could see the relationship blossoming into love. Always, however, when she was about to capitulate to his expert foreplay and clinch the deal, she shrank back, somehow fearful he would perform some of the acts Trevor had so brutally forced upon her which even now she did her best to block out. She was still terrified that she might flip out. And so Don remained – if not at arm's length – at least unfulfilled and for this she was sorry.

Removed from any real sex, their relationship had developed on an intellectual level. From that first song, from 'Annie Get Your Gun' they had often sung together, sometimes in parts, sometimes in harmony. Don had been a lead performer in a Gilbert and Sullivan society, and Jessica had sung at her school, later in the church choir. Neither had done any real singing, though, the past couple of years, so this melody-making when the spirit moved them was a delight to both.

One afternoon they were returning from a walk in Central Park, just turning down 88th Street. Jessica had inspired to start the words from 'My Fair Lady' and, without any preamble opened her mouth:

"I have often walked down this street before,
But the pavement always stayed beneath my feet before...."

Don rose to the challenge:

"All at once am I several stories high
Knowing I'm on the street where you live."
They joined hands and continued in unison:
"People stop and stare, they don't bother me,
For there's nowhere else on earth I want to be..."

A couple passing by indeed stopped to stare, seeing these attractive young people skylarking on 88th Street singing a love song. But the woman just tucked her arm into her husband's and drew him along, smiling all the while.

They paused just before reaching Jessica's canopy, greeted the doorman, and fled toward the elevator. They did not complete the song until they reached the safety of Jessica's apartment, where they trilled the final chorus:

"Let the time go by, I don't care if I
Can be here on the street where you live."

Jessica kicked off her shoes and gave a little twirl. It was almost heaven being here with this charming man whom she just might like to make her own...forever.

Things limped along through the summer and into the fall, and still they had not made love, not gone all the way. Jessica was amazed that Don had not pushed her, but wisely kept her counsel. What she did not know was that Don had a string of girls, none of them of much importance to him, who were always happy to go over to his apartment and service him, whatever the hour. And so, when he was spending the weekend at someone's house with Jessica in the next room, he would call Alice or Gail or Sally over Thursday night and give them a thoroughly good fuck, and get his rocks off for a couple of days. None of these woman was possible marriage material, though none was a professional either. They were women he had met in bars, who had given him their numbers, and one, Sally, was a junior clerk in his office, proud of being able to sleep with the boss. Around the office the girls whispered behind their hands in the lunchroom imagining his magnificent prick, or his inventive love making, but only Sally knew for sure, and she kept her counsel, afraid of losing the wonderful evenings in Don's apartment giving and receiving spectacular sex. She even dared hoped, on occasion, that she might become Don's girlfriend.

On the Thursday before Labor Day weekend, Don had a particular need for Sally. He and Jessica had indulged in some pretty heavy petting at her apartment, giving him a huge boner which he had not been able to use. He had left early, around ten, since they were both getting ready for the weekend in Darien with John and Sarah Cunningham. They had tickets for the Westport Playhouse and there was a clam bake on the beach planned for Sunday night. But it would be three long days without any possibility of sex, so Don pulled out his cell phone while the taxi drove away from 88th Street, and called Sally, hopeful she was home – and free. She was. He settled back into the taxi, happy he would soon be able to relieve the dreadful tension that had built up in his loins.

Sally was buzzed up almost as soon as Don walked in his front door, and he met her, trousers unzipped, his erection proudly standing at attention through his fly.

"Gosh, hon," she exclaimed. "All ready for me, aren't you?"

"You better believe it," Don said. Without any preliminaries, he took Sally's arm, drawing into her into the living room, where he positioned her over the arm of the couch. He flipped up her short skirt, exposing her naked buttocks and her soaking wet crotch. As expected, she was wearing no underwear and was primed and ready to go.

He spread her legs apart with both hands, then positioned himself over her, bracing himself either side on the arm of the couch. She reached behind her and expertly guided him into her willing snatch, then bent farther over so her face was squashed into one of the cushions.

In this position she was both tight and foreshortened, and he thrust deeply into her, moaning his pleasure into her hair. She grunted her assent to his onslaught, her voice muffled by the softness of the down.

Like a teenage boy he ejaculated into her, almost instantly, so primed and ready had he been since grappling with Jessica only an hour before on another couch, in another apartment. He gave a triumphant shout as he came, arching his back and throwing back his head. Below him he heard Sally give a short whimper. He pulled his now flaccid penis from between her legs, giving her a friendly pat on the behind.

"Ok, Lover," Sally said. "Now it's my turn. Into your bed, please."

Replete, satisfied, Don almost said no, told her to go home. But that would no doubt cancel out any future privileges from Sally. So he allowed himself to be led docilely into the bedroom, where she threw herself down onto his pristine bed and held up her arms.

"Come to me, Lover, I want you. Now."

"Sure, sure," he said. "But let's get into the bed first." He had no intention of getting stains all over the expensive duvet quilt, made from the finest Egyptian cotton. Sure it washed, but it would never look the same.

Reluctantly she came to her feet and helped him take off the cover and fold it neatly on the bench at the foot of the bed. She flung back the sheet and thin summer blanket, and again positioned herself, spread eagled, on his sheets. At least the bed linen could go in the laundry tomorrow and Mrs. Sprague came Fridays and Tuesdays. She could change the bed, and she wondered why there were so many days the bed was stripped for changing, well, let her think what she would. Hell, he paid her enough.

Sally drew him down to her, and pressed her mouth over his, forcing his lips apart and delving deep with her tongue. Clearly, she wanted to make this a night of long, passionate, love, but Don was tired and his mind was on tomorrow. He gave a couple of fast thrusts with his own tongue, tangling with her in the hot recess of his mouth, then turned his mind to how to get her to come as fast as possible.

He had many a trick in his sexual repertory, and quickly ran through the list, mentally weighing one against another.

He skipped the upper half of Sally's voluptuous body, concentrating on her core, further down. No need for cunnilingus tonight, he decided. It would take too long and his fingers could do the work of his tongue. Without any preliminaries, the fingers of one hand parted the curly bush guarding the more intimate delights beyond, and he thrust one long finger onto her hot, dripping cunt, massaging the willing clitoris with the heel of his hand. His other hand crept around behind her, the middle finger stroking the opening to her anus, tickling and stroking with an ever increasing rhythm, while the other hand kept pace in her vagina. She arched her back and moaned, the almost unearthly sound telling Don she was almost ready to climax. He congratulated himself in doing his work so well, then found, to his surprise, that he had another erection, certainly firm enough to ram home where his finger was now giving her so much pleasure.

He ceased his ministrations to her anus, after thrusting his finger gently into that orifice, then withdrew both his hands from their labor and, after popping on a condom, flipped himself on top of her. This time it was he who guided himself inside her, helping the not quite firm prick into her pulsing, wet cunt. Because he had come so recently, he had to work harder to achieve another orgasm, which gave her time to achieve her own. Together they rode the waves of desire, higher and ever higher, until she crashed down to the rocky shore, with Don crashing down right after her. All in all, he thought, a most satisfactory ending to what had promised to be another frustrating evening at Jessica's. He was so pleased with Sally's performance, he even let her spend the night, sending her off the next morning with the promise of more to come.

Of course there was many a Saturday night, especially when away for the weekend with Jessica, that he went to his lonely room and jacked off, stuffing the sheet into his mouth to stifle any noise, knowing Jessica was in the next room, dying to fling open her door and go to her, fill her up with his manhood and his sperm. Each time he jerked harder and longer and longed for her more. Each time he vowed there would be no more Sally, Gail or Alice. The very next time it would be Jessica and he would bring her to gasping, screaming orgasm, an orgasm such as she had never had before. He even started compiling appropriate quotes in his head; Jessica was a pushover for quotes from famous books and poems. Somewhere in his repertoire must be something that would turn her on sufficiently that she would – finally – lie down and let him overwhelm her.

In spite of his firm resolve, the desired seduction did not take place, so it was back to Alice, Sally and Gail, never putting one over the other; the idea was to simply get his rocks off and – at last – fuck Jessica so hard and with such finesse that she would never look at another man. And then goodbye to the others. Well, maybe not entirely. It was always useful to have an extra girl or two in the stable.

And so the summer passed and September came and Don decided to ratchet up his pursuit of Jessica. He arranged with his florist to keep fresh flowers streaming into East 88th Street, and bought her love songs by Frank Sinatra and Neil Diamond which he played both on her Boise and his car stereo whenever they were together. He looked up endless love poems which he joyed in reciting to her of an evening, when dusk was falling over the city and lights were coming on up and down the avenues and side streets to mark the beginnings of evenings of cooler nights and high, black skies. He insisted they read sexy books – separately – then discuss them when together: The 50 Shades of Gray trilogy, The Joy of Sex, in which he made her look at the pictures, but nothing seemed to work. Perhaps he was being too direct. At Halloween he thought perhaps he had hit on the right formula. They were invited to an annual costume party by a couple they both knew: she from college, he from work, who had married two years before and even now were expecting their first child. He bought her a copy of Lady Chatterley's Lover, the first 'dirty' book either had probably read under the sheets with a flashlight when teenagers. It had always seemed to titillate the women he knew, with its romantic overtones of the Lady in the Castle – okay, Midlands's estate – and the lowly gamekeeper, distant and mysterious in his lair. He decreed that Jessica and he would go as

Constance Chatterley and Oliver Mellors to the party, then come home and discuss the book. Daily he called to make sure she was reading, fast, and would finish by the last day of October. Being a quick reader, Jessica complied, wondering as she read what all the excitement was at first reading some years ago.

Halloween night arrived, and Jessica was waiting at the door in a 1930's vintage evening dress, silver strappy sandals on her feet, hair bound up in a snood. She had found some junky rhinestone jewelry in the local thrift shop, and sported a pair of clips on the square neck of the bodice and some dangly earrings to match. Don arrived attired in a ratty old tweed jacket, from the same thrift shop, old jodhpurs with a rip in the knee, and green Wellingtons. He carried a shotgun, broken, over his arm, and had topped the get up off with a deerstalker a la Sherlock Holmes.

'Evening, m'lady," Don said, sweeping off his hat.

"Good evening, Mellors," Jessica said with her best English accent. "I trust the trip to the house was not too taxing?"

"Not at all, m'lady," her gamekeeper told her. "Shall we go?" He held out his arm and she threw her short train over her arm and prepared to step out with this disreputable man.

They made a splash at the party, and danced and drank with a mob of men - in everything from loincloths (Ghandi) and satin knee britches (George III) - to woman in Wonder Woman outfits and French maid uniforms to – spectacularly - someone who had come as Marie Antoinette, replete with wide panniers, laced underskirt and a towering white wig, atop which, rather unsteadily, was an array of nodding feathers. Her skirt was so wide and her wig so high she had trouble going through the doorways, and had to bend and bob to not squash her skirts or lose her feathers.

The unexpected fun of being someone else made most of the guests pretty uninhibited, and there were quick forays into the apartment bedrooms when a jocular clown desired a tete a tete with a gypsy fortune teller. That the couple emerged straightening their costumes, told volumes, though they were not the only couple to disappear for a period of a few minutes to over half an hour before somewhat sheepishly rejoining the throng.

It was just the atmosphere Don had hoped for to put Jessica in the mood, and, when they took their somewhat unsteady departure, long after midnight, he had every hope that tonight would be the night.

The party was only a few blocks from Jessica's apartment, and they wobbled somewhat loosely down the street, finally arriving at the building and bowing their way past the night doorman, who looked vastly amused.

Upstairs in the dark foyer, Don stopped Jessica from turning on any lights. "Let's pretend we're walking over the estate and have come to a clump of – oh what? – moss under a spreading oak and stop for a rest. He drew her into the living room, tore the cushions from the couch, and made a nest of them up against a wall. Throwing himself down onto his home made moss patch, he reached up and drew a willing Jessica down beside him.

"Well, m'lady, and what did you think of the party?"

"Oh, Mellors," she sighed, "such fun. But I do fear I am a bit tipsy."

"Me, too," he agreed solemnly. "Just tipsy enough to want to tup you, m'lady."

"Now when did Mellors read 'Othello'?" Jessica inquired. "Since this afternoon m'lady. You know I am in charge of all the game on the estate, so why not the rams and the ewes, m'lady?'"

"Goodness, Mellors, I had no idea you were such an intellectual," Jessica said with mock curiosity. "Just what else do you know that I am not aware of?"

"Well," said Don slowly, "perhaps instead of telling you I could show you. Would that be agreeable with you m'lady?" He leered into the dark at his companion.

"I think that might be very agreeable," agreed Jessica. "How to best begin?"

100

"Perhaps best like this, m'lady," said Don, tipping up Jessica's face and brushing her lips gently with his.

"Yes, please," Jessica melted into his embrace.

"Do you like my bed of moss, m'lady?" he inquired?

"Oh, yes, so bucolic."

"'Come live with me and be my love,'" he quoted

"'And we will all the pleasures prove....'"

Jessica quoted right back:

"'If all the world and love were young,

And truth on every Shepherd's tongue

These pretty pleasures might be move

To live with thee and be thy love....'"

"Would you really?" Don murmured into her hair. "...live with me and be my love."

"Maybe," Jessica snuggled into his embrace and prepared to – finally – allow a man to make love to her again. She drew his head down to her breasts.

His hand thrust down into the low cut bodice of the vintage dress, and Jessica could feel a seam give way. No matter. Perhaps the dress had done its work. She lay back on the cushions, giving herself over to Don's ministrations.

"Do you like this, m'lady?" inquired her game keeper.

"Oh, yes, Mellors, just keep up what you are doing. It is quite satisfactory." She gave a little moan as his thumb and forefinger rolled the tender nipple between them, causing desire to start building up between her legs. She pushed his hand down, ever downward, to the pulsing heat in her loins, arching her back and thrusting her hips up at him. He became tangled in the long, full skirt, causing a short pause in their fondling of each other.

"M'lady, the damn dress is in the way," he said.

"Well, Mellors, let's get the damn dress off." She sat up for a moment, found the side zipper and pulled it down, releasing the tight bodice and pulling the whole cascade of lace and satin over her head.

She was wearing an old merry widow underneath, with lacy garters holding up real stockings, 1930's style and he gasped in pleasure at the sight.

"M'lady does indeed wear finery," he quipped, in his best imitation of a Midlands accent.

"Well, Mellors, do you know how to unfasten a lady's garter?"

"I can but try." His fingers fumbled for a moment, then released the garters and peeled her stockings down her legs and over her ankles, tossing them aside. He groped up under the lace ruffles of the merry widow, encountering a band of silk covering her labia and pulsing clitoris. His fingers swept the strip of silk, evincing a moan from Jessica and a further thrusting of the hips.

"M'lady, you're going to have to help me with this. My – uh – country lasses do not possess such fine undergarments. And John Thomas would like to meet Lady Jane with nothing between them when they – uh – join."

Jessica obliged, with some difficulty for a merry widow is not the easiest thing to remove in a hurry, but finally managed it, leaving nothing on but a beautiful triple strand of pearls.

"Oh, God, m'lady, what a lovely sight." Don/Oliver was breathing hard now. "Let me look at Lady Jane, let me feel her."

Obligingly Jessica spread her legs, exposing her vulva to her lover.

He had not touched her below the waist yet, but he judged she was ready and he shed his clothes as quickly as possible, exposing his full erection. In the dark living room, it was hard to see anything more than dimly, and it was a matter of feeling more than seeing which was turning these two on.

Don raised himself to her face and took her lower lip in his, sucking gently then giving a quick bite, which caused a sharp intake from Jessica, who opened her mouth to receive his tongue. A few moments of intense kissing and sucking of the tongues, and both were more than ready to go forward. Don trailed his tongue down over her breasts, then across her naval and almost down to the triangle of black hair, covering the delights he was about to experience. He remembered another line from *Lady Chatterley* and proudly recited it.

"Here's where tha' pisses," he said, laying a finger within the sopping wet labia, "and here's where tha' shits," he put his other hand between her cheeks and inserted his middle finger, not very gently, into her anus.

Jessica totally freaked out. She jerked away and jumped to her feet, screaming. Don was so surprised it took him a moment to gather his wits together and even then he had no idea what was happening. Jessica fled the room so fast he could not even get to his feet and, in the dark apartment, he could not find her. Finally, after turning on most of the lights and searching both the bedrooms, the living and dining rooms, he heard wild crying coming from somewhere near the kitchen. He found the kitchen lights and switched them on, but still no sign of Jessica. Her wails came from a room off the kitchen, and he rounded the refrigerator and followed the sound into what must be a maid's room, a tiny chamber with a half open door into an equally tiny adjoining bathroom. Here he found Jessica, still stark naked, crouched on the cold, tile floor, jammed between the toilet and miniature sink, with her knees drawn up to her chest, tears streaming from her eyes and running away over the so pitiful body which, only a moment before, he had held with such rapture.

He remembered to throw on some clothes and get a blanket with which to cover Jessica right after he called 911.

After being carted off to Lenox Hill Hospital, where she was heavily sedated, Jessica's mother and father managed to have her transferred to New Canaan, Connecticut, to the world famous psychiatric hospital, Sylvan Glade. Founded seventy years before, mostly as a drying out place for famous people, over its many decades of experience., Sylvan Glade expanded and grew, treating all manner and condition of mental illnesses, on its lovely, large New England 'campus' which flowed into two towns, from the gracious Colonial Main House on the crest of the hill, across Valley Road and down to the Sylvan River at its farthest extremity. It contained different houses for various stages of psychiatric ailments, from mild to severe, a detox unit, a special house for adolescent patients – most of whom were on drugs – a special house for recovering alcoholics, and a large building housing the main hall. Here AA meetings were held several times a week, here were the occupational and recreational facilities, including a large, indoor swimming pool. The ratio of staff to patients was extremely high, and everything was laid on, at an enormous cost, for people trying to become well and function independently in the real world.

To this bastion of hope went Jessica Alden Jellingdorf, frightened, it would seem of her own shadow, unable to face the terrible ordeal her former husband had but her through, which ordeals had unwittingly been laid raw by her session with Don after the Halloween party.

She was assigned a room in Small House, one of the most secure of all the various houses on the campus, with few patients and many highly trained psychiatric nurses. She was also assigned a series of "constant companion": her very own duty nurses, who were literally with her twenty four hours a day, even sitting up all night in her private room in case she woke and needed anything.

It took her the better part of a week to manage to go out into the main hall of Small House, which served both as lounge and dining room, then she timidly forked up her food, or at least some of it, tasting nothing, talking to no one and scuttling back to her room, followed by the day's "constant companion" as soon as she could. The only other place she went was to see her assigned psychiatrist, Dr. Consuelo, but always accompanied by the ever watchful "constant companion" who only left Jessica alone with the doctor.

Dr. Consuelo was perhaps a decade older than her patient, with long, ash blonde hair which she wore loose over her shoulders, and huge, round glasses, through which she peered, with uncommon compassion, at her newest patient.

104

For several sessions, Jessica was barely able to speak, answering some of Dr. Consuelo's questions in monosyllables, not volunteering any information whatsoever about herself or why she had so flipped out that night back home on 88th Street.

The doctor was patience itself, realizing that Jessica had to come to a place where she trusted herself enough to open up, even a little bit, and say what was troubling her to such an extent.

One late morning, the two women sat together, Jessica on the comfortable sofa in the doctor's office, Dr. Consuelo adjacent her in a club chair. The doctor had her pen poised over her open notebook, and attempted once again to lead her patient out of the dark labyrinth into which she had fallen.

"Tell me about your mother," the doctor urged gently. "I met her you know when you came up here and she seemed so very concerned with you. I know she loves you very, very much. Can you tell me some happy times you had with her during your childhood?"

Somehow this simple question seemed to register with Jessica. She came out of her slump a little and even looked over, briefly, at the doctor.

"She was always encouraging me," Jessica said slowly, a very small smile starting – then disappearing – at the corner of her mouth. "In reading, in sports, in interests I had like ballet. I read, you know, when I was about three. And one morning...I must have been five....mother came into my room and found me with a Shakespeare play propped up on my knees. I think it was Henry V. She went out and rented the movie for me, the Laurence Olivier one, and I fell in love with Shakespeare. And with him."

"With him?"

"With Olivier," said Jessica solemnly. "He was my ideal all my growing up years. Until I found out he and Vivian Leigh had split, years before, and I lost my interest."

"And did anyone else interest you then? A man, I mean?" the doctor asked gently.

"Well, that took awhile," Jessica said. "You see there was an incident when I was a child, which made me think all boys were dirty creatures." She stopped suddenly and looked down at her hands.

"And..." the doctor prodded.

"And I don't want to say any more. I want to go back to my room."

The doctor knew when to stop. "I'll call your 'constant companion'," she told Jessica. "We have plenty of time to explore whatever it that is distressing you," she said gently. "Don't think you have to force yourself in any way. Now go and enjoy your lunch." She ushered Jessica to the door and handed her over to the woman who was waiting for her, to escort her the short distance back to Small House.

Pausing for a moment before calling in her next patient, Dr. Consuelo made a note in Jessica's file. Of course, her problems stemmed directly from a bad sexual encounter. It was so very often the situation in such cases.

At their next session the doctor brought up the childhood incident. Jessica seemed to have turned a corner and was now sitting up straighter on the couch, not hiding her face behind her hands or staring down at the floor.

"Do you think you can tell me more about the childhood incident? Where you thought boys were all filthy creatures?"

"I was about nine and it was the boy next door. It was at my grandparents' house in Maine during the summer. I used to go up for at least six weeks every year and next door was a boy called George. We sort of grew up together – at least in the summers. We called ourselves kissing cousins, though we weren't related at all. Anyway, one day we had been out to the point, fishing or just messing around, and went back to my house where I asked if George could stay for lunch. Grandmere said yes and to amuse ourselves for a half hour or so and she'd call us when the food was ready. So we went out to my tent in the backyard to hang out." She paused, remembering that hot summer day and the light falling through the open tent flap to spill over her and George and her pile of Nancy Drew books. Somehow, sitting her safely in the doctor's office all these years later, made Jessica want to understand what had truly happened to her that day.

"Well," she continued slowly. "George wanted to play doctor and I didn't see why we shouldn't. I mean, I didn't really know what he meant but I usually went along with his plans. So he got me to take off my clothes and he pretended to examine me. It was kind of fun. And tingly."

The doctor managed to hide a smile.

"Then he got out of his clothes and he had a sort of – " she paused, embarrassed even now.

"A sort of?" the doctor prodded.

"A sort of erection. I mean he was only about eleven and it wasn't a very big one, he wasn't fully developed, you know." She paused again, eyeing the doctor.

"Yes, I know what you mean. Do go on."

"Well, he had this little one, sort of half stiff, and he asked me to touch it and I wanted to so I put out my hand...."

Jessica stopped, looking down again at her hands, which were folded in her lap.

"My grandmother chose that moment to come get us for lunch, and when she saw what I was about to do she let out a screech that could probably be heard to the end of the road and she hauled George and me out of that tent so fast it was amazing."

"What did your grandmother do?"

"Her scream got George's father over from next door and she turned George over to him, demanding he get the whipping of his life. Me, she hustled upstairs to her bedroom where she got out a special wooden spoon I had never seen and beat me with it until I screamed. She sent me to my room for the rest of the day telling me to think of my dreadful wickedness. So I went to my room and looked over at George's yard. He was hauled off into the stable and his father beat him with a stirrup leather. I saw him run across the lawn to his house, blubbering. But what happened next was even worse."

"What happened?'

"George's father, Mr. Parsons, came out of the barn a minute later and he looked almost – well – elated. Certainly he looked excited. And he got himself behind a big tree where he couldn't be seen from his house. Though he didn't realize I could see him from our house." She paused, turning red in the face. "It seemed so disgusting at the time, though of course I realized later that men did it all the time. But after beating your son to within an inch of his life..." She paused again, breathing hard.

"Tell me what Mr. Parsons did," the doctor urged. "I really need to know so I can help you." She guessed of course what came next, but needed to hear it from Jessica.

"Well," said Jessica, not looking the doctor in the face. "He took out his penis and it was enormous, red and ugly." She grimaced at the memory. "And he proceeded to masturbate until he ejaculated...right into the tree. I had never seen or imagined anything like this in my life and it revolted me. Maybe," she continued in a whisper so low the doctor had to lean forward to hear her, "it still does." She stopped suddenly, her whole body shaking at the remembrance.

Calmly, Dr. Consuelo passed her a Kleenex and waited until Jessica got herself under control. "I think that's enough for today," she said. "Certainly you were too young to witness such an act but, in normal circumstances masturbation is not revolting. I hope I am going to be able to convince you of that as we go along."

Again she ushered Jessica to the door to her waiting "constant companion" and added notes to the file before seeing her next patient.

Having finally opened up to her psychiatrist, Jessica also found she could participate more fully in the life of the patients at Sylvan Glade. She started swimming in the pool, late each afternoon, returning to Small House to change and eat dinner with the other residents. Soon she found herself 'promoted' to a room on the ground floor of Main House, where she joined a large number of the other residents for meals in the main dining room, a big step up from the very few diners in Small House. Here in the spacious room, conversation flowed and friendships were formed, at least the kind of friendships that lasted for the duration of the various lengths of the treatments the people were receiving. Here, also Jessica could also receive guests, reserve a small table for herself and her family members and those friends she had chosen to let know where she was when she had so abruptly disappeared from New York. Her mother had passed around the news that Jessica was exhausted from the divorce, and was coming to terms with her new life as a single woman, and needed a place to rest and recuperate and decide the future course of her life. If people were somewhat skeptical, so what? Sylvan Glade was famous for 'rest cures' --- whatever larger mental problem that might blanket and no one thought the less of Jessica for being there for a few months. For months it would become, as she delved deeper and ever deeper with Dr. Consuelo into her sexual fears.

Marcia was one of the first to take the train out from New York and the expensive taxi ride three or four miles out of the village to the lush and perfectly tended grounds of the hospital. She arrived just before lunch one Saturday, and was greeted on the steps of the Main House by Jessica who was actually looking forward to the visit.

She paid off the driver, wincing slightly at the cost, and tripped up the steps lightly. Marcia had debated what was an appropriate costume to visit the country, and had settled on leggings with a very short pea jacket and knee-high boots. She wore a bulky sweater that could have been a few inches longer, and carried a gigantic hold all,

"Whew," she exclaimed, "they sure keep this place a secret, don't they? I thought we'd never get her, but the cabbie seemed to know the way. Some posh digs you have her." She surveyed the expensive mahogany furniture and tasteful neutral colors of the room, and ran her hand over the exquisite fabric of the curtains. "I wouldn't mind being incarcerated myself in a joint like this."

Jessica was amused at her friend's exuberance. "Well, join me anytime," she said. "I'd love the company."

"Any available guys in here?" Marcia asked, examining her perfectly made up face in the mirror over the large bureau.

"Not so I've noticed. Anyway, who wants to hook up with a nut?" The 'like me' hung between them.

"At least any male nut here would have plenty of dough. Doesn't this place cost a fortune?"

"I don't know," Jessica answered truthfully. "My father's arranged all this, through insurance and I don't know what else."

Marcia had a pretty shrewd idea what 'what else' meant. Mr. Alden was footing the astronomical bill himself. But why not? He could afford it and Jessica was his only daughter.

"Let's take a walk before lunch," Jessica said. "I'll show you the campus."

"Campus?" asked Marcia.

"That's what we can the grounds," Jessica said. She ushered her guest out the door and through the hall.

"We're now in New Canaan," Jessica said. "But the other side of the road – where you turned in earlier – is actually Wilton. Makes for some confusion."

"New Canaan? Wilton?" Marcia was unfamiliar with Fairfield County.

"Two very conservative towns years ago," Jessica told her. "Very WASP fifty years ago. Not any more though."

Marcia wisely held her counsel. WASP seemed a very antiquated way of looking at the world, though, with her affiliation with the Episcopal Church, she realized that a lot of conservative people in New York wished that things were still as they used to be ... Louis Auchincloss style. She had read some of his books prior to her attempt, through Jessica, to break into what she perceived as New York 'society'.

Jessica took her around the buildings on the New Canaan side of the property, pointing them out as they passed: North, Small House, the doctors' offices building, then they carefully crossed the road to the Wilton side, where Jessica proudly showed off the building housing the recreational and occupational rooms, the huge main lounge and the indoor pool. "We all spend a lot of time here, it helps pass the time." In one of the occupational therapy rooms she showed Marcia a decoupage box she was making as a present for her mother. "I do a lot of needlepoint, too," she told her friend.

Needlepoint, decoupage, even with an indoor swimming pool Marcia was beginning to feel claustrophobic. "I'm starving," she announced, 'do you think lunch will be ready soon?"

"Right about now," Jessica told her. "Let's get back to the dining room. I've reserved a table for two so you don't have to talk to the other nuts here."

Marcia had to allow, when they had finished lunch, that at least Sylvan Glade had good food, though a Cosmopolitan first and a decent glass of wine would have helped. No such libation, however, was offered, for the obvious reason that so many residents were recovering alcoholics, and Marcia had to make do with iced tea. After wishing Jessica well and telling her to hurry back to town; she was sorely missed, Marcia breathed a sigh of relief as the taxi she had called arrived at the door. She waved happily to Jessica as it turned out of the grounds and headed back toward the charming village she had seen from the taxi window. As it bore her out to this godforsaken place where Jessica as incarcerated for heaven knew how long, Marcia decided she'd look into some of the fancy shops then catch the next train back to New York and civilization.

Having opened up to Dr. Consuelo about that long ago day in Maine, Jessica was now anxious to share more of her confused sexual hang ups with the doctor and began to look forward to her sessions. None of them seemed long enough; there was always something else to add, but at least the lines of communication were finally open between the doctor and her patient.

Monday morning they took up again in Maine.

What repercussions do you think this all had?" the doctor asked Jessica. "Where did things go from there?"

"Well, there was no one I could talk about it, no one I could tell," Jessica said slowly. "I mean, I was nine; who was I supposed to tell? My grandmother? In any case I was glued to the window. There was no way I could not have watched."

"Why do you think Mr. Parsons was masturbating after just whipping his son?" the doctor queried.

"I'm not sure. He looked – well – almost happy. Happy he had hurt George so badly that it aroused him. How could he have been happy?"

"Pleasure and pain often go hand in hand," the doctor explained. "Arousal can take place when someone causes great pain to another, as Mr. Parsons did to George. Or he could have been fantasizing about someone beating *him*, arousing him sexually."

"Well, it surely didn't make Grandmere aroused sexually, beating me I mean. She was the last person I'd expect to take any pleasure from this; unless you count doing her duty. She always did her duty and she had a very strict code of conduct. I just didn't know about the sex thing...I really didn't know I was doing anything wrong wanting to touch George."

"But you certainly knew your grandmother thought it was wrong," the doctor said, "or she would not have punished you so severely."

"Yes, and for years, literally years, she made me think sex was dirty...and bad." Jessica hung her head for a moment.

"Did anyone try to convince you otherwise?"

"Well, my mother did, a few months later. She called me into her room one day after school and tried to tell me that sex was beautiful, that if two people loved each other everything was alright, it was a really pleasurable experience for both partners and that she and my father had such a relationship."

"And did you believe her?"

"Not really. All I could think about was Mr. Parsons and his great red --- *thingy*. I just couldn't visualize my father pushing his own *thing* into my mother. It seemed too disgusting."

112

"Why do you refer to the penis as a *thing?*" the doctor wanted to know.

"Dunno." Jessica was clearly embarrassed.

"Okay, let's go on. When did you have your next sexual experience?"

"A few years later," Jessica said. "At a teenage dance in someone's party barn." She went on to describe the boy who asked her to dance, then led her to an empty box stall and tried to rape her. It all came back to her: the scratchy feel of his tweed jacket against her bare skin, the indignity of his getting his finger inside of her, his sour breath and raspy voice promising to make her come....she recoiled from the memory.

"He didn't manage to rape you?" The doctor was genuinely concerned now. Teenage gropings in a barn were one thing, but rape of a teenage girl was quite another.

"No, I was saved. And by guess who?"

"Who?" asked the doctor.

"By the boy next door in Maine. George Parsons. He happened to be at the party and knew the boy who took me into the horse stall was a rotter. He had a terrible reputation. So George thought to save the girl who had been chosen for that night's victim, never realizing it was the little girl from that long ago summer when they had played doctor in the side yard." She paused and a smile flickered at the corners of her mouth.

"So the same George who got you in so much trouble actually was the knight who saved you from a possible rape? How did that make you feel?" asked Dr. Consuelo.

"Like there was someone who actually cared for me. Who was there to protect me." Jessica thought for a moment. "Actually, it felt wonderful."

"And what happened to George?" asked the doctor.

"His girlfriend came up to collect him and he vanished into the crowd. I didn't see him again," she said quietly.

"And did you want to see him again?"

"Yes, I did."

"And did you ever? See him again?" the doctor wanted to know.

"No, and I never knew why he was at the party that night and whose guest he was. I mean, it was in Darien and George lived in Boston. He must have gone with someone whose family actually lived there. But I don't know who."

"Did you ever try to find out where George was?" asked the doctor. "You seem to have had a connected circle of friends."

"I sort of hoped George would find me," Jessica said. "And he never did, so I thought he wasn't interested."

The session ended, only this time Jessica could walk by herself back to the Maine House; the "constant companion's" duties had ended a few days before, which as a sign of much progress Jessica's recovery.

The following day Dr. Consuelo decided to confront this dichotomy of pain/pleasure with her patient, so when Jessica was comfortably seated on the sofa, she plunged in.

"Jessica, have you ever thought of the relationship to pleasure and pain? Sometimes they turn out to be the two sides of the same coin. If the seat of pleasure starts in the groin and the seat of pain on the buttocks, can you see how closely connected these two places are?"

"Yes, I guess so," Jessica said. "I know some couples enjoy spanking and even caning each other during sex. I never understood why, though."

Dr. Consuelo smiled encouragingly. "I think I can explain this to you," she said. "And maybe this will help you understand why you seem so afraid of sex. You have experienced the painful part only, but pain can bring pleasure and pleasure, pain."

Jessica regarded her doctor expectantly. Maybe finally she would understand what her friends took for granted: loving and healthy and yes, hot, sex too. She sincerely hoped so.

"Your grandmother caused you great pain in conjunction with your first sexual curiosity, trying to touch George's genitals. So, as a child you perceived all sex to be wrong, dirty and, due to the beating, painful.

114

You connected your punishment as the outcome of your experience with George; hence, all such experiences would never bring any pleasure but only pain. And your experience in the barn took a similar path: you didn't want the boy to touch you sexually but he did anyway, and you experienced great shame, which you equated with pain. Then the same George came along and gave you pleasure by saving you from almost certain rape. But he went away, making you feel pain again at what you perceived as his abandonment. Does any of this make sense to you, Jessica?"

"I think so," Jessica said. "But keep going, please. I still don't see the connection between pain and pleasure, I really don't."

"Why don't we explore this as a fresh topic tomorrow," said Dr. Consuelo. "I want to have enough time to go into it thoroughly." She ushered Jessica to the door and watched, through a window, her swing down the path back to Main House.

The next morning Jessica was early for her appointment and when ushered into the doctor's office settled herself immediately on the couch, looking expectant.

Dr. Consuelo took her usual chair. "The sensations of pain and pleasure are very closely related," she began, "and they tie into love and sex and sometimes even violence, which is not a good thing. But all these are stimulants which cause the release of chemicals and hormones in the human body, which in turn affect how we perceive these sensations. Sometimes endorphins which are released during periods of pain turn these sensations into feelings of pleasure, just as epinephrine and melatonin in pain can also cause a kind of rush that the body perceives as pleasurable. Biological responses in humans are actually very similar in both pleasurable and painful experiences, hence are very closely related."

"I guess I see what you are getting at," Jessica said, "but so far I haven't experienced any of the pleasure you describe through pain. It's really been pretty much all pain. Is there something wrong with me?"

"Not at all," the doctor was hasty to confirm. "We just have to tweak your responses as it were, and find out why anything sexual seems to cause nothing *but* pain. Was your husband considerate of you sexually?"

Jessica's mouth twisted into a wry grimace. "Anything but. It was all for his pleasure, and he didn't care how much pain he caused me. He was a homosexual, you know."

Dr. Consuelo did not know, but she kept her face impassive. Here, finally, was the cause of all of Jessica's lack of sexual interest, her remembrance of nothing but pain in both punishment and sexual encounters. "Tell me about it," she said gently. "All about it. Take your time." She sat back, pen poised over her pad.

"I guess it all started right after we met. A lot of boys had sort of pawed me...not really knowing what they were doing, I guess...but Trevor seemed different somehow, only I didn't get just how different he really was. He didn't paw at me, he was smooth and experienced and somehow very respectful."

"Respectful?"

"Sort of restrained, as if he didn't want to hurt me or frighten me ..." Jessica paused not quite sure of what she was saying.

Dr. Consuelo did not interrupt again, leaving Jessica time to gather her wits and continue on with her story.

"We met skiing in Stowe," she said, "but he lived in New York and I was at Barnard, so when we got back we started seeing a lot of each other. He told me I was just what he wanted in a wife: beauty, brains and breeding. I think that's a line from *Rebecca*. Anyway it as flattering to me and I really liked him. So his campaign to get me worked, and all along I waited for him to make his move...you know, sleep with me, but it didn't happen. I was too embarrassed to tell this to anyone, not my mother or any of my friends. They all seemed to be having great sex and all I was getting was a sloppy good night kiss and some pretty intense stimulation below the waist, never intercourse. I waited and waited, but nothing more."

116

"Did you want to have sex with Trevor?"

"I'm pretty sure I did. I figured he was going to ask me to marry him sometime and we ought to know if we were compatible sexually. And he did ask me and I said yes and I asked him if he was going to sleep with me now. He said he wanted to save that until we were really truly married but he could satisfy me without intercourse. It was all so unromantic it turned me off, but I agreed." She gave a disgusted moue and stopped speaking.

"And how did he satisfy you? Did you enjoy it?" the doctor prodded.

"He put me on the couch, no preliminaries really, just a squeeze of my boobs, sort of perfunctorily, then he flipped up my skirt and pulled down my underwear. He took two fingers and pushed them inside of me and used his thumb to rub my – uh – clitoris. He knew exactly what he was doing and it didn't exactly hurt, but it wasn't very pleasant either. But he gave me a sort of orgasm, at least I guess that is what it was. I'd never had the experience before so I didn't really know what to expect. But as soon as it happened he flipped back my skirt and told me that we still had the real thing to look forward to, and I must be patient. I thought it was because he loved me." She snorted. "Some love. But I found that out later."

"What about Trevor? Did he satisfy himself?"

"Oh, yes," Jessica said. "He took his penis and put it in my hand and made me masturbate him until he came. He even got out his handkerchief and covered himself. Guess he didn't want his sperm all over the couch. It was all so clinical, there was no feeling attached at all."

"There was nothing mutual about any of this," the doctor observed.

"Exactly. But I still thought he really wanted to save the best for the night we were married. Little did I know."

"Tell me."

"Well after the reception we went to the Plaza. He had been drinking pretty heavily at the reception, but I thought that might be wedding nerves. Anyway, he had French 75's at the hotel, no food, and he soon staggered into the bedroom and passed out across the bed. That was my wedding night." She paused again, remembering the disgust with which she had viewed her groom, snoring on the satin spread, still fully dressed in cutaway and gray silk tie.

"Did things get any better after you got off on your honeymoon?"

"No," said Jessica flatly. "It took him three more days to get up the nerve for the big act, then he just sort of shoved it into me one night when I was least expecting him. I didn't even have time to protest. It hurt like hell. I was dry, not expecting him, and he broke my hymen sphincter right away, which bled pretty badly. He looked revolted at the sight of that blood and got a big towel from the bathroom to put over it. I guess that was our official wedding night."

Dr. Consuelo looked sympathetic but said nothing, waiting for Jessica to tell more of the story.

"I kind of hoped things would get better, but instead they got worse," the young woman continued. "There was almost never any face to face interaction; he always wanted to take me from behind, and made me bend over everything from the side of the bed, to chairs and even once on his office desk. That one was probably to prove to his fellow workers what a big stud he was. I'm sure everyone in the office knew what we were doing behind that locked door. He liked to give me a few good slaps on the backside while he was doing all this, even in the office, which I am sure could be heard through the door. It was like he was saying 'mine, all mine, and I can do anything with her I want.' I still didn't know that he was homosexual, I just thought he had some pretty kinky ideas about sex."

"It all sounds pretty bad," the doctor observed. "Did you ever think of getting any sort of help, talking to someone?"

"I asked him once or twice if we couldn't go to a marriage counselor," Jessica said, "but each time he said our sex life was none of anyone's business but our own. Though it was really his own. I wasn't really any part of it; everything was for his pleasure.

The doctor made a cluck of sympathy."

"Wait," said Jessica. "There's more."

The doctor waited patiently.

"He seemed to take such pleasure in humiliating me. He bought me the most outlandish clothes, things I would never have bought myself, and made me wear them. Awful dresses that were cut down practically to the naval in front or showing the beginning of my crack in back. None with any underwear. Then he'd put his hand down my front at a party so everyone knew he was fondling my breast, or down my backside. It was almost like having sex in public."

"He wanted to shame you to prove his dominance over you," said the doctor.

"And how. He'd take me into peoples' bathrooms, bend me over the tub and give himself a quick orgasm, then stroll out calmly doing up his fly, once again so everyone would think he was a big stud. Back at home things got even worse. We'd come in from a dance or a party and he'd make me get naked and get into the tub. It was so cold, but I soon found out what was coming! He'd take out his cock, oh so casually, stand over me and let loose, in my face, in my hair, everywhere. When he was finished he'd stroll out and after I cleaned myself and the tub, I'd find him snoring away in bed."

Even the doctor grimaced.

"I'm actually coming to the piece de resistance," Jessica continued steadily. Once having gotten started she was determined to get this over with, tell the doctor everything and hope it would somehow diminish in the overwhelming hold her husband's sexuality had had on her.

"One night, I think we had been married for only a few months," she began, "he came home from the office and he seemed really horny. He barely got in the front door when he grabbed me and marched me down to the bedroom. I had no idea what was coming but I knew it wasn't going to be good. He made me undress him, admiring him all the way, then demanded I get out of my clothes and lie down on the bed,

119

which I did. He told me to flip over on my stomach, which I did also. Then…" she paused, almost unable to go on, then finished in a rush, "he slammed his enormous hard on, with no preliminaries whatsoever, into my anus. I thought I was going to pass out from the pain and naturally I started bleeding all over him and the bed, everyplace. He pulled out in a hurry, which hurt as much as going in and actually looked just a little chagrinned. He grabbed a towel from the bathroom and shoved it up against my backside, and I told him to call 911. That I needed to get to the hospital. I could tell he was scared, but he did what I asked. Then he told me that if I ever said how this had happened he would kill me. That I was to say we had been fooling around and this was a big mistake. We were just experimenting and things had gone wrong. And he went out of the room and waited in the front hall for the paramedics and the ambulance which came and carted me off to Lenox Hill where they stitched me up and kept me overnight. They tried to get me to say my husband had abused me but I didn't, for some reason. Maybe I was afraid it would get out how badly he had been treating me, I don't know. But the doctor told me if I came in again in this condition he would file charges against Trevor himself. When I got home again I told this to Trevor, and he never did it again. But when he was pissed at me he'd finger my anus and tell me if I didn't fly right he'd cornhole me just like he had before. I had no way of knowing if he meant it or not. Then a few months later I came home unexpectedly and found him in bed with our best man. And that was when I finally got the message." Jessica was ashen faced, but still calm as she finished her story.

Dr. Consuelo was pretty white herself as this frightening story of one human being's inhumanity came to a close. She reached over and took one of Jessica's hands in her own, and held it tightly for a moment.

"Are you alright?" she asked gently.

"Actually, I feel better. I've never told that story to anyone before. It's been like a dank miasma hanging over my head but now you know, and nobody else does, I actually feel a little better.

120

"Catharsis," murmured the doctor. "But Jessica, you *can* overcome all this. You can make a loving connection with a man. They aren't all like Trevor, believe you me. You just need to find someone you trust completely, someone you could love. I'll be here every step of the way to help you along."

Jessica's eyes were glistening with unshed tears. "Thank you," she said simply. "You have no idea how much this means to me."

Today, after seeing Jessica out, the doctor held up her next patient for fifteen minutes while she sat alone in her office. Inwardly she was railing against the monster that had so injured this fragile young woman.

Thanksgiving had come and gone again, and New Yorkers were gearing up for Christmas. Granted, the store windows had been full of yuletide goodies practically since Halloween, but in the brisk days of early December New Yorkers seemed to have even more spring in their step, even more verve and enthusiasm as they charged up Madison and down Fifth in search of the perfect Christmas presents.

Marcia had gone out to a very expensive and not very good Thanksgiving dinner with some women friends from her office who, like her, were not going home anywhere for the holiday. Now Christmas loomed like a blank day in the middle of the festive season. Jessica solved that by inviting her for Christmas dinner at her parents' Gracie Square apartment, though not for present opening in the morning and the midnight church service Christmas Eve, both of which were strictly family events. But Marcia was grateful to be included at all, happy that Jessica considered her a good enough friend to share the holiday with the Alden family especially as Jessica was still a patient at Sylvan Glade, albeit with going home privileges.

Though told not to arrive with presents, she pondered long and hard about some token to give, something to show how much she appreciated the hospitality being extended to her. Finally she came up with just the right present: monogrammed bridge cards from Tiffany and matching score pads. Even though she figured the Aldens probably had masses of cards, since they played bridge almost constantly according to Jessica, another set would not go amiss. And so, that cold and blustery Christmas Day, when the taxi turned into the charming little dead end street running past the three large apartment buildings down to the East River and let Marcia off, she was swinging the unmistakable robin's egg blue shopping bag over her arm.

She wasn't sure whether she should wish the doorman a Merry Christmas; maybe he wasn't Christian and it would be rude? So she confined herself to a bright 'good morning' flashing her best smile as the man helped her out of the taxi.

Upstairs, the Alden apartment was a riot of Christmas decoration but all of it, Marcia noticed, was real. The pine garlands, twisted around red ribbons, gave off a sharp scent of the woods, twined up the staircase and draped over each doorway on the main floor. Placed before the long windows in the living room was a giant Norway spruce, rising from floor to ceiling, decorated with hundreds and hundreds of ornaments which, to Marcia's untrained eyes, looked somewhat tatty and old. There was not a single glass ball, not one piece of tinsel, though there were several long paper chains of various hues. Stars were cut out of silver paper and hung here and there, haphazardly all over the tree, and red and green lights twinkled through the branches.

Marcia was greeted cordially by both the Aldens, then introduced to Jessica's brother and sister-in-law, in from his bank job in London for the holidays, together with their two enchanting little boys, who were tussling over the ownership of a large fire engine.

Jessica drew her friend to the tree and started pointing out some of the ornaments: "I made this in second grade," she said, indicating a lopsided star. "And Matthew," she gestured toward her brother, "made this shepherd in shop about age ten." Her fingers caressed a little wooden man, obviously a shepherd, painted garishly in fading paint. "I got these in Austria when I was skiing," Jessica pointed to a set of somewhat ratty straw ornaments, "and this coronation coach I found in London." She pointed out a replica of he coach, made of cloth of gold.

Suddenly, Marcia got it. These ornaments had been collected over the years, and probably came from many countries around the world, all beloved souvenirs and remembrances of Christmases past. If she had to do a tree she probably would have gone out to Duane Reed or someplace and bought boxes of cheap Christmas balls and hung the tree with foil tinsel. Not p.c. she realized, but how long would it take to collect the sort of ornaments on this tree? Probably several lifetimes.

The Tiffany bag was presented to Mrs. Alden, who drew forth the cards with exclamations of delight. "See, Spencer," she said to her husband. "We can throw out those disgusting cards now to which you seem so attached. Clean cards at last! Thank you Marcia." She gave the young woman a quick hug, which thrilled Marcia down to her core. She was being accepted, by Jessica's parents. Truly this was a special Christmas.

Cocktails were served before Christmas dinner, martinis for Mr. Alden and Matthew, while the ladies all contented themselves with a glass of fine white Burgundy. They chatted over pate and a selection of cheeses, then Mrs. Alden announced lunch, and led the way into the adjoining dining room.

Here, too, Christmas decorations proliferated, with the piece de resistance being massed red roses, in a silver bowl, set off by delicate sprays of baby's breath and white orchids. Marcia vowed to take a flower arranging course in the New Year for surely flowers expressed one's personality and dedication to the art of entertaining. This Christmas was another eye opener to her somewhat arid life, one she hoped to bolster as time went on.

Christmas dinner was a bountiful meal starting with chowder, followed by a rib roast, surrounded by roast potatoes, onions and carrots, with a side dish of fresh peas, a large knob of butter melting on top, and creamed spinach. Fluffy rolls protruded from a pristine white napkin, in a filigree silver basket, and horseradish sauce was passed in what surely must be a very old gravy dish. Chateau Petrus was served with the meal, a wine with which Marcia was not familiar. When she priced it a few days later at Sherry's, she almost fainted, glad she had not gulped it down like Yellowtail. Indeed, throughout the meal she took her cue from Jessica, to her right, and Mrs. Alden, at the head of the table, wiping only the corners of her mouth daintily with her napkin, placing her knife and fork at exactly the five o'clock position when she had finished. Her offer to help with the serving and, later with the dishes, was refused: she was a guest and was only there to enjoy herself. She sank back in her somewhat creaky chair with its needlepoint cover, and gave over to the pleasure of this special afternoon.

Dessert was plum pudding, flamed in the kitchen and brought in burning, apple – and for some reason – key lime pies.

Jessica explained the rather untraditional dessert. "Some guest brought one many years ago and it sold better than all the other desserts combined. That's why we sill have it," she explained, as she put the pie before Marcia. "Would you cut it for us? And who wants a piece?" Several hands went up and Marcia carefully cut the pie, making sure all the pieces were more or less equal and not too big.

They adjourned for coffee in the library, and Mrs. Alden brought out a tray of liqueurs. "I know no one drinks this stuff any more," she said, "But once in a great while I like to offer these. They seem to go so well after such a small meal." She laughed, having made a little joke.

"Some small meal," Barbara, Joan Alden exclaimed. "But as long as you've brought out this stuff I'd love Benedictine."

"Coming right up," her father in law announced. "And what about you, Marcia. Can I sell you some of this poison, too?"

I'll have Benedictine, too," said Marcia, careful to imitate Joan's pronunciation. She took the tiny glass and brought it up to her lips, taking a small sip. Sweet and sticky, but not unpleasant. She was unfamiliar with most of bottles on Spencer Alden's tray; the people she knew drank brandy – she corrected her thinking: cognac – after dinner, if they drank anything. But live and learn. She had certainly learned a

124

tremendous amount from her friendship with Jessica; now Jessica's parents had given her a glimpse of how the upper crust must have lived twenty five or thirty years ago. She filed away this knowledge for future reference, wondering if this style of life was familiar to Pedro, then realized with a start she had not given Pedro a thought until this very minute.

The luncheon broke up around five, and Jessica offered to walk Marcia back to her apartment, before going returning to Gracie Square for the night. She certainly could use the exercise after the huge meal they had just consumed. Everyone kissed everyone else goodbye and the two young women turned out of the building and strolled over to East End Avenue.

"That's the Chapin School," Jessica told her, pointing to a large and handsome brick building across the avenue. Years ago, so Mother tells me, the building next door wasn't there and it was the school tennis court. Can you imagine? And behind the buildings on Gracie Square were empty lots which used to be frozen for skating in the winter. Must have been a whole different world then."

Marcia gave a little sigh for the world that had been, then matched her stride with her friend's as they continued west toward home.

At Marcia's building they paused. "Want to come up for some coffee? Or some tea? Or even another drink?" she asked

"Not another drink," Jessica laughed. "I'd fall over for sure and you'd have to put me to bed. But I'd love to come up for a few minutes."

Upstairs Jessica threw herself dramatically on the couch, while Marcia checked the answering machine on the kitchen counter. There was one from a man with a smooth, sexy voice, traces of a Spanish accent overlaying. He wished Marcia the best Christmas ever, saying he could not wait to see her early in the New Year.

Jessica was intrigued. "That the mystery man? He sounds like sex on wheels."

"You better believe it," Marcia told her. "But, oh, Jessica! I want to be with him all the time and that is not possible. He's married and he's from Colombia. But he and his wife have an arrangement, so he tells me. And he's never going to be available; they are ardent Catholics."

"Can you bear to have him, sometimes rather than never, knowing all this?"

Marcia thought for a moment. "Yes, he means everything to me. I can't wait for his visits, can't wait to tear his clothes off, and have him tear off mine. But there's more than that. It isn't just sex," she added defensively.

"Well, I'm hoping to find my long ago 'kissing cousin'. You seem to be hoping for someone special. We both want something we don't have."

"And how."

"And I hope I'm not expecting too much," said Jessica. I mean, George may be married and have three children by now. Or be bald. Or have no interest in me if we do meet up again. But somehow I hope none of those things is true." She stared pensively out of Marcia's window, where snow was just starting to fall over New York.

"Oh," breathed Marcia, "how romantic. Snow on Christmas night. Wouldn't it be wonderful to be walking through it somewhere with a man you love?"

"Yes, it would," agreed Jessica.

When she left for home a half hour later, the snow was still falling, silently, peacefully, covering all the grime and dirt of the huge city with a clean and shining mantle of white. Jessica walked slowly along, trying to feel what it would be like if, by some miracle, George should appear and she would stroll home, hand in hand, with him. And when they got home they would.... Her musings, as always ended here. They would do what? Make out? End up on the living room couch having sex? Would it be any different for her than any other time? And would Marcia really find fulfillment with someone who was, after all, the property of another woman? She continued to turn all this over in her mind as she trudged through then now swirling drifts toward home.

.

Chapter Eight

After Sylvan Glade

Having finally opened up to Dr. Consuelo, and told her of all the degradation suffered at Trevor's hands, Jessica started to get well. She looked forward to the activities offered by the hospital, and thought about leaving and going out into the real world.

While pleased by her patient's progress, the doctor had reservations about sending Jessica forth to live on her own and cope with whatever life had in store for her. True, too much time within the safety of the hospital, where the real world was not allowed to intrude, was not good. Nor was dismissal too soon. At least Jessica's family had the funds to keep her here as long as needed, so Dr. Consuelo laid her plans and conferred with the board of psychiatrists who met weekly to share their respective patients' progress.

One Monday morning the doctor shared the results of the weekly meeting with Jessica.

"We think you have made wonderful progress," she said, "and we are all proud of you. We do think you need some time to ease back into the world, which, as you know, can be a dangerous place. Especially for people like you who are extremely trusting of those around you."

"And how." Jessica tried to make a small joke.

"We want you to carefully evaluate all your friendships, both old friends and any new ones you may make, and ensure they are not out to use you or get anything from you. We don't want you wounded again, especially not the way you were by Trevor."

"I must have been a fool to trust him at all," Jessica said. "But he seemed to caring, so loving...at least at the beginning."

"So are a lot of people, sadly," said the doctor. "So many want to form relationships for what they can get out of them, not for what they can put in. Sometimes it's hard to tell these people from real friends."

"I'll be careful," Jessica promised.

"I know you will," Dr. Consuelo said. "So what I am going to suggest is that, for present, you remain a weekly resident here, and go out on weekends. You might want to start by going home to your parents. I know how much they love you and how supportive they are of you. They only want the best. You are indeed lucky to have two parents like yours."

"I know," Jessica whispered, looking back over the years, remembering the many wonderful things her parents had done for her. She was indeed lucky to have them, and would be happy to go out of Sylvan Glade for weekends at the spacious apartment on Gracie Square. It was late winter and New York would soon be shaking off the long drab days and preparing for spring. There would be new exhibits at the museums new plays would be opening on Broadway. There were new restaurants to be tried and, even new friends to make. She would draw up a list of all friends and acquaintances, maybe run it by Dr. Consuelo, see who she would contact once she was out again in the real world. And if things got rough, she always had the safety net of her room back here in Main House, and the familiar routine of the hospital to give structure to her days.

Barbara Alden drove up the following Friday after lunch to take Jessica back with her to New York. Her heart was lighter than it had been in many months; Jessica was getting better. She would make it. Mothers always knew these things. She pulled up in the parking lot adjacent to Main House and stood for a moment, surveying the acres of the campus that has housed her beloved daughter these last several months, drinking in the peace and quiet of the Connecticut countryside pristine under a white mantle of late winter snow.

Jessica was waiting, small suitcase packed, eyes bright.

"Hey, I'm getting sprung. At last!" She said, greeting her mother with a hearty kiss. "Can't wait to get back to civilization."

Her mother hugged her, hard. "I can't wait to take you there. Shall we?" She led the way out the door and back to the car.

All the way back to New York on the Merritt Parkway mother and daughter chatted animatedly, Barbara telling her child what was going on in New York and what she had planned for the weekend visit: dinner at home, tickets to 'Jersey Boys' for the Saturday matinee, with lunch first or dinner afterward at Sardi's, Jessica's choice. Sunday she had left free for Jessica to invite any friends over for brunch at the apartment, which would be a special meal of eggs Benedict and mimosas, both family favorites. Barbara hoped the weekend plans met with Jessica's approval, which the daughter heartily agreed to. Mother, it seemed, had arranged a perfect weekend. It only needed Jessica to decide who, if anyone, she wanted to have over Sunday. Perhaps Marcia, who had been kind enough to visit her, and perhaps Debbie Coates as well, an old friend from her school days who had emailed and sent cards, but not visited. Let her other friends – if indeed that is what they were – wait awhile to be invited. Few had contacted her during her stay at Sylvan Glade; were they the false friends about whom she and Dr. Consuelo had spoken? She would think about that later. Right now they were pulling up to the canopy of the building and John, the faithful man who had guarded the door since Jessica's youth, sprang forward to open the door and welcome her home.

And welcome home it was! From the shepherd's pie for Friday dinner – a favorite since childhood – to lunch at Sardis where she and her parents were given their usual table, through the spectacular production of 'Jersey Boys' which somehow she had missed seeing, everything went like clockwork. Jessica began to realize how much she had missed, both as Trevor's wife and as a patient at Sylvan Glade.

Sunday morning Spencer Alden made himself scarce, driving up to Riverdale for a tennis game and lunch, figuring he would be blight on a ladies lunch. Barbara and Jessica happily repaired to the kitchen to make the eggs Benedict, Jessica whipping up a large pot of hollandaise, Barbara laying out the English muffins and sautéing some ham slices to put under the eggs. They put out the orange juice and champagne for the mimosas, as well as a large pitcher of iced tea for those who preferred not to drink at lunch. When the doorbell rang, at precisely twelve thirty, they had the table laid with the beautiful organdie mats and napkins, brought back one Italian trip from La Perla on the Island of Burano, off Venice, silver, Baccarat wine glasses and a centerpiece of early spring tulips, beautifully arranged by Barbara.

Mother and daughter went to the door together to greet their guests.

Both young women blew in on clouds of scent: the more delicate Miss Dior for Debbie, more sophisticated Fracas for Marcia. They embraced their friend, then, more gingerly, her mother, who, surprisingly, hugged back – hard. Marcia had only met Jessica's mother at the wonderful Christmas celebration, while Debbie had grown up with Jessica, and their families were firm friends. Both had thought Barbara Alden somewhat standoffish, but in the instance of welcoming Jessica home from Sylvan Glade, all were true sisters under the skin.

In the living room, over the mimosas, conversation flowed freely.

"You look wonderful," Jessica, Debbie exclaimed. "Maybe we all need a trip to Sylvan Glade. God knows, I could use some down time." She was newly admitted to the bar and way down at the bottom of the totem pole at her enormous law firm, where her father had gotten her a place on graduation. She worked long, hard hours, and this lovely late winter afternoon was happy to relax in the Aldens' spacious and beautifully decorated living room, away from the rigors of the law for a few hours.

"Mrs. Alden" she almost gushed. "You've changed the color of the curtains. I really like that salmon. Makes the whole room look different."

Marcia, who had never seen the room with any other curtains, remained silent. Always she felt left out when Jessica and her crowd discussed events, people and places in which she had had no part. They were a close knit group, as most of them had known each other since childhood, visiting each other's houses, going to each other's parties, in general, traveling around in one large crowd. The crowd to which Marcia so desperately wanted to belong.

Barbara Alden sensed the young woman's exclusion, and sought to change it.

"Marcia," she said. "You haven't seen the whole apartment, just these few front rooms when you were here for Christmas. That made Debbie sit up and take notice: a Christmas guest had to be a very special friend indeed. Can I show the rest to you now? And maybe you'd help me get lunch on the table, while these two flutterbudgets talk."

Marcia rose, glad to be of help and thrilled to be given a tour of the home where Jessica had grown up. She made polite murmurs while Barbara led her through the dining room, up the curving stairs of the duplex and down the long bedroom hall where Marcia counted at least four bedrooms – maybe one was a maid's room? But no: that chamber and small bath were off the little hallway that separated the dining room from the huge kitchen, gleaming with the most modern of appliances and spotlessly clean. You could eat off the floor here, Marcia decided, so unlike her own Pullman kitchen in the walk up only a few blocks away, always with counters in need of wiping off and often dishes were left in the sink. She vowed to do better in the future and was pleased she had been selected to carry in the beautiful Spode plates, the chilled bottle of white wine and the large wooden salad bowl, seasoned to perfection with many years of use. She noted again, she had at Christmas, the quality of everything she saw and touched, awed by the way in which Jessica had been brought up. The settings for the dining room table had been even more formal for Christmas dinner. Maybe someday she, too, could have some of these lovely things. In the meantime, she was simply happy to be included in this intimate lunch party.

132

"Hey," said Debbie when they were seated and the salad was going around. "I'm having a few people for lunch next Saturday, then we're going to that new exhibit at the Morgan Library. I'd love it if you can come, too," she hastily added, turning to Marcia. "Let me have your email, will you, for future use." She turned to Barbara Alden. "I bet you think we are really lazy, not sending real invitations for anything these days. But email's so much quicker and we can send to a lot of people at once."

"Not at all," Barbara replied. "I use it myself for almost everything, too. Except sympathy notes. And wedding invitations." She added the last almost reluctantly, thinking of the high pile of ivory invitations, with double envelopes and reply cards from Cartier, which she had painstakingly addressed in her flowing script only a few years before. Invitations to Jessica's wedding to Trevor. She hoped bringing this up was not upsetting to her daughter.

Jessica surprised her. "Yup, the marriage from Hell. But Mother did a spectacular job on the wedding, didn't you, Mum? It was one over the top party. If ever I marry again it will be off to a Justice of the Peace. No more big weddings for me!"

Barbara breathed a sigh of relief. Maybe Jessica really had turned the corner. Maybe soon she would be out of Sylvan Glade for good.

Debbie had to leave soon after lunch, telling everyone she looked forward to seeing them the following Saturday, and, when Jessica and Marcia volunteered to clean up, Barbara retired to her room. Let the girls chat without her hovering over them. At first she had been somewhat wary of Jessica's new friendship with a young woman whom none of them knew. But it was the 2010's and it was time, she, Barbara, caught up with the ways of this new world. Certainly Marcia had given Jessica every encouragement while in Sylvan Glade. Maybe she would be good for her daughter now she was about to be discharged.

In the kitchen Jessica speedily and carelessly piled the dishes in the sink and turned on the hot water. Marcia would have given more care, had the lunch service belonged to her. Maybe this is the way really rich people operated, things were just things and expendable. Maybe she should watch and learn.

"Your mother's great," she told Jessica. "She seems really nice."

"Oh, she is," Jessica agreed. "We are good pals. She never bugs me and she's always on my side."

Marcia thought of the drunken sot who had raised her, in a shabby, dirty house on a back street in Detroit, and shuddered slightly. Why had not she had the same privileges as Jessica, who seemed to take them so lightly and for granted?

"You're lucky," Marcia said. "And your mother was so nice to me…I mean showing me the apartment and all."

"I could tell she liked you," Jessica said, "and you were dear to put up with the guided tour. Everyone doesn't get that, by the way, only people Mother thinks would appreciate seeing the place."

"Well, it was fun seeing where you grew up. Debbie seems nice, too, and I appreciate her including me next weekend."

"Debbie's always entertaining. Get on her guest list and you are bound to be kept busy. I don't know how she does it what with the new legal job. But she does, somehow. I think she had a direct line to Dean and DeLuca and they just send everything up, ready to go."

From what little she knew of Dean and DeLuca, Marcia realized she was a long way from being able to 'order up' anything she wanted; it was much too expensive. And her apartment was not up to much entertaining. She'd have to think of a way to repay invitations; she'd put her mind to it.

"Hey, Jessica," she said, changing the subject. Any neat guys at Sylvan Glade? Any nooky going on behind the doctors' backs?"

Jessica actually smiled. "Not for me. I don't know about other people. Lots of them were on tranquilizers and probably that kept down their libidos. And there were masses of staff people wandering around all over the place. I don't think there was much privacy anywhere."

"You must be awfully horny," Marcia observed.

Jessica turned from the sink to face her friend. "Actually not," she said. "And please don't repeat this to a soul. That's partly why I am in there," she told Marcia. "I've got sexual hang-ups that really need to be taken care of. Dr. Consuelo and I are working on them."

Having admitted this much, she turned back to the sink, and sank her rubber gloved hands back into the soapy water.

God almighty! thought Marcia. *Who would have known?* But it went a long way toward explaining Jessica to Marcia. She put her hand, reassuringly, on Jessica's arm. "Cross my heart and hope to die," she said, "I promise never to let on what you just told me." And she never did. Being so closely in Jessica's confidence meant the world to this woman, who had once meant to use Jessica to her own advantage, now counted her as a dear friend. And if she didn't like sex now, well, maybe there was hope for her down the road. Marcia inwardly shrank, remembering the bridge game at Marvin's and the trio she had tried to arrange for afterward. In future she'd keep her sexual desires to herself and let Jessica do the same. Maybe the poor woman would get lucky and find the right man. If she, Marcia, had wanted to hook up with most of the men she met, it was entirely her own business. That, however, was before the advent of Pedro. But Jessica's lack of any such desire was also her own business and Marcia vowed, in future, to keep the two entirely separate.

During the following week at Sylvan Glade, Jessica explored with Dr. Consuelo how best to find the friends who would be supportive, and jettison those who were not. She told the doctor about the Sunday lunch party, describing the two friends whom she had invited.

"Debbie, you know, and I have been friends forever. Since first grade, maybe even before that in the playground. Yes, she was one of the only little girls I knew when I was deposited in that homeroom for my first day of school. All those other little children running around in their uniforms, and me standing at the door afraid to go in. Then I saw Debbie, and she came over to me and took me over to join in a game, and I was okay. We've giggled over boys and hair and argued about what to wear to which event and even been bridesmaids in each other's weddings. She's that kind of friend. I think she has my best interests at heart. If she doesn't she's sure making an effort to be kind. She invited me to a lunch party next weekend, Marcia, too."

"Tell me about Marcia."

"She's certainly a new friend. She was nice enough to invite me to lunch right after I was divorced. Some of my other friends, I think, were trying to decide to go with me or with Trevor. But she jumped right in and offered me her friendship. She came to visit me, here, a few weeks ago. None of my other friends made the effort. Too busy I guess."

Dr. Consuelo had some thoughts about 'friends' who were too busy to visit, but kept them to herself.

"And she started me back on bridge. She got up a game at a man friend's apartment with an older woman in the building. It was a good game but the man seemed to think Marcia – and I – wanted sex afterward. I left in a hurry, believe me, and Marcia came right behind me."

"Does this Marcia seem interested in men?"

"Very," Jessica actually grinned. "And she seemed to hope I'd go along, but I haven't --- yet," she added slowly.

"Does Marcia's obvious interest in sex bother you?" the doctor asked.

"Not really. Not if she doesn't try to involve me. She can do her thing and I can do mine. I actually told her I was in here for sexual hangups when we had lunch last week."

"Then she must be one of the people you trust," said Dr. Consuelo.

"You know, she must be. It's kind of nice that I think I can."

"I hope so," said the doctor.

The next Saturday dawned crisp and clear, a perfect day, thought Jessica, to walk the fifteen or so blocks from her parent's to Debbie's in Turtle Bay. She swung off down Gracie Square toward East End Avenue, striding confidently along, as if she owned the world. It was a heady feeling, one she had not experienced for a long time.

At Debbie's, her husband, Blake, was just leaving as Jessica rang the bell.

"Thought I'd leave you girls to gossip without me around. I'd hate to think what you might be saying about me! Gosh, Jessica, you look great! Hope we see more of you now you are back in New York." And, with a gentle kiss on each of Jessica's cheeks, he made his departure.

"Nice husband," Jessica commented to her hostess.

"Yup. I did well. And there *will* be someone for you, I'm sure of it. Hey, we all make mistakes sometimes."

"I sure made a huge one."

"Well, it can be rectified." She led Jessica into the large living room, where a group of six young women, all of whom Jessica knew, awaited her. There were cries of delight all around, with much air kissing of cheeks. The bell went again, and Debbie opened the door to Marcia, who stood, a bit uncertainly on the mat, a florist's bunch of roses in her hand.

"Oh, how lovely!" exclaimed Debbie. "You shouldn't have. But thank you, just let me put these in water. Please go on in." She indicated the archway to the living room then vanished into the kitchen, leaving Marcia standing uncertainly in the front hall.

From across the living room, Jessica remembered her own first day of school and her heart went out to Marcia. She crossed the room in a few quick strides and, taking her friend's arm, led her into the throng in the living room.

"Susan, Bonnie, Grace, Babs, Jeannie, Ronnie," she said, "I'd like you to meet my dear friend, Marcia. And Marcia, this is – heck, repeat your names, please for Marcia." Obediently, the other guests repeated their names, each grasping Marcia warmly by the hand as they did so.

A surge of happiness swept over Marcia. At first she had wanted to befriend Jessica for what she perceived the other could do for her.

Now she realized that she had been accepted, at least tentatively, and just wanted to be good friends, with all that meant.

Walking homeward in the late afternoon, Marcia tried to convey to Jessica how much it meant to have become buddies. Jessica brushed off her enthusiasm gently. "Hey, I like being your friend," she said. "You certainly bring much needed new blood into the group and I'm sure these women like you. Just be yourself and all will be well."

At that moment they passed a familiar man: Mickey Gold returning home to his apartment after an afternoon of errands.

"Hey, Ladies, imagine running into you here," he exclaimed, transferring all his packages to his left hand, leaving his right one free for shaking. "Any interest in a drink? I live right around the corner."

"Well, I am expected at home," said Jessica. "But maybe a quick one, if you'll come too, Marcia."

Arm in arm in arm, taking up most of the pavement, the three rounded the corner and went in under Mickey's awning.

At six o'clock, having downed one fairly strong scotch, Jessica rose to leave. "Don't let me take you away, Marcia," she said. "But I am expected at home. Thanks, Mickey for the drink. It was nice to see you again." Marcia rose too, much to Mickey's dismay. Politely Jessica held out her hand, which Mickey grasped, pulling her into the circle of his arms. He planted a smacking kiss on each of her cheeks, then grazed her lips.

"Wonderful to see you again, too." He released her and stepped back, loathe to let her go. "Sure you can't stay, Marcia?"

"Sorry," she replied, "I have things to do at home." She embraced Mickey and planted a chaste kiss on his lips. "See you around, Mickey." She and Jessica swept out the door and leaned against it. With two such good looking broads for a drink he had hoped at least to detain Marcia for a quick fuck. He was certainly ready, as the bulge in his trousers indicated. He definitely did not want to go into his bathroom to jack off, watch his sperm sluice down the sink. He wanted to stick it into a willing cunt. Well, there were other girls with cunts around town, He'd call one of them. A quick perusal of his little black book brought one to mind, and he punched in her number. With any luck Darlene would be home and willing to come over to service him. Hell, he'd even buy her a hamburger afterward. Why spend another evening alone?

He was in luck; is quarry was indeed home and more than willing to walk the few blocks to his apartment.

He was waiting for her behind the door, and swung it open even before she rang the bell, pulling her into an embrace as soon as she got through the door.

"Hi, ya, Darlene. Glad you can come. I'm horny as hell," he said, leading her over to the couch that had so recently been vacated by Marcia and Jessica.

"Slow down, lover boy," Darlene said. "I'm not going anywhere anytime soon."

"Never fear, I know what to do," Mickey announced with all the sophistication of a fifteen year old.

"You betcha," said Darlene.

Mickey shed his jacket and pulled her into his lap and started nuzzling her neck, which he knew she loved. She purred into his ear, taking a brief nip at the lobe, then letting her tongue dart in and out briefly. Mickey felt his hard on enlarging even more. "You really turn me on," she murmured.

"And how. Now shut up and let's attend to business.

And attend to business they did.

Darlene undid the small buttons down the front of his shirt, and slid her hands inside, tickling the curly chest hair and thumbing his nipples until they firmed up under her ministrations. At the same time Mickey got his hand inside her camisole, slid around her back and, showing much practice, unhooked her bra with one hand, no mean feat. He lifted up the cups in front, letting her small, perky breasts bob free.

"Lift your arms," he commanded in a hoarse whisper. She complied and he slid the bra and camisole up and over her head, tossing it to the floor.

Darlene realized this would necessitate a trip to the cleaners for the garment, but what the hell? She had no intention of spoiling the mood as desire flooded her groin and crept up to the breasts, which he was now kissing and sucking with abandon.

She pushed his shirt back off his arms, and he shrugged out of it, exhibiting a broad chest, flowing into a trim waist and all that lay below it. Not for nothing was Mickey a regular at his gym.

Darlene tugged at his belt, unbuckled it, then worked at the clip on his trousers, finally managing to get it apart. Only the zipper now stood between her and her desire, which was straining the crotch of his trousers, threatening to burst through the material if Darlene did not manage to free it soon. She pulled away from him, with a loud sucking sound, and bent to the task at hand.

Down came the zipper and into his shorts went her hand. With some urgent tugging and pulling she managed to free his erection, which she stroked and pulled gently, running her fingers under the head of the glans. He groaned his pleasure, lifting his hips so she could slide down both the trousers and the shorts, exposing him fully to her view. The offending garments got tangled at his ankles, and Mickey found it almost impossible to move.

"Lie back and take it," muttered Darlene into his crotch. "I'm going to do my worst to you, like it or not."

"I like it, I like it," gasped Mickey, totally in her thrall. He lay back on the couch, ankles still tangled in the offending trousers, and Darlene knelt over him, planning her strategy.

"I'm going to stroke you like this," she purred, running her fingers lightly up the insides of his thighs, bringing waves of pleasure to each of them. "Then I'm going to follow with my tongue," she demonstrated, with short, darting strokes where her fingers had just been. "Now my mouth." Her head had disappeared between his thighs and she took his swollen schlong between her lips, which were carefully spread over her teeth. She had no intention of hurting him, no nips in this department; they were much too dangerous.

He plunged into her the warm, willing orifice presented to him, thrusting and withdrawing in a rhythm designed to bring him to a shattering orgasm any second.

Sensing his heightened mood, Darlene gently withdrew her lips, and took the engorged penis between her breasts, holding herself together as she formed an alternative vagina for his especial pleasure. She was kneeling on the floor now, the better to envelop him in her cleavage, the head of the penis now peeping out, now disappearing between the two perfect mounds of flesh.

Mickey was practically salivating with expectation and, just before he actually climaxed, Darlene rose from the floor, straddled him on the wide couch, and lowered herself, oh so slowly over his mighty manhood.

It was but a moment of thrusting and parrying and, together, the dam broke and both thrashed in a monumental, shattering orgasm, which seemed to go on and on and on, until Darlene literally thought she might faint. Certainly she ceased all conscious thought as she rode the enormous wave which crashed and broke, unceasingly, on the rocky beach.

They finally rolled apart each breathing hard enough to be heard above the whir of the air conditioner, pumping away in the living room window. Dusk had fallen outside, though neither had noticed, and neither spoke until, several minutes later, the breathing slowed, allowing some gulps of air to penetrate the throbbing chests.

"My, God," exclaimed Darlene, 'You are one helluva lay, let me tell you."

"And you're the best, Darlene," rasped Mickey. "There's no one like you, no one."

"Any time," Darlene told him. "You know I enjoy you any time."

"Well, how about another time, right now. You're here, aren't you? We might as well take advantage of the fact. And you said you didn't have to be any place special any time soon. On my bed this time. In my

bed. All night." He kicked off the garments wrapped around his ankles, stood up and offered her his hand.

"Anything you say, lover," said Darlene, allowing herself to be led, stark naked, into the other room and the warm confines of the king size bed which, with its wicker headboard, and closet full of silk ties, offered all sorts of interesting possibilities. She hadn't been laid in awhile and Mickey was here and always ready. So why not take advantage of him?

Jessica continued as a weekly patient at Sylvan Glad for another three weeks, then was deemed capable of living on her own by Dr. Consuelo and returned to her own apartment, to begin her life in earnest as a single woman. She found things were not as hard as she had once anticipated, and even thought about going back to school for a graduate degree, perhaps in education. In the meantime she volunteered, giving her time to substitute teaching in the New York Public School system, a job she found rewarding if limiting. The curriculum was set in stone as far as she could see, and any supplemental books or extra material she wanted to include was not possible. Library Science was another field of possibility, and she gave more time to the local branch of her library, where she helped shelve the books and did intake for the annual book sale, categorizing the donated volumes as they came in. After Christmas, a job for a temporary French teacher in her old school came vacant, and Jessica was surprised when she was chosen to fill in for the teacher leaving for maternity leave. At least it would keep her occupied and off the streets for a few months, and she threw herself into the project with gusto.

January found her enroute to the school by eight o'clock each morning, Monday through Friday, with little time to think of other matters but her students and the class, which she taught to a group of fifteen eighth graders. Weekends she corrected papers, chose additional material for the class and, occasionally, went out to lunch, a movie or a bridge game. It was far more satisfactory a life than being a young society matron and going around to various committee meetings, such as she had experienced with Trevor, giving her a feeling of fulfillment the other life had so lacked. There were no men in her life at this time, though Marcia frequently volunteered to get Jessica a date, to double date with her and Pedro when he was in town. Jessica just brushed off such suggestions, preferring to hang out with her women friends so Marcia often turned down a Friday or Saturday night date in favor of spending the time with Jessica.

Dr. Consuelo had recommended a doctor in New York, one Jason Wright, who had late office hours on Thursdays, so Jessica continued exploring her life and her motives on those evenings. But she never formed such a close bond as she had experienced with the good doctor at Sylvan Glade. The two doctors had conferred and had come to the conclusion that perhaps Jessica should try to track down the elusive George Parsons, and needed to continue to explore her sexual hangups with him back to that fateful day during that summer, so long ago, in Maine. Maybe she could relate to him, as she had not been able to do with either Trevor or Don. Maybe.

At first she was reluctant. Perhaps George was married. Perhaps, even if she did find him, he wouldn't want to see her. Perhaps, perhaps, perhaps. But finally she was won over and decided to discuss this new venture with Marcia.

She chose a snowy winter afternoon, and invited Marcia over for a drink before going out to a movie. The two women settled comfortably in the living room before the fireplace, blazing with apple logs from Connecticut, which threw out a gently spicy scent, redolent of autumns past.

Jessica began without any preliminaries. "Dr. Wright and Dr. Consuelo have come up with a scheme in which I am supposed to track down a long lost friend...someone actual_y from my childhood. See if he can help me get back on track with this sexual hangup thingy." She was embarrassed being so childish as to use 'thingy' but every time she remembered that day in Maine she froze up, reverting to childish language, unable to call a spade a spade.

"What happened back then?" Marcia leaned forward, all ears.

"I was playing doctor with the boy next door and my grandmother caught us. She hauled me upstairs to her room where I got the beating of my life, and turned the boy over to his father for a similar punishment. I couldn't sit down for a week. Nor, I expect, could he."

"What happened after that?" Marcia wanted to know.

"Well, they separated us for the rest of the summer. I really missed him. We had played together since we were infants...in the summers, I mean. He didn't live in New York but his family had the house next to my grandparents in Maine where I spent most of my summers. It gave my parents time to have together and to travel. I was really too young then to go along on some of their vacations; they went all kinds of special places like Africa and India and all over Europe. Later, of course, they took me along on their jaunts, but back then I would have just slowed them down. I was nine the summer this happened and things changed right after." She paused, remembering the last summer of her childhood spent in the special place in Maine and how the awful punishment had somehow negated most happy thoughts of her grandparents' big, comfortable house, slumbering on sunny days at the head of the point of the harbor.

"Did you miss Maine...and George?" asked Marcia.

"I didn't really think much about it at the time," Jessica said. "My grandfather had a stroke that following winter so there was no more Maine for me. In any case, my parents decided I was old enough – at ten – to join them, so we used to go away together. And George's parents sold the house that winter as well. I think his mother wanted to be someplace more convenient like Cape Ann – they were a Boston family."

"So you never saw George again?"

"That was the odd thing. I did see him again, he rescued me from some randy boy at a teenage party in Darien when I was fifteen. I was visiting a friend from school and she took me to this big party in someone's barn. Anyway, a pretty gorgeous boy asked me to dance and the next thing I knew we were in a box stall in another part of the barn and he was tearing my clothes off me. I didn't know what to do, but another boy came by and threw the guy out of the stall and took me back to the party."

"And the boy was George?"

"Yes," said Jessica. "It was George. My knight in shining armor. I looked for him when we left the party, but he had a girlfriend who was clearly suspicious of who I was and dragged him away. And that was the last time I saw George. Gosh, it was over ten years ago."

"And you think you would like to find him now?"

"Well, both doctors think it is a good idea. And yes, I'd like to see what became of George. He's probably bald and has two and a half children and commutes from New Canaan to some dull job in New York. But I'd like to know." She paused, a faraway look in her eye.

Marcia jumped up. "No time like the present. Turn on your computer. Let's see if we can find George on the internet."

They went down the hall to the second bedroom, where Jessica kept her computer and where she did her correction and any other office work.

"Let's try Zabasearch," said Marcia. No luck. "How about Peoplefinder?" She typed in George's name but still no luck. Another twenty minutes of searching still brought no results. Marcia was stumped.

"I can always put out a search among my friends," Jessica said. "I mean, if he was at that party someone must know him, where he went to school, what happened to him. Just my luck he's posted to Beijing. Or Cape Town or someplace. We can but try."

Marcia was impressed by the network of people with whom Jessica had grown up. They went to the same schools, the same camps, fanned out to the Ivy League colleges, and many of them kept up after graduation. Someone would know the whereabouts of George MacIntyre.

Jessica got the ball rolling by having lunch the following Saturday with Debbie, Babs and Grace, all childhood friends, all with many connections in various places. They had brothers, cousins, club memberships which might help. If only George's family was in the Social Register, it would have been a snap. But they were not so it was necessary to use secondary sources such as personal contacts. Somewhere, somehow someone would find George for Jessica.

Chapter Nine

Finding George Parsons

Marcia was unable to help with the tracking down of the long lost George Parsons, and found herself a bit on the outs with Jessica's school friends, all of whom operated in the same network. Marcia observed somewhat sourly that these women, and the men they had married, all seemed to be cut from the same piece of cloth: privately educated, well versed in the many sports which filled their year, from tennis and golf to riding and sailing, even to croquet, which they played with gusto, all in white, in Central Park during the summer weekdays. They belonged to the same clubs and societies, pretty much shopped for their clothes in the same stores, even favored some of the same breeds of dogs: Golden Retrievers, Labradors, Boston Terriers and the lovely long haired Cavalier King Charles Spaniels which shed all over everything and everybody. When they traveled they seemed to stay in the same hotels, or the same affiliated clubs to which they belonged in New York. All in all a pretty closed society, to which she so desperately wanted to belong. And Jessica had given her the 'in' at that ladies lunch at Deborah's. Now, however, she was unable to join in on the networking that was going on among Jessica's friends, networking designed to bring forth the whereabouts of the long lost George.

She suffered in silence for a month or so, pretending to listen rapturously when anyone thought she had any new information. But all leads went nowhere, and Jessica assumed that perhaps George had gotten totally away, after all.

Finally, when all of Jessica's contacts seemed to have come up dry, Marcia enlisted the help of Mickey Gold, whose work often involved tracking down people and who had a small coterie of investigators at his finger tips. She put her request to him over lunch, not at Mickey's apartment, where he had wanted to schedule the meeting. She knew what that would entail: a request for a wild romp in his bed lasting most of the afternoon. No way, not with Pedro in the background. Mickey promised to put his best man on the job, and reassured Marcia that this PI always got his man – or woman, as the case may be.

Reginald Katz sat in one of the client's chairs across Mickey Gold's fake mahogany veneer desk. Square of jaw, massive through the shoulders, Reggie Katz sat ramrod straight, exuding confidence. His pepper and salt hair sported the perfect amount of whitish sideburns, matching his military style moustache. Reggie might have come from Central Casting, so perfect was his image of the quintessential private investigator. He had been a lead detective in a Brooklyn precinct for most of his working life and, a few years ago on retirement had hung up his police badge for a PI license. He claimed he could track anyone down, anywhere in the world and had case histories to prove it. One of his best stories involved a breeder of racing camels in Australia, though the man was originally from Germany. Far flung connections and favors called in had taken Reggie just ten days to find this man, winning him the approval of his clients and bringing in many future cases. Now he was being primed to find the elusive George Parsons, lately of Maine and Boston, who, seemingly, had vanished overnight.

Mickey had every faith in the PI. He had called him in when Marcia had enlisted his help in finding the long lost white knight of Jessica's barn party, at least ten years ago. He would be around thirty now, and might be anywhere, in any country around the globe. No one seemed to have heard from him since he abruptly left school, well over a decade ago, and no one seemed to know who might be a contact now. His mother, too, seemed to have vanished in the night, though his father had been easily tracked down: to a state penitentiary for embezzlement of funds from his former company.

"Think you can find this guy?" Mickey wanted to know. He had used Reggie before with great success; he always got the goods on a cheating spouse – not that anyone cared about that any more – and he had tracked down some pretty reluctant witnesses for Mickey's cases. But George Parsons looked like a challenging case.

"Who wants him? Some dame owed child support?" asked the detective.

"Nothing like that," Mickey told him. "I guess it's a case of lost love. The woman is someone I got unhitched from a ho....uh, horrible husband." Almost he had slipped. "Looks like she is trying to find her first love."

"How romantic," jeered the PI. "Well, as long as she pays me I don't care who the dude is."

"Uh, she's not paying you. I am."

"Huh?"

"Let's just say it's something I'd like to do for her. So please go easy on me; you know I give you a lot of business," Mickey said.

"Sure, sure. Well, first let's meet this dame; see what she might know. Okay by you?"

"Yes," said Mickey. "In fact we're taking her to lunch, her girl friend, too, who's also a friend of mine."

"Dames. Lunch. Gosh you're going soft in the head, Mickey," said Reginald Katz, but he smoothed his moustache as he said it and Mickey knew he was as anxious to meet the client as he, Mickey, was to have a chance to see her again. However much it cost him.

They took a taxi across town to Sardi's, which Mickey figured would be filled with tourists and they could slip in unnoticed. Somehow Reggie always stood out in any crowd and his company manners left much to be desired. Sardi's was noisy enough and crowded enough, particularly on a Wednesday with the theater crowd, to absorb someone like Reggie Katz.

Jessica and Marcia were already seated at table 16, eyeing the entrance for the arrival of the two men. Marcia waved enthusiastically when she saw Mickey and Reggie. Jessica, so much more reserved, sat politely waiting for the men to go over to their table.

"Hi ya, Marcia," boomed Reggie. "This must be your girlfriend. Introduce us." He held out his hand before Marcia could say a word.

Mickey stepped into the breach. "Jessica, I'd like you to meet Reggie Katz, who is going to help find your friend, George. Reggie, Jessica Jellingdorf."

Jessica put out her hand, to find it engulfed in Reggie's huge paw. He squeezed just a little too hard, making her wince, but she kept a smile in place.

"How do you do? I am so glad you will help in our search." She indicated the banquette by her side, and Reggie slid in beside her. Mickey took the head of the oblong table, with Marcia on his left.

"Drinks, girls?" Reggie took the lead, snapping his fingers for one of the red jacketed wait staff, which brought another wince from Jessica. Marcia caught the grimace out of the corner of her eye, but pretended not to notice. Once, however, a well set up man like Reggie would have gotten her undivided attention, no doubt leading to a later afternoon matinee in his hotel room or her apartment. Now, newly entwined with Pedro, he was just another man, and a pretty loud one at that. But if he could help Jessica, she was all for him.

The waiter, who had tried to ignore Reggie's finger snap, now arrived at their table, pad in hand.

"Martinis all around?" asked Reggie jovially.

"I don't think so, not at lunch. Perhaps a glass of Chardonnay for me," said Jessica.

"Same for me," echoed Marcia who might have liked a martini but decided to emulate her friend.

"Just a coke," said Mickey. "I have work to do back at the office."

"Well, then I'm the only martini man," said Reggie, and proved his point by having two more with lunch.

150

"Tell me about your friend George," he said, turning to Jessica.

"There's not much to tell," said Jessica. "But he did me a big favor some years ago and I just want to find him so I can thank him." She hoped this loud, vulgar man would get on with his investigation and she would not have to see him again. After all, what could she tell him about George? That they lived next door to each other her first nine summers, then she didn't see him again for six years after which he disappeared again? It made her sound like a romantic fool, searching everywhere for her lost puppy love.

Yet Reggie made her go through just these facts, and where he went to school, and if they had any mutual friends. He took all this down in a spiffy little leather notebook, then snapped it shut and turned to the cannelloni – a specialty of the house – which he had ordered. "This looks good," he announced to the table in general, when all their food had been delivered. "Boune appetite," he said, mangling the French badly.

Jessica was too polite to correct him, but merely picked up her fork, delving into her chicken salad.

They sat around over coffee as the restaurant emptied of theater goers, all hastening to make two o'clock curtains, until only a few tables were left with diners around them. Mickey had to excuse himself, leaving Reggie to pick up the check, which he did with a flourish. What the hell! He might as well impress the ladies, especially as the check, and a hefty tip, would go onto his account to be settled later on with Mickey.

From Sardis Reggie returned to his own tiny apartment, on the ground floor of a pretty good building on East 72nd Street, and packed a bag for a few days. He's take the Accela train up to Boston, rent a car, then continue on to that quaint little town in Maine where his client and her lost boy friend had spent so many childhood summers. It was always fun going out of town and if he picked up some useful information, all to the good. Though he wondered why that good looking broad, his client, was so distant to him at lunch. Somehow he had hoped she was a good time girl, one who would have happily accompanied him home for a quick roll in the hay. He'd have to ask Mickey about her. Maybe he'd have better luck when he was back in town.

Jessica and her charms went right out of his head as he met a good looking blonde on the train, who was also headed for Boston. When they detrained together, he gallantly offered her a ride to her destination, which ended up being his same hotel. He could swear she really was going someplace else, but why call her on it? A little sex before starting his search for George would not go amiss and he could always wait until tomorrow morning to start. The evening was young and it looked like he had made a good hookup. He helped the girl out of the taxi at the Copley Plaza and ushered her up to his third floor room. He wondered if he'd have to buy her dinner after fucking her. Somehow he hoped not; he'd like to look over his notes before he started out in the morning and dinner with more martinis and wine might sap his concentration.

Inside the standard room, with its mini bar housed in the giant cabinet that also held the TV, its matching Queen beds with the dark red spreads, the hangers secured around the rod so they could not be removed, and the glasses, each wrapped in its sanitized paper were so much of a piece with so many other hotel rooms he had occupied. Even the blonde somehow seemed familiar. He sighed softly as he slung his suitcase onto the rack.

"Anything to drink? I'm – uh – Roger by the way. What's your name?"

"Sue," the girl answered.

"Well, Sue," said Reggie. "How about it?   No time like the present." He started unbuckling his belt.

Sue followed suit, shucking off her jacket and unzipping her skirt. She looked around for a place to put them, and decided on the bed nearest the window. Reggie threw back the covers on the matching bed, and continued disrobing. Dressed only in his shorts, he inserted himself under the covers and waited for Sue to join him. She only had her bra and panties on, of plain white cotton. Maybe she had not expected to meet a man on the train, but what the hell. They all felt the same way naked. He beckoned, and she came to him, lying down next to him and waited for Reggie to take the lead.

He put one arm around her back, thrusting his other hand down the elastic waistband of her panties, thrusting his fingers into her curly black bush. Sue arched her back a little, giving Reggie permission to go on. And go on he did, thrusting his middle finger down between the hot juices seeping out of her cunt, thrusting into her, bringing her to almost instant readiness. He pushed the knit cotton knickers down over her thighs, leaving them dangling between her knees. Pushing down his own shorts, he snapped on a condom and mounted her, entering her with no further preliminaries. He liked his sex plain and foreplay kept to the minimum and he pumped away happily, knowing his climax was not far off. As to Sue, if she got her rocks off too, good, if not, so what? This was for his pleasure, after all, something she should understand. A moment later he gushed out his semen into the tight condom, thrust wildly for another moment, then subsided, rolling off her to lie on his back in the bed, a satisfied smile on his face. Thankfully, Sue made no sound. Sometimes they expected to get it up again and satisfy the woman. Not this time, though. He had picked well.

Ten minutes later he saw her off in a taxi to her own residence, tucking a fifty dollar bill into her hand, 'for the fare'. She really hadn't been staying at the same hotel, something he has suspected all along. He gave a brief wave as the taxi pulled out into the main traffic, then returned to his room for a clean shirt and underwear. He liked to shower after having a broad, change and go out for a good dinner. Tonight it would be a steak, the next day on by rented car to Lilac Knoll, the distant Maine town where George Parsons had summered with Jessica Alden so many years before. Hopefully he would pick up the scent of the elusive George, and run him to ground. He was good at this, he knew. Humming lightly under his breath, Reggie departed the hotel and went in search of his good steak.

The drive to Maine was uneventful, if long. He had forgotten how far away was this state which so many city people loved for its summers. For Reggie, a city street, a good dinner and a quick lay was his nirvana. But what the hell; he was a top investigator and his work often took him far afield. He hadn't realized quite how far afield Lilac Knoll really was.

He kept to the Maine Pike past Old Orchard Beach, Cape Elizabeth and Portland, to the Freeport exit at Brunswick. He might as well drop into L.L. Bean and stock up on some casual, country clothes. He'd see if that little greasy spoon around the corner was still there; they had the best fried clam bellies in the whole state, as far as he was concerned. He could always suck some Tums afterward to get the heavy, gassy feeling out of his stomach. But those clams were worth a little discomfort once in a while.

Lunch over, Reggie sped on to the turn off for Route 1 and continued up the coast past Bath and Boothbay Harbor, through the charming towns of Rockland and Camden, and to the top of Penobscot Bay to Bucksport, where he dropped down the rocky peninsula that would lead him past Castine and on to the point that was Lilac Knoll.

He pulled up in front of the Seagull Inn just about cocktail hour, and carried his bag into the quaint parlor of the only accommodation in the town. He had called ahead, but probably need not have done so: there were but a few patrons sitting in the wicker chairs on the broad porch, overlooking the harbor, or in the small, paneled bar, which held photographs of some of the great sailboats which had plied these waters over the years.

Just his luck, thought Reggie, all by himself in this backwater burg, probably not a single girl in the whole village to solace a lonely traveler. He heaved his suitcase onto the chenille bedspread of the double spool bed, cursing under his breath. Though the view from his windows was over the sparkling waters of the harbor, with all manner of pleasure and fishing boats bobbing on the gentle waves, Reggie was unimpressed. He hated the country – or any suggestion of it – and hoped that, like Boston, he wouldn't be stuck here too long.

Sighing, he went back down to the lobby, and entered the bar. An elderly man, gray haired and somewhat stooped, was behind the counter, polishing its shining surface with a bar cloth. What'll be your pleasure?" he asked politely, as Reggie mounted one of the four stools in front of the bar.

"Martini. Straight up. Olive." He watched as the bar tender took down a bottle of Sapphire Gin, and commenced to fill his cocktail shaker carefully. At least this dump had decent booze. He wondered what might be on the menu for dinner.

"You serve dinner here?" he asked abruptly.

"Certainly, sir," came the ever polite reply. "We serve from seven to nine. Let me give you a menu with your drink so you can have an idea what you might want to order."

Well, okay. No need to drive up and down the peninsula looking for someplace to eat. At least they served here. Probably slop, but he wouldn't have to go out and there was plenty of good booze right in this bar to help him while away an otherwise dull evening. He picked up his martini and took the first sip. Perfection. Maybe this wouldn't be such a bad evening after all.

Two martinis later Reggie was feeling far more mellow. And it looked as if his luck was about to change as well. He saw a low slung sports car pull up to the front of the inn and a leggy blonde of about thirty get out. She strode across the porch with tremendous purpose, and went up to the front desk of the inn. From his perch at the bar, Reggie could hear her conversation with the clerk behind the counter.

"I'm on my way to Campobello," she announced. "And I just can't drive any farther. Do you have a room for tonight? I don't have a reservation."

"Yes, we can take you," the clerk told her. "Just sign here please. I'll get someone to take up your bag."

Reggie realized he had his opening. He gulped the rest of his martini and strode out into the hall."

"I'm just going upstairs myself," he announced, looking over the new arrival with pleasure. Great boobs, pretty face, longish blonde hair. He bet she would be a good lay. "Why not let me take the lady's bag to her room?" He gave his best subservient smile.

"Why, thanks," said the clerk. "Martin's out doing the lawn, but I could call him in...."

"Let Martin keep doing the lawn," said Reggie politely. "It's no trouble at all. I was just going up to my own room."

He was rewarded by a smile from both the desk clerk and the new hotel guest.

The clerk handed over an old fashioned key, which Reggie saw had the number '6' on it. Right down the hall from his own room, number '10'. With a little luck only one of these rooms would be used tonight.

They climbed the stairs to the second floor and Reggie led the way down the corridor. "I'm right here," he announced as they passed his door. "Just in case you need anything, or something frightens you in the night." Almost he leered at the woman behind him.

"Probably not necessary," the woman said. "But thanks."

"Any time." They had come to her door, and she inserted the key, swinging open the portal to exhibit her own room, with the same spool bed and chenille bedspread.

"Quaint," she remarked. "But fine for the night. Thanks for bellboying. It was nice of you."

"No problem," said Reggie. "I was coming up anyway for – uh – my cell phone. I forgot it earlier."

"Ah your cell phone," said the blonde.

"I'm on my own here," Reggie told her. "Just like you. If you'd like to have a drink with me it would be nice."

"Why not," said the blonde. "I could use a drink. Just give me ten minutes to freshen up and I'll join you. Did I see the bar downstairs?"

"Yes," said Reggie, "right off the lobby. I'll be waiting." He tipped an imaginary hat and left the room. He paused in his own room just long enough to gargle with Listerine and pat some aftershave into hit armpits and, as an afterthought, into his pubic hair. The sting almost felt good, and a prelude to what he hoped would be a night of great sex. Hey, things were looking up. Maybe this burg wasn't such a backwater after all.

The woman's name turned out to be Helen Mulberry, from Philadelphia, and she was on her way to Campobello to scout out one of the locations for an upcoming film about Roosevelt and his summer home. Reggie was impressed: a looker and in films. He mentally polished off his meager knowledge of the movie industry then thought to quiz her about her participation in this particular project. He knew people liked to talk about themselves, and had spent many hours in his profession drawing such people out. First it had been in interrogation rooms in the precinct, later in all manner of places, from parks to drawing rooms, when he was investigating a case for a private client. Helen turned out no differently. When led into a topic, she was happy to expand on it, taking the lead and talking easily on everything from initial idea for a movie, through its production with all its ramifications, through the final distribution at the actual movie houses.

Actually, Reggie was impressed by her knowledge and obvious intelligence, and strove to keep his voice as accent free as possible, his own profession somewhat shrouded in mystery. They repaired from the bar to the charming dining room of the inn, all done up in lavender cloths with fresh flowers on each table. The menu was classic Maine: they each chose seafood chowder and a lobster, with cole slaw and fries, cooked to perfection and served with expertise by what were obviously local students, well trained by the inn to take good care of the guests.

Two hours later, replete with food and drink, they decided to take a stroll through the streets of the now quiet village. They walked past Colonial houses, many with gardens and picket fences, by the town tennis courts, onto a lonely road that seemed to lead out to the farthest point, reaching into the now wine dark sea.

Helen threw herself down on a flat rock and leaned back on her elbows, contemplating the scene before her.

157

"Sometimes, when life gets so hectic at home," she told Reggie, "I like to think of just such a night as this, all peaceful with the stars above and the waves lapping at my feet. But I know I'd go stir crazy if I really lived in a place like this." She laughed, tilting her face up in the moonlight.

It was the obvious invitation to a kiss, and Reggie obliged easily, pressing down on her warm lips then nudging them with his tongue until they parted, leaving him access to her mouth. He probed deeply and she returned his ardor, circling his tongue with her own then taking his lower lip, gently, into her teeth.

Reggie was not one for romance, but the night and the sweet scented girl on the rock below him did something to the detective; he took her head in both his hands and gently pulled her closer to him. Their kissing became erotic now, less gentle, more savage, with each trying to devour the other solely with their mouths.

Panting, they lay down side by side on the rock and began to explore other parts of each other's bodies. Reggie ran his tongue down under Helen's ear, causing her to moan, then darted his tongue into the opening itself, which made her cling more tightly to him.

"Hey, lover," she whispered into his own ear, "this isn't the most comfortable place, is it? Let's get back to the inn where we can really get into each other."

"I'm all for it." Gallantly he extended his hand and helped her up from the rock, then flung his arms around her and pressed her to the length of his body as if he would never let her go. How well they fitted together! Her breasts pushed heavily into his chest, his burgeoning erection pressed up between the sweet v of her legs. He slid his hand under her skirt, coming up against the softness of her labia, now dripping wet for him. He could hardly wait to get her back to the inn, strip her and push into her hot cunt, come in a huge burst of sperm swimming up into the ever present condom.

158

Together they almost ran back to the welcoming porch, pushed through the front door, waved to the receptionist and headed up the old fashioned staircase.

"Your room or mine?" he breathed into her soft, fragrant hair. What was her scent? He was good on women's perfumes, then it came to him. Helen was wearing Eternity. He hoped their coupling would be an eternity, that he could stay inside of her for hours, give her as good as he was going to get, an unusual thought for him. But something about the girl and the night and the tremendous pressure building up in his loins....he didn't stop to analyze. He just wanted to get on with it.

"My room," she gasped.

She fumbled with the key in her door then, blissfully, they were alone with the spool bed, the moonlit night coming in through the open windows and the waves lapping on the shore below them.

Reggie turned to her, expecting to undress her and get her immediately into bed, but Helen had other ideas.

"I want to tie you up to those lovely spools," she murmured into his ear. Then have my way with you, no hands, no movement from you. You submit to my ministrations. I promise you won't regret it."

Under normal circumstances, Reggie might have demurred. He liked to take the lead in sex, have the upper hand. But this night, the incredibly sexy Helen and his own desire had rendered him incapable of saying no. He stood on the braided rag rug at the side of the bed and waited Helen's instructions. They were not long in coming.

"I'm going to undress you," she said. "And tie you to the bed. Then I'm going to fuck you to my heart's content and you are going to beg for more. That I can promise you."

Reggie managed to nod.

"First some bonds." Helen rummaged around in her open suitcase and drew out several scarves. An involuntary shiver ran through Reggie; what was she going to do with them and how would he feel? He did not have long to find out.

"Put your hands over your head," she commanded and he did as he was told. Helen expertly bound his two hands together at the wrists, then passed the long scarf around the first spool of the bed's headboard. She fastened him loosely.

"Sit on the bed"

He did as she said. Helen knelt down on the floor before him, and thrust his legs apart with one hand. The other moved to his zipper, and she drew it down, then reached into his shorts and pulled his erection out from his fly, leaving him almost completely dressed. She manipulated it with firm strokes, up and down the shaft, around and around the head, flicking the ridge with a snap of her thumb and forefinger. He gasped in pleasure, and tried to reach out to touch her. Alas, the bond held firm and he could not use his hands.

"Not allowed," she said. Swiftly she undid a few buttons on his shirt, pulling the sleeves over his arms, making any motion even more impossible. "You are in my thrall," she told him, "and any insubordination will be severely dealt with. Do you understand?"

"Yes," he breathed, "I understand."

"Good," said Helen. "Now lie down on the bed. Swing your legs in."

Reggie obliged.

Helen bent down and slipped off his loafers, then his socks, tossing them under the bed. His upper body was completely immobilized between the shirt and the silken scarf around his hands. Now Helen bade him lift his hips, at which point she slid down his trousers and underwear, removing them quickly over his feet and tossing them with the rest of his clothing under the bed. His torso was exposed, as was all of him from the waist down. She spread his legs apart, then bound each ankle with another scarf to the footboard of the bed, leaving him in a perfect 'Y' spread out before her.

Casually, slowly, she removed her own clothes, dropping each garment over the footboard of the bed, until she stood, naked and beautiful in the moonlight. Her bush was of burnished gold, matching

160

the long hair that swung over Reggie as Helen bent over him. He could hear his breath coming raggedly in his ears, drowning out all other sounds from outside: the waves, the cicadas chirping in the grass. All as focused now on Helen and her ministrations.

She cupped her perfect breasts, one in each hand, pushing them up and together, running her tongue slowly over her lower lip.

Reggie was practically salivating now.

With total abandon, Helen mounted him on the soft bed, one knee each side of his quavering hips and the huge erection that bobbed between them. She lowered herself onto him, full face, letting the shaft of his throbbing hard-on on slip between her legs, but not not letting him enter her, and started writhing on his chest and hips. Up and down, around and around, never quite letting even the head slip into her willing snatch, teasing and tormenting him until he thought he could stand no more.

She flipped herself around, until her mouth was poised directly above his schlong, her cunt directly over his face, but too far away for him to reach her with his willing tongue.

Slowly, slowly, she lowered herself until she could take the full length of him into her mouth, licking and sucking the rock hard shaft of his manhood.

Reggie thought the top of his head was going to explode. The tantalizing cunt dropped lower and a little lower until, at last, he was able to insert his pointed tongue into the hot, throbbing opening, flicking it up and down her labia and around her enlarged clitoris. He heard her gasp and doubled his efforts, drawing forth from her a series of moans that surely could be heard all the way down the hall and into the lobby. Just when he thought he would ejaculate into her mouth, she pulled back, taking her beautiful snatch with her. He flailed at the bonds, wanting to touch her, knead her willing flesh into submission, flip her over and jam his throbbing dick into her beautiful, hot cunt.

She lay on the bed beside him, stroking his inner thighs, running her tongue around his ear and down his neck, now speeding up, now slowing down, now stopping entirely. Reggie writhed and twisted on the bed beside her.

At long last she took pity on him. Turning her back to his face, she again positioned herself over him, taking his willing prick into her from the rear, then knelt firmly on his thighs as her internal muscles clamped and loosened on the throbbing center of his existence. The eruption that occurred a few seconds later sent him far, far up into to that night sky they had glimpsed from the rocks, way above the stars, over the moon, up and up until he thought he actually was going to die. Astride him he heard Helen scream, almost in triumph then they crashed together back down to earth, leaving them both limp and totally spent.

Helen got up from the bed, went to the bathroom, and returned with a warm washcloth and a hand towel. She carefully cleaned Reggie off, dried him, then did the same for herself. She returned the towel and cloth to the bathroom, came back to bed, and untied Reggie.

"How was that, lover?" she asked as she climbed in beside him.

Reggie, for once, was at a loss of words, but only could grin at Helen and take her in his arms.

"I thought so," she said, allowing him one goodnight kiss. "Now roll over and go to sleep. I have a long day tomorrow." Without further ado she pulled up the covers and turned her back to him.

He drifted off, thinking that tomorrow would bring him more bliss than he had ever thought possible.

When he woke, it was to the screech of gulls and full sunlight streaming through the wide windows. Checking his watch, he saw it was past nine. Where was Helen? A quick survey told him her luggage was gone and the only reminder of that mind blowing night was the indent of her head on the pillow next to his own.

Sadly, Reggie gathered up his clothes and put his head out the door. The coast was clear and he ran down to his own room in his shorts, hoping no one would come out in the corridor until he made it safely in his door. No one did and he gained his room, throwing his clothes on the chair and sinking down on the bed for a few minutes. Last night's sex had been beyond incredible and he had hoped to have more time with the elusive Helen, but she was gone. Maybe, just maybe, it had been the best sex Reggie had ever experienced in his life. He stepped into a hot, hot shower, still pondering this question.

The dining room served a huge breakfast of oatmeal, ham, eggs and pancakes with blueberries, with real maple syrup and Reggie ate his way through it all with evident pleasure. New York breakfasts consisted of a cup of coffee from the corner Dunkin' Donuts, sometimes with a bagel, more often not. Now he lingered at the table over his third cup of coffee, planning his day to come. He had the address of the Alden house, and asked at the desk for directions. Finding it was but a few streets away, he decided to leave the car where it was and walk. You could often get information along the way, or at least get the feel of a place where a subject had once lived. Granted it was a long time ago, but the Alden house was still in the family and the new owners of the Parsons home might have information.

He strolled out into the perfect spring morning. The sky was a high, taut blue above the harbor and the tide was coming in. Seagulls swooped and cried above and from somewhere nearby was the sound of a lawn mower. As he drew closer, he smelled the wonderful aroma of fresh cut grass. A youth was pushing the lawn mower and Reggie stopped across the picket fence to ask directions.

"Pardon me, young man," he called above the noise of the mower. "Do you know the way to the Alden house?"

"Up to the corner, turn down the harbor side and it's two more streets down. But no one's there, no one has used the house in a couple of years, I guess."

"That so?" replied Reggie. "Interesting. Do you happen to know about the people who lived next door a long time ago? The name was Parsons."

The youth was happy to cease his mowing and talk to the stranger. "Sure. My parents often talk about the family. Mr. Parsons went to jail for stealing money from his company."

"Embezzling," Reggie corrected him.

"Yup. Anyway, he went to jail; think he's still there. There was a wife and son and they were up to Boston. I think they moved somewhere else and no one around here has heard from them since."

That made sense. No one anywhere had heard from them. But Parsons being in jail held out a promise of finding George. He'd find out which jail and perhaps pay a visit. Or maybe he could get the information in this little town instead. The long trip was beginning to pay off. And the sex with Helen.... Sternly he told himself to drop this line of remembering. It would only cloud his primary purpose.

He turned back to the youth. "Do you think your parents might have any idea about the family? Would they talk to me?"

"Sure," said the boy. "My dad runs the boatyard." He pointed down the harbor to a clump of old, gray shingled buildings. "There. Jackson's Marina. M'dad's Tom Jackson. Just ask for him."

"I'm obliged." Reggie put his hand across the fence and Tom Jackson's son gave him a ragged shake.

He headed in the direction the boy had indicated and soon found himself surrounded by all manner and condition of boats, from sleek yachts and clumsy fishing boats to sailfish and sunfish and a large number of dinghys, some with sails. A class of children was about to take to the water in these dinghys, and Reggie stopped to watch. His own childhood had been spent in public parks and swimming pools in Brooklyn and he had never had a summer on the water. Obviously these children of Lilac Knoll had been on the water from birth and now sailed smartly away from the dock in their small craft, followed by a committee boat calling out directions.

A crooked sign on one of the smaller buildings read 'office' and Reggie pushed open the screen door and entered.

"I'm looking for Tom Jackson," he announced to a man at a littered desk.

"You found him."

Reggie put out his hand and put on his best smile. "A nice young man directed me here," he said. "Your son, I think? I'm a PI and I'm looking for information about a young man who used to live here, George Parsons." He had always found it good policy to announce his profession and his quest at the onset of any conversation. If the other party didn't want to talk there were various ploys to get him to do so, but very often people wanted to spill the beans, to make themselves seem important to have privileged information. Jackson might fall into either category. Reggie put on the charm.

"Mr. Jackson," he began. "I'm here trying to track down a boy who used to summer here with his parents. The boy is a man now but a girl who was his friend many years ago has lost touch and really wants to get in touch with him."

"You don't say so," was the taciturn answer.

"Yes. Jessica Alden. Jessica Jellingdorf now. She married a few years ago and is divorced. But she and George lost touch and now she has sent me to try to find him. Can you help?" He thought a direct approach to the other man's sense of friendships from long ago might resonate."

"Well, you won't find no Parsons here now," Jackson informed him. "He went to jail; seems he stole some money. And all the family funds were used up by lawyers trying to defend him down in Boston. Mrs. Parsons had to sell the house, and I heard everything else they had, too. But he went to jail just the same."

Bingo! Reggie was sure he was getting closer to his quarry. "Do you know what happened to Mrs. Parsons? And George?" he asked eagerly.

"I know they had to sell up in Boston. My wife heard from her cousin that Mrs. P. didn't want to show her face anywhere around where she had lived; changed her name and took George and moved away. I'm not sure where."

"What did she change her name to?" George inquired.

"Why, she took back her maiden name, it was MacIntyre. I know she changed her name and think she changed George's too. George had to leave his fancy school in Boston, too. They were left with just about nothing." Jackson leaned back in his swivel chair.

Reggie pumped the hand of this man who had given him the lead he needed. "Thank you so much, Mr. Jackson. You've been a tremendous help."

"Warn't nothing. I remember Jessica Alden. Cute little girl. She and George were thick as thieves, but that last summer something happened and the families were never friendly again."

"Do you know what happened?" Reggie asked.

"Nope, nor does anyone else around here. But it had to be something bad." Jackson stood up and ushered Reggie out of his office. He had perhaps said more than he meant, but if little Jessica wanted to find her childhood playmate, for whatever reason, who was he to stand in her way? And this guy looking for him certainly seemed like a professional. He turned over in his hand the embossed card Katz had presented to him. 'Reginald Katz'. P.I. He had never met a real private eye before. Sort of like Magnum. Something to tell the wife about tonight. He gazed after Reggie as he swung out of the boatyard and headed back to the inn.

A short ramble through the town brought him to the white clapboard house of the Alden family. He admired the Colonial structure, so foursquare and solid, seemingly there forever. He noted the shades were down, though the yard looked trim and the paint was obviously fresh on both the house and the shutters, so dark green as to look black. He opened the swing gate in the picket fence and passed under an arbor which displayed a tracery of vines over his head and continued up the brick walk to the front steps. The door was painted a welcoming shade of red (he would later learn it was Chinese red) and the knocker, in the shape of an anchor, was brightly polished. Repeated knocks did not bring anyone to the front door, so he strolled around the side of the house and mounted a porch, wide and welcoming, though devoid of furniture. Here the windows were not shaded and he peered in through the glass, old and streaky and not too clear, into what must be the dining room. A massive mahogany table was surrounded by a dozen chairs, with intricately designed backs; probably old too. Indeed, the whole house stunk of 'old', not a period that particularly interested Reggie Katz. He liked his furniture sturdy and functional, with no need to polish or shine it. Here, the housekeeping must be a nightmare. He looked up at the porch roof, noting a wrought iron light fixture above his head and the ceiling, painted a particular shade of robin's egg blue. It seemed New Englanders used this exact shade for all their porch ceilings, but he had no idea why. The place obviously had an excellent caretaker, though Jessica had told him that the family rarely used the house these days. It belonged jointly to her father and his brother, and was available to the family at any time. It just seemed that the various members were more wedded to other places to vacation: Palm Beach, Southport, Connecticut, Watch Hill. So the house sat and waited…for someone to come, let up the shades and throw open the windows to the ocean breezes.

Reggie tramped through the back yard and leaned over the stone wall that separated this property from the one behind. Surely the former Parson's place, though now in the hands of another family. He tried to picture that long ago summer day when both children had been so severely punished for playing doctor, but found it hard. He himself had been the recipient of his father's belt on his backside and thighs on many occasions, and it hadn't scarred him for life or turned him off sex. Far from it. To each his own, he guessed

Returning to the inn, Reggie paid his bill, took his car and headed back down to Boston. It should be fairly easy to find George and his mother now. At least he had the right name.

He arrived late afternoon and checked back into the Copley Plaza in a standard queen size room. No need to impress anyone this stop, and the wild sex he had enjoyed last night in Maine would do him for at least two or three days. Gently rubbing his sore pecker he thought it might even be a couple of days longer. But nothing like a good workout to sharpen the wits and give vigor to the day. He took a quick shower and ordered a burger and fries from room service. He always traveled with his own bottle, so set this up on the bureau, within easy reach of the wrapped glasses. A night in would do him good, maybe even get to bed early.

He propped his computer up on the desk and went to work, looking for any internet site that mentioned George, or any newspaper articles that would lead him to George Parsons – now George MacIntyre. A thorough search only brought up one small item: a Jonathan Parsons had been sentenced for embezzlement....blah blah. Nothing about a missing wife – soon ex-wife – and son. Hum. He'd have to dig deeper. No MacIntryes, Grace or George, listed in the Boston phone directory, or in information. He'd have to hit the library tomorrow, check out old phone records. Maybe he'd done enough for one day. Reggie flipped through the channels and hit a reality show. Blank out the mind, veg out a little. Idly he fondled his penis through the twill of his trousers, surprised it showed some life. Maybe a quick hand job would settle him down. He unzipped his trousers and went to work. Maybe he wasn't sated after all.

The next day he found an address a few years back for a G. Parsons, and, a year or so later, nothing. The new MacIntyres, George and Grace, seemed to have vanished without a trace. They seemed to be flying under the radar.

Nothing loath, he tried the public schools in the suburb where Grace had moved after the trial, pretending to be a prospective employer checking references. Here he did a little better, finding out that George had transferred to Staples High School in Westport, CT. With a sigh for another long drive, George decided to motor to Connecticut, staying in the only hotel/motel listed for that town: the Westport Motor Inn. He was passing by Sturbridge just around early dinner time, and stopped to treat himself to a chicken pot pie and a beer at Ebenezer's Tavern in the Publick House, one of his long time favorites. He always stopped here when at the junction of Massachusetts and Connecticut, figuring it was less than three hours to New York, two to Boston. Westport should be an hour short of New York; he'd be there in time for early bed and a reconnoiter around the town tomorrow.

The beds in Westport were comfortable, the curtains thick, and he had been given a room at the back, away from the noise of the traffic on Route 1. He had a decent breakfast and set off to discover Westport. He thought he had taken some girl to the beach here many years before, but his memory was hazy. Was she the blonde in the red bikini or the brunette in the black Speedo? It hardly mattered all this time later. He called the admissions office at the High School, and this time he hit pay dirt. Yes, a George MacIntyre had been a student there, but he had left at the end of his junior year, and moved to England with his mother. He apparently had also returned to the United States after an absence of four years and attended Architecture School at Harvard. His GPA had been high and he had excelled at sports. They wished him well and hoped he'd get the job Reggie was calling about.

England, and another name. No wonder he had been running around in circles. Reggie next put on his most posh accent and called Harvard. He met with some resistance here, but finally convinced the broad on the other end of the line to look up George's file; he had a really important commission for him and would be devastated not to get in touch with such a budding young architect. A few minutes wait finally gave him what he wanted: an address someplace in Oxfordshire, at a company Called High Gate Associates. Bingo. He turned to his computer screen and almost instantly came up with a list of websites for the firm. He opened one at random and found himself staring at a picture of a good looking bloke called Bevington. His biography was lengthy and impressive, with many awards to his credit and even an OBE (whatever that was). At the end was a short personal note: Bevington, first name Malcolm, was married to a Grace MacIntyre. He had two children by a previous marriage. Reggie scrolled down and there, eyes looking directly into the camera, was his quarry. George MacIntyre was pictured full face, unruly hair falling across a high forehead, likeable smile turning up one side of his mouth. George, the budding young architect was living in Oxfordshire, working for his stepfather. There was no mention of a wife, or any children. Reggie could only hope.

Glancing at his watch he noted it was lunchtime, so he headed into downtown Westport – what there was of it – looking for a place to eat. On a street behind the quaint main street, called, most unoriginally, Main Street, he discovered a handsome Colonial building done over into a restaurant. Outside tables sat under brilliant orange umbrellas, most of which were filled with well dressed people, all in animated conversations. Maybe Westport wasn't such a dull berg after all.

He ate a steak salad with relish, washed down by a St. Pauli Girl beer, then strolled down toward the river. He found a row of comfortable benches along the shining water, and parked himself on one, pulling out his cell phone. It was one thirty on the east coast, six thirty in England. With any luck he'd get George's number and find his subject at home.

The overseas information operator couldn't have been more helpful and, only a few minutes later Reggie found himself dialing a number three thousand miles away. The double ring, peculiar to England, dinged once, twice, and someone picked up. A male voice, definitely Boston but with a trace of posh overlaying it picked up.

"Seven seven two three oh two four," it said.

"Good evening." Reggie put on his best accent again. "This is Reginald Kavanaugh of – ' he slurred a name that ended in 'architecture magazine' – "and I'm calling for George MacIntyre."

"This is he." It was a phrase that often puzzled Reggie who certainly would have said 'this is him'. "I'm doing a piece on up and coming young architects, and your background interests me. I mean, aren't you American?"

"Yes," said George, "but I did A levels here in England and went to Oxford before grad school in the United States."

"Yes," said Reggie. "Harvard, I think. And you now work for your stepfather?"

"Yes, that's right," said George. "Tell me your name again, please. I didn't quite get it"

"Reginald – uh – Kavanaugh." Reggie often used different names when tracking people down. He was glad he remembered this time who he was supposed to be.

"Well, Mr. Kavanaugh, I haven't really done many interviews, but if you'd like to meet with me sometime next week I'll be glad to show you around the firm and answer some questions. Which day is good for you?"

Reggie wasn't about to let an opportunity like this pass him by. "I plan on being in London next Wednesday," he said. "And could travel out to Oxford perhaps Thursday. The twelfth? Would that work for you?"

"Fine," said Reggie. I can meet you at the Old Bank Hotel on the High Street. Any taxi driver will know it. I'll leave my name at reception. Why not call me from London the night before and let me know what time you are arriving."

"Terrific," Reggie replied. "Until next week then." He hung up, spirits soaring. He probably didn't really need to go to England, but it was the surest way to get the best possible information, from the client himself. Humming, he returned to the lot where he had parked his car and headed back to the hotel/motel for his bag. He'd drive down to New York and be back in his apartment by cocktail time. Maybe he could convince Marcia to come over, if not, there was a stable full of other girls in his little black book. He'd already forgotten his vow to lay off the broads for a few days. He had a lot to celebrate: his quarry almost run to ground and a quick trip to England next week. Things were looking pretty good for Reggie Katz.

Chapter Ten

Reggie Goes to England

Reggie leaned back in his coach class seat as the Virgin Atlantic flight took off from Kennedy and headed out across the Atlantic Ocean to London. This would be the last leg of his search for George Parsons MacIntyre, whom he was meeting in Oxfordshire the day after tomorrow. His plan was to skip London entirely, take the inter city bus from Heathrow directly to Oxford and arrive there before lunch. He had a reservation at the Old Bank Hotel, where he was meeting George the following day. It would be a long first day abroad, but better this way than a night in London then an early trip up to Oxford the following day. Besides, he liked to acclimate himself to new places, sort of get the feel of things before starting his investigations.

On most flights Reggie chatted up at least a few girls in his immediate vicinity, picking one to share transportation in from the airport to whatever city he was visiting, offering her breakfast or a drink – depending on the time of day the flight arrived. More often than not these girls proved willing bed partners as well, getting Reggie's rocks off before he settled down to work. But on this particular trip he felt the effort would have been useless. How many single women going to London were also planning on traveling up to Oxford the day he landed? He'd wait until he hit the university town and see how pickings were there. There were bound to be plenty of coeds, if not hotel staff as well, or women drinking in the hotel bar. Reggie pushed the call button, ordered two scotches to be brought to his seat together, downed the little bottles of amber liquid, and put his seat back as far as it would go.

With any luck he'd get a few hours sleep before arriving at his destination.

Heathrow seemed particularly jammed the morning of his arrival, and Reggie took an inordinate amount of time clearing passport control, getting his one bag and strolling out through customs. He caught the express bus to Oxford and gazed out at the English countryside as the bus drove north-east to the university that had been operating for the last thousand years, a fact that impressed even the jaded Reggie. At the terminal he caught a taxi to the hotel, and marveled at the yellow sandstone buildings as he drove past, serene under their mystic spires. No college in the United States could possibly rival this, even though Reggie was not familiar with most of the higher seats of learning. He had joined the Police Academy right out of high school and had worked his way up in the ranks to become a detective before he was thirty. Those years on the Brooklyn force had led to his present career, sometimes dull but on a case such as this one, absolutely fascinating. And he was good at what he did: he almost always found his man – or woman, as the case may be.

The hotel assigned him a large and comfortable room and bath, done up in muted shades of beige and cream. Across the street was an incredible view of the Radcliffe Camera, as pointed out to him by the obsequious bellboy. Reggie tipped him generously; hey, you never knew when someone on the bell staff would come in handy, then disrobed and stepped into a comforting hot shower. He dried himself carefully, slipped into clean underwear and dove into the queen size bed, almost immediately falling into a light slumber. He slept for five hours, and was awakened by the late afternoon sunshine pouring over him. He had forgotten to draw the curtains but what the hell, it was time to get up anyway. Get dressed, go downstairs and find a drink and something to eat. Maybe pick up a girl, too. It would be interesting to bed someone with an English accent.

Downstairs he found the bar only about a quarter full, mostly small groups of business people with only one woman on her own, sitting at a small table just inside the door. He casually took the table next to her, ordered a whisky and took a couple of sips before pretending to notice her for the first time. She was a good looking redhead, grey eyed with a sprinkling of freckles over her high bridged nose. He wondered how many freckles resided under her somewhat stern gray suit and felt the familiar stirring between his legs.

"Excuse me," he said in his most ingratiating voice. "I just arrived here in Oxford, from New York, and wonder if you know the lay of the land." He allowed the word 'lay' to linger on his lips just a bit longer than usual. He was rewarded by a smile, and he returned it in full force. This was almost too easy.

"I'm a graduate of Lady Mary College," the redhead told him. "I'm just here for a dinner in hall. Whiling away a couple of hours before I have to get over there."

This was an invitation if ever he heard one! Reggie motioned to the empty place at her table, and she patted the chair beside her.

"Come on over," she said. "I'd love some company for a bit."

It took less than fifteen minutes for them to finish their drinks, which Reggie put on his tab, then together they left the bar and went up to his room.

"Care for another?" he asked, indicating the mini bar which he had flung open on their arrival.

"Just a quickie with you," the girl said. "As I told you, I don't have much time."

"Whatever you want," said Reggie gallantly.

"How about a little bondage? I'll go easy on you."

Reggie was breathing harder now. He had heard these English girls could be down and dirty, but this one lost no time.

"Me in bondage or you?"

"Oh, you of course," she said coolly. "Now get out of those clothes. Do you have some neckties?"

174

Dumbly Reggie indicated the open suitcase on the rack at the end of the bed. '"Help yourself." He dropped his clothes in a jumble and lay flat out on the bed.

The girl was over him immediately, tying loose knots around each wrist and looping two ties together to make a longer bond. Reggie soon saw why. The headboard was upholstered, with no place for her to affix the ties, so she took the extension of each tie and knotted it to a leg of the bedside tables, left and right. His legs she left free.

Reggie felt his prick standing to full attention. This was just like that incredibly hot girl in Maine. Was it only last week? He wondered if women were more and more interested in taking the upper hand these days, being the dominatrix while the man had to play the subservient position. His semi-helpless position excited him more than he would have thought possible, and he anticipated her lowering her oh-so-hot cunt over him, taking him into her slippery snatch inch by inch. Desire flooded over him, almost engulfing him. He closed his eyes, anticipating his upcoming pleasure.

Nothing happened. After a moment Reggie opened his eyes. The girl was in his trouser pocket, lifting his wallet out. He struggled against the silken bonds, but they held fast. She rifled the bills, removing all the sterling he had, strode to his bed where she gave his engorged penis a painful flick with her forefinger.

"Bye bye, asshole. Thought you had me, didn't you? Well, I had you instead." She moved to the door, opened it and was out in a second, closing the portal gently behind her.

On the bed, Reggie squirmed helplessly. What in God's name was he supposed to do? He twisted and turned, trying to slip his wrists from his own ties, to no avail. He did the only thing possible, jiggled the bed from side to side against the bedside table until it knocked the phone from its cradle and, when he heard a disembodied voice asking how it could be of help, had to shout over toward the receiver to explain that someone needed to come upstairs and untie him. A few minutes later there was a discreet tap on the door, then the lock clicked open and a valet type stood over him as he lay there naked as the day he was born, a half assed hard on waving above him.

"Let me get you untied, sir," the valet murmured. He soon had the bonds off Reggie's wrists and had the good taste to throw the sheet over his nakedness. "Will there be anything else, sir?" he asked with aplomb.

"Not now, thank you," Reggie managed to mutter. "What's your name?"

"Alastair, sir."

"Well, Alastair, I want to take care of you later. Please go now."

"Certainly, sir." Alastair even managed to execute the smallest of bows before letting himself out.

Even Reggie, for all his experience, was totally embarrassed at the plight the girl had put him in. Maybe another time he should be more careful. But he remembered a twenty pound note for Alastair, slipped into an envelope with no note and left at the desk. Reggie figured Alastair would know who had left it for him. And, when he checked his wallet, he found the girl had relived him of only about a hundred and fifty pounds. All his American cash and his credit cards were intact. Thank goodness he had not changed any more money in New York. He had been advised that the best rate of exchange came through the ATM's of the major British banks and there was no lack of such ATM's throughout England. But a hundred and fifty pounds for no sex seemed somewhat excessive. Well, he could always take care of himself. As his hard on had not totally diminished, he sat down before one of the windows and, as he jacked off, gazed out over the spires of Oxford, dreaming in the late afternoon sunlight.

The incident with the redhead put paid to any further philandering Reggie might have wanted, at least for the rest of the evening. He ordered roast chicken in his room, watched a couple of dull programs on the television, sent an email to Mickey Gold telling him of his meeting with the elusive George the next day, but not that he was in

England. Shortly thereafter he turned off his lift and settled in for the night.

Next morning he ordered a full English breakfast in his room, marveling at the amount of food that arrived on the rolling tray, covered by a pristine white cloth. There were eggs and ham and some sort of odd bacon, sausage, fried eggs, rolls and croissant with little pots of jam, honey and marmalade, even a broiled tomato to lend color to the plate, he supposed. How did English people stay trim with all this food, much of it fried, Reggie wondered, as he poured the first of several cups of rich, dark coffee from a silver pot. Ah, this was the life. He hoped some future assignment would bring him back to England someday.

His meeting with George was for eleven, so he selected his tan poplin summer suit, with brown oxfords, a white shirt and a tie from Vineyard Vines, a shop he has just discovered, courtesy of Marcia who had been taken there by Jessica. He thought it gave just the right hint of jauntiness, without being too effete. He hated effete. He inspected himself in the full length mirror on the bathroom door and, at five to eleven, headed downstairs. No need to look too impressed with the meeting.

He inquired at the reception desk for a Mr. MacIntyre, and a tall, youngish man rose from a leather easy chair in the lobby and crossed the few feet between them to shake Reggie's hand. George Parsons MacIntyre in the flesh.

Reggie noted he had a firm handshake and an honest gaze into the eyes, then realized he had overdressed for the meeting. George wore perfectly pressed designer jeans, loafers without socks and an impressive linen shirt, obviously fresh off the ironing board. His genial, open face gleamed with good health, overhung by a somewhat messy head of hair the color of dark wheat.

"Mr. Kavanaugh. Glad to meet you. Shall we have coffee here, or would you like me to show you one of my best projects?

"Whatever you like," Reggie answered genially, warming to this large, exuberant American in such a British setting. He took out his wallet and carefully extracted the card that read Reginald Kavanaugh, and handed it over to George for inspection.

"Well, it's off we go then. We can have coffee or a drink when we get there." He ushered Reggie outside to where the valet was keeping George's car, a long, low slung model, top down on this perfect early summer day.

The car swing out of town on the motor way, but turned off in twenty minutes to a secondary road which soon gave way to a narrow lane.

"Close, but still private," George commented. "It rarely takes me more than a half hour to get to work and I have the pleasure of country all around me and even some vestiges of village life."

"Reggie had no idea about village life, so simply gave an approving grunt.

They came on an imposing pair of stone gateposts, topped by figures that looked like something out of someone's outrageous imagination. "Gargoyles," George announced. "My stepfather's idea of a good joke."

Since Reggie wasn't quite sure of what a gargoyle was, either, he wisely kept his mouth shut.

They were running along open pastures now, dotted here and there with the large and dirty fluff of ewes with their lambs, the little ones mere puffs of the snowiest white. Reggie decided it was time to comment.

"Quaint," he announced, waving toward the flock. "Do you raise them to eat?"

"Not very many," said George. "We raise them mostly for wool. My mother is fond of reciting Blake's poem about the Little Lamb. Do you know it? She says it's a direct counterpart to Jerusalem.

Reggie was nonplussed. Blake? Lambs? Jerusalem? He was a long way from Brooklyn.

"Do you like poetry, Mr. Kavanaugh?" George inquired politely.

"Oh, sure," Reginald said heartily. "Why don't you recite one of those poems for me? Maybe the one about the lamb?" Anything to keep this man agreeable to Reggie's scheme: to find out all he could about him.

George Parsons began:

'Little lamb, who made thee,
Doest thou know who made thee?
Gave thee life and bid thee feed
Beside the stream and o'er the meade?
Gave thee clothing of delight,
Softest clothing, wooly bright,
Gave thee such a tender voice, making all the vales rejoice?"

"An I boring you?" asked George.

Reggie had no idea what the poem meant but politely replied, "Please go on."

George continued,

"Little lamb, I'll tell thee
Little lamb I'll tell thee.
He is called by thy name
For he called himself a lamb.
He is meek and he is mild
He became a little child
Little lamb, God bless thee,
Little lamb, God bless thee!"

"Gosh," Reggie managed to say. "You sure know your poetry." And that, he hoped, was the end of any more recitations.

Ahead, was an enormous stretch of lawn, dotted here and there with ancient trees. An avenue of some flowering variety pointed straight at a manor house, of mellow brick, sleeping in the sunlight. It was something straight out of a Masterpiece Classic program, and Reggie realized he was in the presence of true success and gentility.

"My mom and stepfather live there," George announced, then veered off onto a side lane, not much more in reality than a cow path. Giant hedgerows reared up on either side of the narrow way, obscuring any views of what lay beyond. Reggie wondered what happened if a car was coming the other way but, before he could find out, they drew up into the forecourt of one of the most unusual buildings Reggie had ever seen. The walls were of a rough and seemingly unfinished material, resembling mud and twigs, with a lot of pebbles thrown in. The huge rectangle was flanked by three separate round towers, almost dwarfing the structure contained by them, which rose three stories from the ground. Fields and orchards stretched out beyond this amazing edifice, as far as the eye could see.

The two men stepped out of the car. George announced: "This is my first project, which I did as soon as I qualified: the Oast House. It was on the property and Malcolm - that's my stepfather – gave it to me as a present." He swept his arm toward the unusual structure.

Reggie gaped. He had not counted on being so warmly received, and felt somewhat uneasy about his supposed connection with an architecture magazine.

"Gosh, George," he said. "I really appreciate your taking all this time with me. I don't know if I told you that the magazine is a start up. I mean I'm getting investors, there are lots of interested people and I'm sure we'll have a first issue within the year. I'd certainly like to include your wonderful house and give your background. It's young architects like you that are the future of the profession." There, that sounded sufficiently interested and he had a service back in New York that wore many hats, each connected with one of Reggie's projects. If George had called the supposed firm's number to check, he would have gotten a perky 'receptionist' who promised to pass along any information to her 'boss'. It was all so easy.

"Sure, Reggie," George said easily. "I'd like that. And I'm always happy to show my pride and joy to anyone who's interested. Did you bring a camera? Or do you want me to send a file of shots for the article. If you write it, of course?"

"That would be great," said Reggie with all the enthusiasm he could muster, and was given the guided tour for the next half hour, most of which went over his head.

George drove him back to Oxford, offered to buy him lunch – which Reggie declined, saying he had to get on to London. He did, however, leave with all George's particulars: his business address, his home address, his email and phone numbers, and access to his facebook and linkedin pages. And, almost more important, Reggie discovered that George was still single. George had been nothing but helpful with the supposed article, and Reggie felt a bit of a heel. But, what the hell, he had accomplished his mission. He could now give all the necessary information to Mickey to pass on to Jessica, and this job was done. He had done some pretty underhanded things before to get the necessary; he'd just have to chalk this one up to experience. Oh, and, as he checked out of the hotel, he reflected that this was one town in which he had not gotten any pussy, which was unusual for him. He'd have to make up for lost time when he got back to New York.

Chapter Eleven

George and Grace

The mail waiting on Mickey Gold's desk this Monday morning in April contained a thick brown envelope, bearing the return address of Reginald Katz, PI. Eagerly, Mickey pulled it toward him, taking up his letter opener, a present one Christmas from Marcia. It was a handsome brass and leather piece, suitable for an attorney's office and Mickey enjoyed owning it.

Inside was a sheaf of carefully typed pages bearing the title:

'Search for George Parsons, formerly of Boston, now of High Gate Farm, near Oxford, England'

Huh, thought Mickey. What in God's name was the elusive George doing in England, of all places? Well, he'd better put his other work aside, read the report, and find out. He spread out the pages on his desk, after leaving instructions not to be disturbed and ploughed in.

Jonathan Parsons, he read, had gotten in trouble financially a couple of years after the Maine summer which had severed the ties between his son and the girl next door. While on the surface he was a hail fellow well met individual, he harbored a dark side unknown for years to anyone but himself: he was a secret gambler, risking large sums on everything from the spread in major sports events, to the track and the roulette tables at various casinos he patronized on his many business trips away from home. For awhile his large salary and bonuses from his accounting firm, one of the largest in the country, and his management of his wife's funds in the stock market, saw him through, but then came the economic downturn and Jonathan's luck began to change. The ponies he backed seemed to be running last in the field, the roulette wheel spun up any number but his own and his manipulations of his wife's funds began to go south. In desperation he turned to day trading, buying and selling with wild abandon, until there was no more in the account. Unwilling to face financial disaster, he started to divert funds from his company to straw accounts, set up in the Cayman Islands and Switzerland, until those, too, crashed, due to his mismanagement, and he was faced with total financial ruin.

Parsons contemplated taking his own life, then thought seriously of disappearing to some far flung part of the world where he was not known, and starting over. Leaving his wife and son behind did not seem too high a price for his own safety, for he was, as ever, a totally self-involved man. However, before he could put either of these plans into action, the police arrived at his home in Beacon Hill early one morning and took him away in handcuffs. It was the first time either his wife or his son had any inkling that their comfortable life was built on the thinnest layer of sand, not on the rock solid foundation they had always thought.

Jonathan Parsons, after a year in jail and a two month trial, was sentenced to 5-10 years in federal prison. Grace Parsons (wife) and George Parsons (son) were left destitute after paying the attorney fees.

Grace Parsons, at first, took this total change of fortune with ill grace, wringing her hands helplessly and taking to her bed for days at a time. What would she and George do? How would they survive – both the financial upheaval and the disgrace? How would she ever face her friends again? How would she pay the bills? The Maine house had been sold some years before, and she had no idea their Boston home was mortgaged to the hilt. She reviewed the years she had spent as the wife of Jonathan Parsons, and bile filled her soul. The absolute cretin, no, the

bastard! How could he have so brought his wife and son to this place of complete collapse? With her anger rising day by day, Grace rose from her bed, faced reality and decided what she would do.

George would have to leave his excellent boarding school and be placed, at least temporarily, into public school. She would have to find a job and a small place for them to live, one she could afford. And it would probably have to be in the environs of Boston, for she knew no other city, had no real contacts anyplace but this metropolis where she had been born and lived all of her life. She put her pride in her pocket and went to various friends, asking them to find her a job. Her job skills were few, but she was determined. Finally, a friend from her school days came up with the perfect solution. Grace knew Boston inside and out, had the kind of knowledge of this cradle of civilization that was afforded few people. She would make a spectacular addition to the concierge staff at one of the large hotels. The friend called in a few favors, and Grace was hired, albeit as a lowly sub assistant and a very lowly salary and became a clerk in a hierarchy that would probably not bring her much satisfaction or many perks.

Grace and George Parsons resided in Arlington, a suburb of Boston, for the duration of the jail sentence and trial. Grace secured a position as assistant in-house concierge of a major Boston hotel.

She found half a two family house for rent, in the suburb of Arlington, making her commute inconvenient but wanting the best possible public education for George. With her wardrobe from her days as the wife of a successful businessman, and her perfect manners and deportment, she brought a certain cache to the department that had not been there before.

Mickey put down the report and scratched his head. What a comedown for a woman who had been used to the best! He had to hand it to her, she landed on her feet. He rubbed his eyes before continuing.

Her first day on the job, Grace was assigned a small cubicle at the end of a long row of similar cubicles and given the job of checking the times of opening and closing of various museums around town, and contacting movie theaters for their upcoming showings. The hotel chain published a monthly magazine for each city, listing all kinds of activities and restaurants for the use of the hotel guests. Grace, surprisingly, found she fit right in. Her many years of volunteer work had made her a stickler for accuracy, and, within a few weeks, her work was praised by the in-house editor of the magazine, and she was given more responsibility. She was soon put in charge of keeping the racks of sightseeing and travel arrangements filled outside the small office, off the lobby, where the concierge actually worked, and she became friendly with this other denizen of Boston, who had almost more information at her fingertips than Grace herself.

As she commuted in and out of the city to her new job, Grace sometimes ruminated on the life she had left versus the new life she had made for herself and George.

Certainly the hours on the job were tiring, and going home to the somewhat depressing half-a-house when she had been used to a spacious ten room dwelling, with lovely grounds and gardens which she gloried in keeping pristine and beautiful. But, she told herself, aside from George, she had felt somewhat useless, estranged as she was from her husband, who spent more time away from home than in it. Plus, she had hated the frequent punishments Jonathan had meted out to George, shouting at him for the least offense and belting him with the leather strap he pulled from his waist. She hoped George was not too upset with their abrupt change of status, but she did her best to give him all the time she had away from the job, hoping it would make up for the life lost to him.

Certainly she did not miss the sex with Jonathan, which had been infrequent, at best. It had been coarse and swift, with no thought given to her pleasure. As long as Jonathan had achieved an orgasm, he was

185

satisfied, leaving her nervous and jumpy for hours afterward. His idea of a 'good time' – his expression – was bedding her in a hurry and retreating in an equal hurry. A typical Saturday night, after several rounds of cocktails with members at their golf club and a heavy dinner, usually took place right after they returned home. They would barely get in the front door before Jonathan would make a lunge for her, often catching her off guard. He'd grasp her buttocks in a vice like grip, and mutter something like, "hey, babe, how's about it? Let's get upstairs and get laid." If he had ever kissed or caressed her, it might have been different, but the sex was strictly functional. He'd remove his clothes upstairs in their bedroom, then lie on his back on the bed, pecker rampant, often with his hand on the shaft, stiffening it further for his entry into her.

Reluctant, Grace would often take as long as possible, hanging up her clothes neatly, placing her shoes in the bags in her closet.

"Hurry up," Jonathan would urge. "My prick can't wait to get into that hot cunt. Wha' do you want me to do? Jack off while I'm waiting for you?" And he'd actually leer at her, thinking no doubt he was making pillow talk.

When Grace finally did approach the bed, there was no foreplay, not even a kiss. He'd reach a finger up inside of her and, if he deemed there was not enough lubricant there, he'd open his bedside table where he kept a large tube of KY Jelly, slathering his finger with the colorless goo, thrusting it up into her, then wiping off any excess in her pubic hair.

"Come to Daddy," he'd moan, "let's get it off." And, spread eagling her on the bed, he'd climb aboard and start to pump, faster and faster until he let out a yell of triumph, then collapsed, full weight on her for a moment before rolling off, turning on his side and snoring. Grace would be left in the dark, sore and unhappy, so miserable that sometimes she shed a few quiet tears into her pillow.

It was even worse when Grace had her period. Jonathan would tell her she smelled like dead fish so it was more degrading during her menses when he wanted to have sex. He claimed he could smell her, and

186

would greet her at the door with 'God, you're bleeding again. Disgusting." As if she had any control over this bodily function. But still he would march her upstairs, often right past George, who gaped from his room or from the couch where he watched television. Once in the bedroom he would not bother to undress, just drop his trousers and shorts, sit on the edge of the bed, and beckon her over to him. "Come to Daddy. Kneel down. Daddy wants a blow job." And he never locked or even fully closed the door during these ministrations.

Inwardly cringing, she would obey, dropping to her knees before him, waiting for him to take her head in a vice like grip and force her down over his swinging penis. She never dared object, simply opened her mouth and let him thrust into her, so deeply she always gagged. Five or ten good thrusts was all it would take for him to ejaculate, sending the sperm gushing down her unwilling throat, forcing her to swallow it at which point he released her head. She would jump up, rush to the bathroom, and gargle madly, anything to get the taste out of her mouth. By the time she returned to the bedroom he had shed his clothes and was snoring on his side of the bed. The one time she had suggested, early in their marriage, that he might want to do the same to her, Jonathan had looked at her like she was crazy.

"God, you think I want so lick your dirty crack? Why would I do that? You're disgusting down there." And that had been the end of any cunnilingus for her. She had learned, over the years, to bring herself off, quickly and quietly, usually on the nights Jonathan was absent, or in the bathtub after letting out the water, and locking the door.

That had been their sex life and Grace was glad to be quit of it.

Several months after the arrest, owing to much publicity in the local papers, Grace Parsons went to court and legally took back her maiden name of MacIntrye for herself and for George. Henceforth they are known as Grace MacIntyre and George MacIntyre.

Soon after the trial ended, Grace (now) MacIntyre secured a position in a Stamford, CT. hotel, and she and George (now) MacIntyre moved to Westport, CT.

Matters accelerated, however, several months after Jonathan's trial ended, with articles continuing to appearing in the local papers. Grace had had enough. Appalled at this invasion of her privacy in her new life, Grace went to court and took back her maiden name of MacIntyre for her and for George. Realizing that in Boston she could never remain anonymous, she went to her boss and asked if there could be a transfer to another city. The concierge, sympathetic to her plight, put the wheels of change into motion and, by the start of the new school year, Grace found herself with a job in Stamford, Connecticut, with the rental of a tiny, run down cottage near the station in Westport and George enrolled in 11th grade at Staples High School. She soon got her bearings and enjoyed her research into the doings and dining around Fairfield County. The rented house even had a tiny plot out back, which Grace soon filled with flowers. Life, if not perfect, at least seemed tolerable and she took pride that she had done all this herself, relying on no one else.

Though Grace worried inordinately about how all these changes would affect George, in truth he took the loss of his father and his father's way of life with more equanimity than his mother had expected. It had been tough when his father's name and his father's crime had hit the Boston papers, and some of the students at school had been cruel indeed to taunt him George with it. But after his mother changed their name and they moved to Connecticut, he settled well enough into his new school and even began making friends. He was an all around good athlete, making the tennis team with ease, and the easier standards of the public school gave him a high B / low A average. College was still two years away and he and his mother would figure out some way to get him there.

He did not miss the father who had so often been absent in his life, and who had punished him so severely, seemingly taking pleasure in the whippings he administered, All that was over now and his mother was the most reasonable of women, seemingly happier now than she had been in the big house in Boston, the fancy cars and the house in Maine. Maybe everything would work out for the best. In the meantime, George enjoyed living in a small town with its proximity to New York. When he could, he went down to the city, to hang out, visit some of the museums and explore the crooked streets of Greenwich Village. He was not a particularly complex boy and did not think to question the events that had brought him and his mother to this entirely new life. There were girls aplenty in his high school class, many of whom seemed to like him and several who liked having sex, in the houses empty of parents in the two working parent families that abounded in Westport, or down on the beach late at night, avoiding the patrolling police. It made things more exciting to know they might be caught. There were back lots and woods and, as always, the back seat of a car, parked on some lonely road. All in all George was having the time of his life.

Occasionally he remembered the little girl he had played doctor with in Maine, all those summers ago, then the barn party where he had rescued her from that creep. But they were vague memories and he did not expect to see her again. Her parents had money, lots of it, and his present circumstances did not permit him to live the same kind of life she must be having, so close down the road in the city.

George noticed, about six months into their time in Westport that his mother had taken on a sudden glow. She took an enormous amount of time with her hair and makeup, and was constantly changing clothes, turning this and that way in front of her mirror, examining herself from every angle. "Uh oh,' he thought, 'there's a man around somewhere.' He was right, of course, but it took quite a long time for his mother to make the introduction.

Grace had been promoted at her job, and placed in charge of certain of the events and conventions that took place at the hotel. Her former life had taught her the fine points of table setting, flower arranging and menus, as well as check lists for invitations, promotions and the like, and she was becoming more and more valuable as an employee. She had a number of night assignments now, especially during conventions and symposiums, overseeing everything from the greeting of the guests at the check in desk, to their accommodation, meals, car hires and even, in some instances, their travel arrangements. One early evening she sat in the lobby of the main ballroom, primed to receive a delegation of international architects, meeting in Stamford to discuss the future of green construction and all its ramifications. It was a subject that interested Grace, and she planned on sitting in the back of the room when the speeches started and reading the material which she was even now handing out to attendees, each sheaf of papers enclosed in a handsome dark green cover, embossed in gold lettering.

Grace gave a ready smile with each folder, indicating the entrance to the ballroom, welcoming the men and women at the seminar. The smile was automatic and the faces passed before her, one blending into the next. Then a man stopped before her and did more than pick up his folder and disappear into the ballroom.

Grace was aware of a well polished pair of black brogues, obviously not new but of the best possible quality, which led upward to a perfectly tailored suit, a pristine white shirt with spread collar, and a natty regimental striped silk tie. Above this was a ruggedly handsome square face, firm chin, hazel eyes, all topped off by a neatly cut head of sandy/gray hair. Certainly a man worth looking at. The smile Grace gave was warmer than usual as she handed him his folder.

"Thank you." The voice was deep and the words s spoken in a beautiful Oxbridge accent. She searched her memory, trying to remember in the guest list who was over from England for the seminar. She could only think or two, or possibly three, architects whom she had registered for the event and this was obviously one of them. She would certainly get it when he gave it to her for the check in, which he did immediately.

190

"I'm Malcolm Bevington, from Oxford. Might you be Grace MacIntyre, the woman with whom I have been corresponding about this event? He put out his hand, the back of which was sprinkled with blonde hair to match his head.

"Yes, I'm Grace MacIntyre. How clever of you to remember." She found herself almost simpering and drew herself up inwardly with a reprimand. He was a client. She was a hotel employee. That was all there was to that.

"I wanted to thank you personally for taking such good care of me prior to my arrival," he said, not relinquishing her hand. "You even remembered to order me a hard pillow for my bed. A most comfortable bed, by the way."

Was he flirting with her? It had been so long since she bantered with a member of the opposite sex, certainly before she married Jonathan, that Grace was not sure.

"Could I invite you for a drink, or lunch, sometime while I am here in Connecticut to thank you? I know the seminar keeps us pretty busy but I was going to stay over an extra day or two. Maybe then?"

Grace knew she was not supposed to socialize with guests of the hotel, but perhaps after the seminar she could manage a meeting with this attractive man.

"Maybe," she said, non committedly.

"Let me call you tomorrow after I see what my schedule is after this seminar," Malcolm said. "In the meantime, thank you again for everything." He flashed her an open grin and went through the double doors to the ballroom and out of her sight.

Grace sat back briefly, savoring the moment. Would he call? Probably not. But she could hope.

Another body presented itself at her table and she handed over yet another green folder, giving her perfect-hotel-employee smile.

Mickey Gold again paused in his perusal of the report. So Grace maybe found herself another man. Lucky Grace. But he felt, somehow,

191

she might deserve it. Let's see how this meeting took things forward. He turned again to the report.

Grace was in her hotel office as usual a little after nine the next morning, and at nine fifteen her first line lit up.

"Grace MacIntyre. How can I help you?"

"Good morning, Grace." May I call you Grace? Or would you prefer Mrs. MacIntyre?" The voice was as deep as she remembered, clipping the words of carelessly, using a tone that would not have been amiss quoting Shakespeare.

Her world brightened a little.

"I find we are being kept extremely busy these next few days," Malcolm told her. "But you already know that. Would Sunday suit you to get together? I haven't seen 'Jersey Boys' yet and hear it's a wonderful show. Would you like to go? And oh, could your office get the tickets."

"I think that could be arranged." Grace was practically grinning from ear to ear now. "Though it will be expensive, I'm afraid."

"Don't worry about the expense, just put it on my bill. I shall ask you to rent a car, too, to drive into New York. I could pick you up at your house."

Grace thought quickly. Much as she was not ashamed of where she and George lived, perhaps it was best not to let this man into her personal life so soon. And George would be sure to be curious to know just who this man was. "It can be such bad traffic," she said. "Why don't we take the train instead? So much easier and no problem parking a car. I am a couple of towns up the line and could save you a seat. Say in the second car?"

"Sounds good," said Malcolm. "Shall we eat afterward? It's always so rushed trying to have lunch before a matinee, don't you think?"

"Oh, I quite agree," said Grace.

"Where could we eat afterward?"

"Do you like Sardis? I mean, it's sort of corny, but it's open and it's right across from the theater, I believe."

"Done," said Malcolm. ""I leave all the arrangements to you. It's nice to have a personal social secretary."

She appreciated the little joke and hung up, happier than she had been for a long while.

And so began the long distance romance of Grace and Malcolm, which was to bloom and blossom as the months passed, even though much of it was conducted by email and Skype.

Grace found herself humming as she went to work, did her tasks at home, worked in her garden, and spent as much time as he had with George.

George, by now, had made his own friends and had a life in Westport that included school and the sports he played there, with weekend parties and dates, summer weekends stretched out on Compo Beach with one bikini clad girlfriend or another and occasional dinners out with his mother. They fell into a workable routine, both living their own lives, but coming together often as mother and son, too. George had completed his junior year of high school, and Grace was beginning to worry about college. She need not have. Fate, in the person of Malcolm Bevington, was about to solve that, and all her other problems for her.

Malcolm had made several trips back to the United States after that first convention, always staying in a local hotel or inn, though, after the second trip, Grace had joined him in his room, once during the afternoon, once after a date to dinner and a movie. She was amazed by the ardor and scope of his lovemaking, and told him so often.

"You're amazing. You seem to know what I want even before I want it," she told him one late afternoon as the sun was sinking over Long Island Sound, throwing dappled shadows from the water on their bedroom walls."

"Like this?" asked Malcolm as he dipped his tongue into her ear.

"Yes, like that." Grace murmured. "And so many other things."

"Like this?" the tongue continued down Grace's neck, over her collar bone and to the rapidly rising nipples of her breasts. He gently took each nipple into his mouth, sucking and tonguing it, causing Grace to arch her back and thrust up toward him.

"Yes," she moaned. "Oh, yes."

Malcolm gave a short laugh, and continued down, down, over her navel, with a practiced flip, down one inner thigh to her knee then back up the other, drawing nearer and ever nearer to the glistening labia. He parted her with two fingers, flicking his tongue over her enlarged clitoris, causing her to moan and grasp his rampant penis in her hand.

He palmed her hairy mound with the flat of his hand, thrusting two fingers into her willing vagina, pressing her clitoris with a thumb. She tightened her grip on his prick, running her finger under the head as he had taught her. Much of this foreplay was new to her, used as she had been to Jonathan's quick entry and exit, and she gloried in all the pleasure she could bring to Malcolm's body, as he did the same to her.

"Now," she gasped, "I want you now." Her knees fell ever further apart and she arched her sex upward ever upward for him to mount her.

Malcolm obliged, positioning himself above her, weight distributed on his elbows. His lips sought hers, as his tongue probed her open mouth, and he gently slid into her, causing Grace to moan with pleasure as her hips performed an involuntary little dance of their own.

"Hold on," Malcolm whispered into her ear. "No need to rush our pleasure."

"But I can't wait," she whispered back. "I'm coming, now." Her body was racked by waves and waves of intense pleasure, her hips thrust faster and faster upward ever upward as she was blown away by the intensity of a gigantic orgasm that went on and on, seemingly without end. Finally, she crashed down to earth again, clinging to Malcolm as if she would never let go.

"That was incredible," she breathed, when she could get her breath. "The best."

"Want another?"

"Yes, please." And, as Malcolm tickled her twitching clitoris, she again felt herself rise and rise and heard him shout as they came together, in one giant crescendo.

Afterward, it seemed natural to be talking marriage. He never really asked her, but they began to discuss where to live and how and when to tell George and how things would work out, quite as if such a change in both their lives was the most natural thing in the world.

They chose a Saturday night to tell George, taking him out to dinner at The Boat House at the Saugatuck Rowing Club. Here they were given a table on the balcony overlooking the river, quiet now in the early evening, with no traffic other than a few groups of swimming Canada Geese, with a pair of swans paddling away upstream.

Grace and Malcolm ordered martinis, George, a coke. He had come to know Malcolm over the past few months, and felt totally at ease with him. He also was happy that this man seemed to be making his mother into a totally different person from the one who had been married to his father: softer, prettier, serene.

Grace took a big gulp of her drink, not her usual way of downing a martini and cleared her throat.

"George," she said, looking him full in the face. "Malcolm and I have something to tell you. Rather, we want to ask what you think...." She trailed off, not sure now to continue.

"You guys getting married?" George asked.

They stared in unison at him. "How did you know?"

"Well, you're always holding hands and gazing at each other. You seem to be happy all the time. Maybe you're just going to shack up?"

"No,"Malcolm said. "I guess we are old fashioned enough to want to make things legal."

"Do you mind?" Grace asked softly.

"I think it's great," George said and leaned over to give his mother a kiss on the cheek.

Tears appeared on her cheek, but she wiped them off with her napkin and clasped George's hand. "I'm so glad you are happy for us.

And don't think it will change the way I feel about you because it won't. The more love there is in someone's life, the more there is go to around."

"Hell, I'm just happy for you."

Malcolm reached across the table and clasped his hand. "I know you've had a hard time of it," he said. "What with all that mess with your father. But I am not going to try to take his place. You're too old for that. I'd like to think we can become the very best of friends."

"I hope so," said George, and his voice shook a little. "I sure hope so."

"I know this is going to change your life," Malcolm was quick to say. "We plan on living in England, but if you want to go to college here, I am prepared to pay for it. I told your mother that, it is the least I can do. Or, if you think it would help your future life, why not take A levels in England. I can get you into sixth form at my old school. It would be an extra year, but if you want to attend university in England, it's only three years. Or come back here if you prefer."

What wonderful options suddenly opened up for George. He knew his mother couldn't pay for college and faced a huge student loan. Everything was changed and in his favor. And all due to this man who was going to marry his mother. For an instant he wondered what it might have been like to have a father like this, but dismissed the thought. He was here now and that was all that mattered.

Together they gazed out over the peaceful river.

Grace MacIntyre met and married Malcolm Bevington, of Oxfordshire, England, in Connecticut, and moved with him and George to England at the end of the summer before George's senior year at Staples High School. They married in a ceremony in the village church in Wytton-Under-Lynchley shortly after arriving in England.

So George suddenly got an enormous boost to his education, Mickey Gold thought as he turned over yet another page of the long, involved report. He wondered which option George took: an extra year in England then college, or four years in the United States at the college of his course. Lucky bastard. But, considering the father who had landed in jail, maybe George deserved this break. He'd find out. Mickey Gold took up another page of the report.

After much consideration and conversation with both his mother and Malcolm, George finally decided to take up his stepfather's option to complete his undergraduate education in England. Since his mother would no longer be in Westport, indeed in the country, there would be no home to go to in the United States on vacations. Plus which, four years of an English education would surely boost his chances in the job market once he graduated. So, with Malcolm pulling some strings, he was enrolled in a top English public school, not too far from his mother's new home outside of Oxford. It was here in the lush green countryside of England, from where Malcolm designed the 'green' houses and public buildings that had made him famous. Home for the new blended family was a mellow manor house, home of the Bevington family for four generations, large enough to be impressive but not too large to be unmanageable. Built of red brick, faded to pale coral by years of exposure to the weather, it sat atop a knoll overlooking a wide valley with a branch of the Cherwell at its base. A few miles down the road, the spires of Oxford, that magical city where higher learning was begun a thousand years ago, lay dreaming, its ancient buildings of pale gold unchanged over the centuries. George realized that when the first scholars took up residence in those hallowed halls, America was populated solely by native Indians, and that the first such educational establishment – Harvard – would not be founded for over six hundred years. It was somewhat awe inspiring to such a totally American boy, but, on completing his Upper Sixth Form and acquiring three A levels for himself, George was thrilled to be accepted by Oxford, and spent his three years there in total harmony with his new life.

George MacIntyre completed his undergraduate education and entered Oxford, completing his three years there before attending

197

architecture school at Harvard. With an AIA degree he returned to
England where he works for his stepfather.

The years in Oxfordshire with his mother and new stepfather
gave George an unparalleled view of architecture in the 21st century, and
it made him want to – if possible – follow in Malcolm's footsteps. He
applied to graduate school in Architecture at Harvard, and was accepted,
returning to America and Cambridge at age twenty two, earning his
degree two years later. England beckoned, and he returned to
Oxfordshire, accepting an entry level position with Malcolm's company
where he started in the drafting department. His fascination with
emerging concepts of energy saving methods of building structures was
in total keeping with the ambitions of the firm, and his first project was
to totally renovate an old Oast house on Malcolm's property, which was
given over to him for his residence in Oxfordshire. The resultant
structure, in every possible way an energy saving residence, with solar
panels on the roof, its own well and massive windows cut into the old
timbers of the building was spectacular enough to gain a mention in
Architectural Digest. George was on his way.

Mickey Gold rubbed his eyes on completion of the report. It had
been painstakingly put together, with many details of the years since
Jessica had last seen George. But the best sentence of all came last:

*Subject George (Parsons) MacIntyre, now age 30, is single,
apparently straight, with no entanglements. He resides primarily in
Oxfordshire at the above address, when not traveling on international
assignments.*

Email and phone numbers were given, also the information that
George was listed on Facebook and Linkedin.

Mickey Gold sat back, satisfied. Now to call Reggie, thank him,
and pass the news along to Jessica. On second thought, he'd invite them
both to lunch, locally, at Hillstone. Let Reggie give her the good news

himself; he had certainly worked hard enough as his bill, enclosed with the report, indicated.

Chapter Twelve

Making Contact

Mickey picked up the phone immediately after reading Reggie's report and first called the detective, then Jessica. Luckily both were available for lunch that day, so he arranged to meet them at Hillstone, a block up from his office, at 12:30 and reserved a back booth where, hopefully, they would have some privacy.

He arrived on time to find Jessica seated at the bar, a glass of whisky in front of her.

"A little early isn't it?" he asked jokingly. "You usually only have a glass of white wine at lunch."

"I'm a nervous wreck about the report," she said. "You didn't say anything on the phone."

"Well, your curiosity will be satisfied in about two minutes," Mickey told her. ""Here's Reggie now. I thought you would like him along, too, in case you have any questions. It's a very thorough report, though."

"Is he married?" Jessica demanded.

"No, he's still single and that's all I'm going to tell you for now."

Jessica's eyes lit up and a silly grin appeared on her face. "Wunderbar!" she exclaimed and slid off the bar stool into Reggie's arms. 'You're a genius," she told him, "and I can't thank you enough for finding George for me. Where is he? Here in New York? Up in Boston? Where?" She sounded like an eager little girl.

"Hold your horses. Mickey will give you the report as soon as we sit down." They were led to their booth and Jessica slid in first, putting out her hand for the large manila envelope Mickey was carrying. She picked up the drink and took a huge swallow, eyes tearing slightly.

Without paying the slightest attention to either man, she opened the envelope and slid out the pages and pages of closely typed notes.

"Oh, England!" she cried. "What on earth is he doing there?"

"Read the report, Reggie told her."

The men were finishing their second drink by the time Jessica's eyes left the last page in her hand, which she added to the pile of the others with a sigh. "Poor George," she said softly. "And poor Mrs. Parsons. I mean Mrs. MacIntyre. Actually, it's Mrs. Bevington now. Lucky woman; it seems she found a wonderful second husband." Why did she sound so pensive?

"Well, look," said Reggie. "He's single, he doesn't seem to have a girl friend, and I've given you lots of ways to contact him. You could call him of course, or email him, or try him on Facebook. Or even write a letter. The old fashioned way."

"Yes, any of those ways," said Jessica dreamily. She gazed at the picture, taken from the Harvard graduating class in architecture. Yes, the same firm mouth, the same unruly hair, the same eyes, framed in blonde lashes. George. Maybe here was her salvation.

She hardly noticed the salad she ordered for lunch, or the wonderful espresso to finish the meal, but she remembered to thank both Mickey and Reggie profusely, before she hailed a taxi and gave her address.

All the way up Madison Avenue she clutched the manila envelope to her bosom, fearing it might take off and vanish into thin air. She greeted her doorman hastily, almost ran across the lobby and willed the elevator to get to her floor faster. Once inside the apartment, she tossed her keys on the hall table, kicked her shoes under the pier table and flopped on the living room couch, where she removed the report again, separating the first and last pages from the rest. George near Oxford. George with both a degree in 19th Century English Literature from Oxford *and* an Architecture degree from Harvard. Good for George!

Plus A levels in History, French and – of all things – Milton. He had achieved the kind of education many people dream of and even now was designing houses, not only in England, but in Europe and the Middle East. Maybe someday he would be in America, designing the kind of houses people would live in in the future. Anything was possible, and he was still single. A miracle.

She went into her bedroom and turned on her computer. She stared blankly at the icons against the blue background, deciding which way to go. Finally she opened her Facebook and, glancing at the address Reggie had given her, sent a 'friend' request to George MacIntyre, Oxford. With fingers crossed she pushed the 'send' button and sat back, wondering what, if anything, would happen next.

Nervously she paced the rooms of her apartment, straightening a cushion here, tweaking a bedspread there. It occurred to her she needed to go to the bathroom and went into her black and white tiled bath, where she peed quickly and flushed the toilet. Figuring a watched computer never brought in a message, she went out to the kitchen and poured a glass of chardonnay from an open bottle in the refrigerator. At this point she would be drunk by dinner time, but far better to be in that condition than to be this jumpy, unable to sit or do anything else. She took the wine back into her bedroom and looked at her computer screen. Wonder of wonders! She had a reply. George Parsons MacIntyre had 'friended' her. It must be evening in England and he must be looking at some digital device, be it a phone, i-pad or his computer.

'*Hey, Jessica!*' the message box read. '*What a wonderful surprise. Do write back and tell me what you have been doing these many years; email would be the best bet. I saw your wedding announcement in the Times a few years ago; how's Mr. Jellingdorf?*' He added his email address, not that she didn't have it already from Reggie.

Realizing she was actually a little tipsy, and that now was probably not the best time to tell her life story to George, Jessica pushed the button and simply wrote '*Tomorrow better for me. Will write at length then. There is no more Mr. Jellingdorf. A bientot.'* and put down the screen, hugging herself as she did so.

The next morning found her up very early, and she took a large lined pad to make notes for the message she would send George at a more appropriate time. God forbid he think she was up at 5:47 a.m. just to write him. She made a cup of strong coffee in her French press, and sat down at the dining room table to make her notes.

Where to begin? Back in Maine all those years ago? No, that was not a good idea. Certainly not the barn dance in Darien. No, maybe she should start now, this very minute, tell him she was making a truly fresh start. She gnawed the end of her pencil, then began writing rapidly.

The message, when it was composed from 7:45 a.m. to 7:50 a.m. and sent at 7:57 and had taken a great deal of thought. It read:

> *'Dear George:*
>
> *I was so pleased to find you online so easily. I have long wanted to get in touch, but thought you were probably married with three children...and bald? Is any of this true? I'm living in New York now, divorced, no children. I teach French to 15 year olds...sometimes great, sometimes a disaster! How did you land in England and what are you doing there? Would love to hear. Do get back to me when you have a chance.'* She thought long and hard about how to sign the email, then just finished simply with *'Jessica.'*

She shut down her computer, threw the multiple pages of notes she had made to type the short message into the wastebasket, then took up her handbag and hurried off to school, where, with any luck, she would arrive just in time to walk into her first class.

Resolutely, throughout the day, she did not check for messages, texts or emails on her phone. She waited until she was back home, back at her own computer, and ready for anything.

A short list of emails popped up, but the one she sought was the only one she opened. George had written

'Hi, Jessica,

Thanks for emailing so soon. I've been in England now these last three years. You may not know, but my father went to jail for embezzlement and my mother changed our names then married a great guy named Malcolm Bevington who lives here in Oxfordshire. He's an architect, so am I and I work for him. Can you call a stepfather's influence nepotism? Probably. But I found the right career for me and love doing what I do. England is far different from America, as you know, though I may take myself and my talents (?) back to the good old U.S. of A. one of these days, but right now I am learning so much that this is my home for the foreseeable future. Any chance you might be crossing the millpond in this direction? It would be great to meet again. Hope to hear from you soon again. George.'

Jessica printed out the email and danced around the apartment, clutching it to her chest. She felt almost delirious with happiness, flimsy though it might be. George wanted to see her. He had actually almost invited her over. Alas, she was going nowhere until the school term was over in June, but, in the meantime, she could at least write George. And he could write her. If he did. If he would. She kissed the email and slipped it under her pillow. Maybe if she slept on his words she would dream about him.

The next morning she woke up with the feeling that all was wonderful and, for an instant, wondered what had happened in her life. Then she remembered: George. She hugged herself, drew the now crumpled email from under her pillow and kissed it, smoothing out the folds and reading the message, which she already knew by heart, again. She opened her computer, put up

To: George@HighgateFarm.com.uk
From: JAJeast88@aol.com
Re: Greetings

'Dear George:

Off to teach the little darlings subjunctive verbs. Ow. Back this afternoon when I will write more. Jessica.'

She pushed the 'send' button. At least George would know she was thinking of him.

The first thing she did when returning home was to open her computer. The screen immediately popped up:

To: JAJeastt88@aol.com
From: George@HighgateFarm.co.uk
Re: Yours of earlier

'Hi Jessica

I trust your little darlings didn't wear you out. I hope you have plans for the weekend. I wish we weren't so far apart. George'

Was this the beginning of something? Or just a little online flirting? She had no idea, so decided to call someone who would know.

The phone was picked up on the second ring: "Hi, Jessica. What're you up to. No, no dates for me this weekend, Pedro's not here."

"Hey, guess what, I'm in touch with George. You know, George."

"What?" Marcia's screech was so loud Jessica had to hold the phone away from her ear. "Why didn't you tell me?"

"Well, it only just happened," Jessica said. "Reggie found him for me, with email address, linkedin, Facebook, everything, and we've communicated – she paused for effect – four times now!"

"Why you little sneak! Imagine all that raunchy prose winging over the Atlantic without me knowing about it." Marcia was only teasing. "What does he say? Has he sent you any suggestive pictures yet?"

"You think he's already sexting me? Marcia, really!"

Marcia thought of the rampant penis that had popped up on her phone screen after the abortive bridge evening with Marvin, but decided to leave well enough alone. "Well, time for that later," she said cheerfully. "Now are you going to invite me over? We can crack a big bottle of that chardonnay you like and have a blast."

"Sure, come on over," Jessica said. "I haven't seen you all week." She hung up the phone, and went out to the kitchen for glasses, humming under her breath. She realized with a start it was the tune of an old, old song: 'You do something to me....' She couldn't remember the words but vowed to look them up on the internet. After Marcia left. A pleasant tingle started in her groin, something certainly unexpected.

Marcia breezed in a half hour later, bearing a bag from the local liquor store containing an extra bottle of the chardonnay she and Jessica liked. "Sounds like you have it bad," she remarked as she brushed Jessica's cheek in greeting. "Well, girlfriend, let's hear all about it."

Jessica ushered her friend into the living room and poured brimming glasses of wine before saying anything.

"I'm in touch with George," she said. "He's an architect now, living in England. His mother remarried and his father's in jail for embezzlement. Gosh, what a lot has happened in a few years. "

"Number one question," said Marcia. "Is he married?"

"No," said Jessica. "Isn't that wonderful? And he apparently doesn't have a girlfriend now either."

"Well, when are you going to see him?" asked the ever practical Marcia.

"No plans yet. Though he did say he wished we weren't so far apart. And he asked how Mr. Jellingdorf was. I was happy to say he was no longer part of my life."

"Sounds like the stage is set for some fun and games," Marcia told her friend. "Question is, where, how soon and how far are you prepared to go?"

"Oh, I'd go to England, if he invited me, like a shot."

"That's not what I meant. How far are you prepared to go sexually? Would you go to bed with him? You've got a trail of disappointed men around New York who'd love the opportunity."

"Marcia, don't be silly. Who – well besides Don – would have me."

"Oh, I can think of several others," Marcia said. "But let's get back to George. Well?"

"Well, yes. I don't know why, probably childhood dreams of the knight in shining armor on the white charger sort of thing. And why George? I don't really know. It just seems like a good idea."

"Are you going to tell him about your sexual hangups?"

"Yes," said Jessica. "Dr. Consuelo told me that when I found a man I could trust I had to open up to him. I couldn't pretend that what has happened to me never took place. And George was there for some of that, remember?"

"I sure do," Marcia reassured her. "Well, on to George then. Have you answered his last email?"

"No."

"Why on earth not? I'm going to finish this wine then leave you to get onto your computer. No time like the present." She gulped down the rest of her wine and stood up to leave.

At the door, Jessica gave her a big hug. 'You're the best friend a girl ever had."

"You'd better believe it," Marcia said as she vanished into the elevator.

Jessica sat down at her computer.

To: George@HighGate.co.uk
From: JAJeast88@aol.com

'Dear George:
Just rummaging around in a box of old snapshots and came up with one from Maine, oh, so many summers ago! There we are on the point and you just caught a fish. You were so proud of it, though it probably wasn't even big enough to eat. I was proud of you, too. Don't know if there is any fishing in our future (are you

hauling in enormous salmon from some Scottish river perchance?). If not what else are you doing? I'm going to scan the snap and send it to you. Jessica'

She scanned the picture, attached it and pressed the 'send' button.

'There, she thought, might as well reel him in a little, reminding him of how far back we go. The pleasant tingle started again in her loins and she reached down to fondle herself. The sensation intensified, surprising her. She went into her bathroom, poured a lot of scented oil into the tub and turned on the taps full blast. As she removed her clothes, she examined her body in the full length mirror on the back of the door, something she had avoided for a long time. She was still in good shape, narrow waist, high breasts, hips which curved a little too much for her taste. She climbed into the hot water of the bath, sinking beneath the foamy bubbles, and her middle finger sought the bush between her legs sliding easily into her warm, wet vagina. The feelings intensified, but only a little, though she continued to thrust and plunge the finger for a few more minutes. All she could bring forth was a pleasant glow. Well, maybe when the time came, George could do more, could bring her to one of those gasping, shuddering orgasms she now felt was her due. She hoped so.

The emailing went on for a week or more, then George suggested they get on Skype, see each other, talk face to face. Eagerly, Jessica agreed, calling in her computer geek to install the necessary equipment. They set up a Saturday for their first communication, ten o'clock New York time, 3 p.m. in Oxfordshire.

At ten o'clock precisely George appeared on her computer screen. Jessica had taken care to look wonderful, but not too well put together. She didn't want George to know she had been up since dawn, trying on different outfits, experimenting with hair and make up. At last she had settled on well cut jeans, a tank top which showed just a little cleavage and a tailored Brooks shirt thrown carelessly over the top. She wore a linked gold chain necklace, and gold shell earrings, but both hands were bare of rings. She wanted George to get the picture that she was relaxed and comfortable in her present life, able to operate without him. --- or, she hoped --- with him.

George, too, was casually dressed, though he had made some effort to slick down the unruly hair.

"Jessica," he exclaimed on seeing her. "You're gorgeous. I always said you'd turn out to be a beauty." He remembered the skinny girl of yore, lanky and awkward, but with the most beautiful skin and a healthy shine on her hair. This young woman on his screen had fulfilled his wildest dreams. He wanted to reach out and touch her and, impulsively, he put his fingers on the computer screen.

"You look pretty good, too," Jessica told him, putting out her own hand and touching his fingers, three thousand miles away.

"What are you going to do, today?" George asked.

"I'm planning on taking my bike around the park," Jessica said. "Then I'll meet a friend for a late lunch somewhere. We haven't decided where yet."

"What's his name?" George asked.

"His name is Marcia and he's a she," said Jessica, thrilled that George might be jealous of other men she knew.

"That's a relief," he laughed.

"And you?"

"I have to drive up to Scotland tonight. A fishing expedition. We actually are going to be fishing for salmon. You hit the nail right on the head and I loved that picture."

"Guess I know your worst vices," Jessica said lightly.

"Oh, you don't know the half of them."

"Why don't you tell me?"

"Well, my worst one is probably Skyping with a beautiful woman from my past who happens to be three thousand miles away. I'd love for her to be three inches away right now."

"Really?"

"Yes, but that may happen sooner than you think. My stepfather is sending me to Boston on a project. He was going to go himself but he's got to go to Dubai. There's a much bigger project there. I just get the little ones. So I'll be in Boston next weekend, can you believe, and I thought I'd go home via New York, if you're free for dinner. Next Monday?"

Jessica could barely conceal her excitement. "Yes," she said. "Oh, yes, that would be wonderful."

"The Harvard Club? Six. Sorry to make it so early but I'm taking the late flight back to Heathrow."

"Six is fine." She hesitated then added, "I can't wait."

"Neither can I," said George. "Until then."

When they hung up Jessica threw herself onto her bed, rolling around in glee. Oh, she was seeing George! And so soon! She couldn't wait to pick up the phone and tell Marcia, but hugged herself for a little longer before doing so.

The next eight days passed in agonizing slowness. She and George Skyped several more times, each conversation seemingly bringing them closer together. Finally, the day arrived. Jessica went from school to the hairdresser, then went home and rearranged the carefully arranged hair in front of her mirror. She wanted to be the carefree young girl of long ago, even though nearly twenty years had passed since that last summer in Maine. She discarded heaps of clothes, then settled on a swingy, dark blue chiffon shirtdress and Tori Burch flats. No high heels for this first meeting. She pushed through the heavy doors of the Harvard Club a couple of minutes past six and into the lobby.

George rose from a chair by the staircase and crossed the few feet to where she was standing.

"Jessica, it's wonderful to see you again."

It was a somewhat awkward meeting, neither quite sure how to greet the other after all this time. George solved the situation by bending down from his six foot one height (maybe the flats had been a mistake

210

after all) and gave her a quick hug, shoulder to shoulder, lower body held back.

"Shall we?" He ushered her into the dining room, wood paneled with wonderful trophy heads adorning the wall, the portrait of JFK on one side of the fireplace, Helen Keller on the other. They were seated at a crisp linen draped table for two under one of the windows overlooking West 44th Street.

"What can I order for you?"

"White wine, please." Jessica had no intention of clouding her wits this of all evenings.

"Did you have a successful trip to Boston?" she asked.

"Yes, I think we will get the commission." His answer was stilted, polite.

"There has been so much water over the dam," Jessica started to say at the same time George spoke,

"We have so many years to catch up on...."

Somehow this broke the ice and they both laughed.

"You first," said Jessica.

"No, you," George insisted.

Their drinks came and it gave them a chance to each take a gulp, gather their wits and begin.

"You know I was married. It didn't work out. So now I'm divorced. Single again." Jessica knew she had already told George this, but somehow it seemed paramount in her mind.

"Any lasting repercussions? I mean you seem to dwell on it. Lots of us make mistakes so I hope you aren't focusing exclusively on this."

"Probably too much. It sent me to Sylvan Glade." There. It was out. If George now despised her at least she had brought things out into the open.

"You poor thing!" He exclaimed. 'It must have been bad. If you want to tell me about it sometime I'd love to hear. Or not. But I had a pretty bad patch, too, when my father was arrested and our lives were totally turned upside down. Mother was amazing, just picked up the pieces and moved to Connecticut. Changed our names, too. I didn't want to make it any harder on her so I did my best to take everything in my stride. It all turned out okay, though. I mean, Malcolm and England and my job. I was really lucky."

"I'm glad for you," Jessica said. "I never thought I'd find you living abroad."

"Find me? How?"

"Well, I really wanted to get in touch again so an attorney I know hired a private investigator to find you. It was that name change that took awhile. I hope you don't think I was prying..." she trailed off, miserably. Maybe this would break the fragile connection she had forged with George.

To her delight, he threw back his head and gave a loud guffaw, causing several other diners at nearby tables to actually turn and stare. The stuffy, conservative Harvard Club didn't get too many guffaws in the dining room.

"Jessica, that's priceless! I bet you know more about me than I do myself. Why am I spouting forth? The rest of the evening is yours." He glanced at his watch. "And, I'm sorry to say, we haven't got all that much time. So we'd better order. The Dover sole is good here. I should know. I live in the land of Dover sole." He wrote down their orders and gave the chit to the waiter, then turned back to Jessica. "Now tell me more about that marriage of yours. What was it? Drugs? Gambling? Another woman."

She looked him square in the face. 'No, none of those things. It was another man."

"Oh, my God! You poor thing."

"He was trying to be straight for his parents' sake. He didn't think they could cope with a gay son. So I was supposed to his beard. I wondered why things were - well – so strange between us. But I didn't know much about sex so I went along with the way things were. Until I found him in bed – our bed – with our best man. Actually, it was on our first anniversary."

"And that sent you to Sylvan Glade?"

"No, it was something some other man did to me about a year later that reminded me of Trevor...of my husband. I guess I was totally suppressing anything that happened between us. I just freaked out. I guess I had to have that time at Sylvan Glade, to examine myself.

"And did you?" he asked most gently.

"I think so. I had the most wonderful psychiatrist, Dr. Consuelo. She helped me put things in perspective."

"And have you?"

"Well, not quite yet. She said I had to find a man I trusted, and tell him everything. If he wasn't appalled she hoped I'd find – uh – fulfillment with him." She cast her eyes down to the table cloth. What man was going to put up with all this crap? Men didn't like women emoting all over the place.

She felt a warm hand grasp hers under the table.

"Well, may I be that man. And I only wish I could start tonight, but I do have to get that plane back to London. We'll take it from tonight, believe me."

Jessica lifted her head, a grateful smile on her face. And throughout the rest of dinner there was much to smile about, many clasping of hands, many stories told. When they walked together out to 44th Street, he paused and, right in the street, gathered her into his arms. His lips sought hers and she responded eagerly, pressing her body the length of his, standing on tiptoe (damn Tori Birch!). His tongue parted her willing lips and for a few moments they were joined, mouth to mouth, tongue to tongue, fingers digging into each other's backs before he released her regretfully.

"Until the next time, Jessica Alder," he told her. "It will be soon, I promise."

Chapter Thirteen

Pedro's Proposition

Pedro had made infrequent trips to New York that spring, and Marcia hoped his ardor was not waning. He was such a wonderful, positive force in her life and she had never felt more alive. She sprang out of bed each morning, refreshed and ready to take the world by the balls. She was doing such a good job at work she got a small promotion with a smaller salary increase, but at least she was going upward. When Pedro was expected in town she was in a fervor of excitement, pacing her small living room, trying on everything in her wardrobe and washing with special care the beautiful undergarments he had bought her at La Perla.

The white pear trees put forth their tender blossoms up Third Avenue and down Second, one of the loveliest sights New York had in its arsenal, and the ranks of spring bulbs popped up in the Park and on the islands in the middle of Park Avenue. It was a season filled with promise, as always, and Marcia joyously rode its waves.

She had hoped they could Skype, as Jessica and George were doing, but their first attempt almost ended in disaster. They had both logged on and Marcia had begun a slow strip tease – virtual sex – when her screen abruptly went blank. All efforts to revive the session were unsuccessful and she had to wait until the next day when an email arrived. Pedro had almost been interrupted by a servant, come to announce a friend had showed up at the door. He had to explain to her that he rarely was alone to the extent he could communicate with her by Skype; he was surrounded by family members, servants in his various houses and, while at work, by associates and employees. He never knew when someone would knock on his door and he might not have time to put down his screen on another occasion. So they would have to stick to email and the occasional call he made. Such was his life in Colombia.

Marcia could not even imagine such a life. She was used to the privacy of her own small apartment and, in other days, the apartments of her various boy friends with whom she had shared such a wide and varied sex life. Now she was celibate, except for Pedro's visits, which gave her a lot of time on her hands. But at least he was in New York this week in May, and, she hoped, they could take up where they left off during his previous visit.

She was not disappointed. She arrived at the Carlyle late the Friday of his arrival in New York and, no sooner had she entered his foyer than she was in his arms.

"Ah, darling," he breathed into her hair. 'It has been too, too long." He kissed her ardently, walking her backward into the bedroom as he did so, where she found herself lying, fully dressed, across the wide bed where they had shared so much passion.

"What have you been doing while I have been away?" he asked.

"Waiting for you," she breathed. "Only for you."

"Then let us not waste another moment. Oh, how I have longed for you." He started tearing at her clothes, pulling each garment off with haste, tossing them aside with total abandon. She groped for his shirt buttons, his belt buckle, his shorts as he did so, and soon they were lying naked together, locked in a tight embrace. His massive erection swung between them, pushing up tight against Marcia's straining crotch, tickling the curly hairs of her pubis, pulsing between her legs.

She led out a long sigh, and gave herself over to his tender ministrations. Somehow, it had never felt so good before. Or maybe it was the hiatus with no sex. Maybe a certain amount of forced abstinence made the joining together all the more pleasurable. Whatever the reason, Marcia's every nerve was zinging with anticipation, shivers of pure lust shooting through her loins. She clutched Pedro harder, loath to ever let him go.

They were ready for each other in short order. He positioned himself over her, guiding himself into her willing opening, propping himself on his elbows so he could look down into her face and, from time to time, explore her mouth with his probing tongue. They climaxed together, easy for two who were so sexually in tune. Cum dribbled down Marcia's thigh and she reached a finger down, wet it and brought it to her lips. Oh, that she might have this man's child! But she knew it was a vain desire. Pedro had made it perfectly clear that his present three children were all he was ever going to have, and his wife would remain at his side as long as she lived. Marcia did not fault him for it; a man who would dump a wife for a younger woman would no doubt dump that younger woman for one even younger. It was the way of the world. She tried to tell herself that what she had with him was enough: his trips to New York when she was the one and only.

He did not remain in bed for another round, but went into the bathroom and she heard the shower running. Almost she went in and joined him, but realized she had not been invited and stayed where she was. He soon emerged from the steam filled room, a towel wrapped around his still trim waist. She knew he played polo at home and spent a great deal of time on the tennis court; it showed in his rippling muscles and flat stomach. She was not quite sure how old he was; judging from the age of his children she suspected somewhere in his early forties, surely the prime of life for a man.

"I'm hungry," he announced. "Where would you like to go for dinner?"

"You pick," she said. "Anywhere you like is fine with me."

"Then how about the Capital Grill?" he asked. "I could do with a big steak this evening."

Marcia went into the bathroom to take her own shower, picking up her clothes from where they lay draped over the chair, the night table

216

and a lamp, hoping they would shake out sufficiently to make a decent showing at dinner.

They were finishing their steaks when, abruptly, Pedro laid down his fork and faced her squarely on the banquette.

'Uh, oh,' thought Marcia. 'Here it comes. I hope he is not going to dump me.' She sat up straighter, determined not to cry, whatever he said.

"You know I cannot marry you," he began.

Marcia nodded.

"But I do not want to lose you. However, what I propose may not be fair to you and I want only the best for you. These last months have been some of the most wonderful of my life. I look forward to seeing you in New York the same way a randy teenager would. It's almost unbelievable at my age."

Marcia relaxed a little, waiting to see what was coming next.

"So I have a proposition for you. I want you to move into the apartment at the Carlyle, be there for me when I am here in New York. I will make every effort to be here as much as I possibly can. And I want you to quit your job and work for me. As you know, I keep a small office in the Graybar building, but I propose to give this up and move my desk and files to the present library on 76th Street. I can put my personal items there, too, so you need not be embarrassed in front of your friends if you entertain anyone there while I am in Colombia. You can simply say you are running the New York office of a multinational company and it comes with living quarters."

Marcia's mouth fell open. Never in her wildest dreams had she expected anything like this. A move to the Carlyle apartments! A job working for Pedro. Having him with her every minute when he was in New York. The word 'mistress' crossed her mind, but she quickly dismissed it. The only man she wanted to be with was Pedro; if it meant not marrying or having children, well, it was worth it. He was worth it.

"Yes," she breathed. "Yes, I'll do it."

217

He took her hand and brought it to his lips. "Well, we would need to make financial arrangements, to your advantage. I'd get my attorney to draw up an employment contract.

"What sexual arrangements would be in the contract?" she asked wickedly.

"None," he said. "That is personal and private between the two of us. "But I do not want you to lose out monetarily. I will include accounts with certain of the hotel services, food and laundry and the like. And pay you a generous annual salary to run the business.

"Is it very complicated?" asked Marcia, afraid this part of the bargain might be more than she could manage.

"Not really. Most of the business is handled in Bogata. You would be here mostly to arrange a few business meetings for me when I am in New York, possibly take notes at some of these meetings. Not much more than that."

"That I could do," said Marcia.

"Good." said Pedro. "Now let's finish these steaks before they become too cold. Would you like dessert?"

"Only you," Marcia said, running her hand, under the tablecloths, from his knee, up his thigh and into his crotch, where an erection was burgeoning under his zipper. "Let's get out of here."

Pedro called for the check, signed it in short order, and they fell into a taxi out front of the restaurant. All the way uptown on Madison Avenue the necked like teenagers, pushing against the floor of the taxi in their haste to get to their destination and out of their clothes.

They greeted the doorman, crossed the lobby and went up in the elevator, careful not to touch any more. Marcia could feel herself dripping into her La Perla knickers, while it was all Pedro could manage to keep his penis safely enclosed within his trousers, straining at the zipper, almost threatening to burst the stitches.

This time they did not even make it into the bedroom, but only to the living room couch where each undressed in frenzy, throwing their clothes every which way, then coming together with the least of

218

preliminaries, Pedro sliding easily into her oh so welcoming snatch, thrusting the length and breadth of his erection into the hot cavern, meeting the rhythm of her gyrating hips perfectly with his own. They were partially sated by their early love making, and parried and thrust with equal expertise, so in tune was each with the other's body.

Pedro slid a hand down Marcia's pulsing thigh, bringing his thumb up into the center of her sex, rubbing the head of her clitoris until she moaned in pleasure and speeded up the frantic motion of her hips, thrusting herself higher and ever higher toward his manhood, pushing and shoving itself deeper and ever deeper into her willing insides. A low moan escaped Marcia's parted lips, rising to a shrill soprano wail as she felt herself climax, then climax higher, and yet higher, riding the waves of pleasure until she crashed back to reality, panting as if she had just experienced a heart attack. Above her, she heard Pedro's answering shout of triumph as he, too, ascended the dizzying scales to heaven.

The three days he had in New York passed all too quickly and on Monday night she rode out to the airport with him, as she now did when he departed for home. They rode with hands entwined, having sated their lust all afternoon, first in the bed, later on the fluffy Greek sheepskin on the floor, later still standing up against the wall in the foyer, where he easily lifted her onto his probing, engorged schlong, lowering her onto its shaft until she moaned in pleasure and quickly climaxed. She was sore from the many times their bodies had come together, sore in a wonderful, beautiful way. If she had trouble walking the next few days, so what? She was a woman who had been well and truly loved.

As Pedro kissed her goodbye outside the terminal, he had one last word for her. "I will instruct my attorneys to draw up a suitable contract for your employment," he said. "It will contain no reference to our private arrangement, so please show it to your own attorney before signing it. It is only proper we conduct this part of our lives in a suitable manner."

She waved him off, then climbed back into the limousine for the return trip to the city.

The promised contract arrived a week later, in a large envelope with the name of one of New York's most prestigious law firms emblazoned on the top left corner. Trust Pedro to do nothing by halves. She drew out the thick, bond paper, and lay the contract out on her small dining table, the better to peruse it. Certain facts and figures leaped out at her: The Carlyle apartment, her new residence. Unlimited room service, charge privileges in all Carlyle restaurants, laundry and dry cleaning, the services of a professional decorator to redo the suite, a salary of $1500 a week, plus performance bonuses reviewed every six months. A signing bonus, to be determined, was also offered. Original contract would run for three years, with additional time to be determined. Etc. etc. The words and typing swam before her eyes. It all looked incredible. Getting out of the walk up she called home. Redecorating the Carlyle apartment. Services galore and a generous salary on top of it all.

Her eyes blurred with the endless possibilities Pedro seemed to be offering her, but she took his advice to share the contract with her attorney. Picking up her phone, she asked Mickey to be her guest at Hillstone for lunch on the upcoming Saturday.

"Love, to," Mickey told her. "What's this about?"

"I have an employment contract I want you to read before I sign it and figure the least I can do is buy you lunch."

"Well, well," said Mickey. "You're coming into the big time. Probably you'll drop me as a friend."

"You know I'd never do that," Marcia reassured him. "How about 12:30?"

"Good oh," said Mickey, "scan that contract and get it to me before then, will you?"

"I'm on it as soon as I hang up," Marcia reassured him.

Saturday lunchtime Mickey walked in right behind Marcia and they took their usual dim booth at the back.

"Whew," Mickey said as he sat down. "Glad I brought a flashlight. He reached in his pocket and drew out a small light, which he switched on as he spread out a couple of pieces of paper before him.

"Looks like you struck pay dirt this time, Marcia," he said. "Who is this guy anyway? You never mentioned him to me."

"Just someone I met casually," Marcia told him with a straight face. "We seemed to hit it off and he needs somebody to run his New York office. He says the work's not too hard and imagine! It comes with a place to live, and what a place. Have you ever been in the Carlyle residences?"

"No," said Mickey, "but maybe you'll invite me up sometime."

"Oh, I certainly will. If I take the jcb. What do you think, Mickey?"

"That you'd be a fool not to. I've been checking out this guy's company, he's in lot of enterprises, shipping, oil, resorts, you name it. I don't think he's running guns on the side."

"Of course not," Marcia was quick to defend Pedro.

"Well, I'd say go for it. I even brought a pen for you to sign. Do you want me to get it back to him with something on my letterhead?

"Yes," said Marcia. "Thank you Mickey. That way he'd know everything was on the up and up."

"Sure there's no more to this than in the contract? I'm asking as a friend."

"No," said Marcia steadily. "Just business. As I said, I sort of fell into this by accident."

"Then how about we go back to your place after lunch? Celebrate the deal?"

"Sorry, Mickey, I've got another appointment," Marcia said. She figured Mickey would get the point.

The only person she knew who had met Pedro was Jessica, and Marcia concluded she had better fess up and tell her the truth. There was no way she could pull off this entire new life behind Jessica's back, nor did she want to. Jessica had to know.

So after lunch she called her friend and headed uptown on the Madison Avenue bus. Probably in a few weeks she'd have a car service at her disposal at the very least. Talk about rags to riches. If only some of her high school friends back in Detroit could see her now! But they'd probably just shake their heads and decide Marcia was doing something sleazy. Well, Pedro was anything but sleazy and, since he could not marry her, he was doing for her all he could.

Once in Jessica's living room, Marcia simply thrust the contract into her hand and sat back, waiting for a verdict. Jessica carefully read it through, then paused for a few moments.

When Marcia could no longer stand the suspense, she inquired "Well?"

"Well," said Jessica slowly. "I can see certain advantages to you. You will have a much better quality and style of life, a wonderful place to live and enough money. But Marcia, doesn't this cut out any other men? Any possibility of marrying? Having children someday."

"Yes, probably," said Marcia. "But Jessica I love him. I adore him. He's everything to me. No man has ever treated me like he does. It's not just all the sex, though that is amazing, too. Somehow I know I'll never find a man like him again. Look, I'm twenty eight. I've knocked around for the last few or so years. Let me try this. It's only for three years. If it doesn't work out, if he looses interest or finds someone else at least I'll have what the contract promises for that time. Then I'll see what happens next."

"Why not indeed?" Jessica and went over to give her friend a hug. "Enjoy while you can. I'll never tell just who this mysterious Colombian is. He's just a rich business man who's given you a spectacular job. Anything else is strictly between the two of you."

Marcia, relieved hugged back. 'You are the best friend a girl ever had," she said.

Mickey faxed the signed contract to Colombia, following it up with hard copies and, within two weeks Marcia was installed at the apartment at the Carlyle. The signing bonus had been a $10,000 gift certificate to Saks, with no note attached. That and the duly executed contract had come express mail form Bogota and Marcia was over the moon. She assumed the gift certificate was to upgrade her wardrobe into suitable dresses and suits in which to accompany Pedro on his rounds to expensive restaurants and clubs in New York. She enlisted Jessica's help and together they combed the better floors of Saks, spending a wonderful day buying, buying, buying. Back at the Carlyle they hung the new garments carefully in the empty closets of the master bedroom. Pedro had been as good as his word and removed his personal belongings to the second bedroom/cum office. So no one need know exactly where he slept on his excursions to New York. That would remain a secret among three people only: Pedro, Marcia, and Jessica, though it was no doubt one shared by the entire Carlyle staff as well. But they would never tell.

And so began a golden time for Marcia, relieved of any financial constraints, living in a luxury apartment in one of the great hotels of the world, with everything possible laid on for her. If she wanted a chicken sandwich, she merely had to pick up the phone and order one. If a dress needed pressing, she could call the valet. Liquor was sent in on request and a car was waiting for her at the door if she needed to go farther than a few blocks from her door. She luxuriated in her new life, spending time with Jessica and living for the times Pedro was in New York.

On his first such visit after Marcia had signed the contract, Pedro introduced Joss Taliaferro, the society decorator, who took her under his wing. Marcia realized this was probably to curb some of her more exuberant attempts at decorating, which tended to run to somewhat bizarre colors and combinations of objects, and only wanted to redo the Carlyle apartment to Pedro's tastes. Together she and Joss attended some of the auctions at Christie's and Sotheby's, combed the antique shops up and down Madison and spent time in the decorators building choosing fabrics. Jessica was often included on these shopping expeditions, adding her superlative taste to what promised to be a spectacular apartment when it was finished.

Pedro seemed amused by all the chaos surrounding this redecoration on his visits to New York, going along with most of Marcia's suggestions and adding a few of his own. One night they came back from lunch and found a large stack of fabric samples had been delivered, put into the apartment by the elevator man. Gleefully, Marcia pulled them all out form their bags, flinging them over the living room couch to see them all together.

"These surely are not all for the same room?" Pedro asked.

"Oh, no, not all for here," Marcia assured him. She took up a mushroom colored velvet, striped in a darker shade of brown. "Maybe this for the living room couch," she grabbed another, a bronze satin and flung it over the first. "Then perhaps this for the curtains," another larger sample landed on the other two, "and these for the curtains in the bedroom and here, and these three for the second bedroom and...." She kept flinging more fabric on the pile until it rose from the cushions, threatening to topple over onto the floor.

"I have a great idea for all of it," Pedro exclaimed. "Let's try it out, right now. No clothes." Together they started to rip off their clothes, until both stood naked for a moment.

Giggling, Marcia got the idea. "Last one in's a rotten egg," she cried, flinging herself down on top of the pile, which, obligingly, slid to the floor, Marcia on top.

"You little devil!" Pedro plunged in on top of her, rolling her over, covering her with pieces of fabric. "Let's see how you look in this one." He draped some satin over her thighs, 'and this one," another sample landed over her shoulders. "And another."

Marcia joined in the game, draping Pedro in other fabric samples until they resembled nothing more than two nude people caught up in a crazy quilt of different colors and textures.

Pedro caught her by the shoulder, turning her to face him. "I love you in this satin," he breathed. "And this velvet."

"And I love you in violet. I must get you a tie this color."

224

The thickness of the samples, on the lush velvet pile of the rug, gave them a sufficient bed on which to assuage their desire for each other, heightened by the silly game they had invented with the fabric samples.

"Ah, love," he breathed into her ear. "I'm going to touch all the seven orifices of your beautiful body, before I enter the one that leads to paradise." He commenced touching her, each ear, then her nostrils, a tender stroke on each, then his tongue found her mouth, probing, exploring. His hand crept down her back, parted her cheeks and, ever so gently flicked a finger over her anus, causing Marcia to twitch with pleasure. She was creaming over the expensive fabrics spread on the floor, hips twitching in the rhythm of intercourse, inviting his rampant prick to split her labia and enter her hot, wet vagina.

She mounted him now, taking him in her hand, guiding him into her, rising on her knees, then lowering herself to take the fullness of his shaft into her deepest region. She sat astride him, flexing her inner muscles until she heard him groan, then commenced her rocking and riding him until, together, they came to an all consuming, shattering orgasm. When she had rolled off beside him, and taken him in her arms, when her breathing had slowed to a point where she could take again, she asked Pedro

"Why is it that it just gets better and better?"

He returned her embrace, fervently. "I do not know, my love, I only know that it is so. Now, are you ready for another round, perhaps on the bed this time? Joss will kill us for spoiling his pretty fabrics."

"Well, let him kill away. You have got to be one of his best clients, so he will just have to put up with it."

Pedro led her across the floor toward the bedroom, admiring the bounce of those magnificent tits. And his own penis was starting to burgeon again, swinging somewhere at half mast as they went. An afternoon of loving was surely turning into a marathon of sex. He led Marcia to the wide expanse of the bed, pushed down the spread and laid her out for his inspection.

"Ah, Marcia," he said, his voice catching. "What you do to me...."
He covered her body with his own. "Now come to me."

Happily she obliged.

Chapter Fourteen

Flow Gently Sweet Cherwell

The school year finally ended and Jessica was booked to fly overnight to London on June 7. The weeks leading up to this oh-so-important date were filled with endless activity: trying on practically everything in her wardrobe, twice daily checking of the weather in England, reading up on Oxford and Oast houses, deciding what to take as a hostess present to Malcolm and Grace, in whose house she would be staying the first few days of her visit.

Marcia though all of this was the soul of tact; not trying to push Jessica immediately into an intimate situation with George, in case things did not work out. But this negative thought she kept to herself, wanting only the best for her friend. She was on hand 24/7 to encourage, give advice on clothes and shoes and handbags, and, as much as possible, convince Jessica that making love was a beautiful thing and she should relax and let things take their course. There was no reason why she could not find the kind of fulfillment Marcia herself had found with Pedro. She even made Jessica buy some new and sexier underwear than her usual plain white cotton, and offered to lend her anything from scarves to handbags, sweaters and jewelry, including her greatly worn copy of The Joy of Sex. The book, well thumbed, had been Marcia's 'constant companion' from about the age of 17, and she wanted her friend to have the same information available that had so helped her along the way of the years of indiscriminate sex with so many men. When Jessica demurred, Marcia simply left the book on Jessica's bedside table one day. She noted a great number of tabs inserted into the pages when she checked a few days later, and chuckled as she tiptoed out of Jessica's bedroom. Hopefully the book might do the trick.

June 7 finally arrived, and Marcia picked up Jessica in a limousine, courtesy of Pedro and the Carlyle, for the trip to Kennedy. They rode out in heavy traffic, clutching each other's hands as the airport drew nearer.

"You will be fine," Marcia said soothingly. "Believe you me. And when you and George finally do it it's like falling off a log. Just lie back and enjoy it."

"That's the advice English mothers used to give their daughters on their wedding day," Jessica said. "Lie back, relax and think of England! Can you imagine? And they didn't have The Joy of Sex to help them."

"So you've been reading it?" Marcia asked.

"You bet I have. Wow! What a lot of information. Seriously, though, how many people go through all those gyrations?"

"Well, you'd be surprised," Marcia quibbled. "Just let George take the lead, find out what he likes. And tell him along the way what you enjoy, and what you don't."

"You make it all sound so easy."

"Oh, it is," Marcia said. "It is."

They drew up to the Virgin Atlantic check in section and the driver unloaded Jessica's two bags, one to check and one to carry on. She had stuffed the latter with cosmetics, snacks and lots of reading material, including Marcia's loaned book, just in case.

The women embraced and Jessica vanished through the glass doors. The great adventure had begun.

It was an uneventful flight, and Jessica managed to catch a few hours sleep, which surprised her. She thought she would be too keyed up to do more than count the passing hours. Perhaps, though, now she was enroute she felt she had thrown herself into whatever would come next.

Early morning in Heathrow. The sky was an overcast slate gray, with rain threatening. A perfect English summer day. Jessica wound her way through the formalities of arrival, pulled her suitcase through customs without incident, and pushed out into the airport proper through the heavy doors. In the crowd behind the barriers, she immediately spotted George, who was holding up a large placard with

'Miss Jessie Alden' on it. Jessie: the name George used to call her when she was a little girl. Her heart gave a lurch and a moment later he had her wrapped in a huge bear hug. Jessica felt as if – finally – she had come home.

The low slung Jaguar, bottle green, purred up the motorway toward Oxford. George drove fast, expertly, passing slower cars but keeping a steady speed of 70 most of the way. They passed Oxford and continued to the turn off for Wytton-Uncer-Lynchlely and the estate of Malcolm and Grace MacIntyre, where Jessica would stay the first day or two of her time in England. Beyond that, she did not know, but appreciated being given this time to settle in without coming to terms with her relationship with George.

They pulled up to the red brick manor house. A man in livery opened the door and hastened out to take Jessica's luggage. And there, in the doorway, was a familiar woman, though Jessica had not seen her in many years.

Grace had aged gracefully, and only showed a trace of white in her hair, becoming among the strands of faded red. She held out her arms to Jessica.

"My dear child," she exclaimed. "You have no idea how happy it makes me to see you after all these years. I don't think we have met since that summer in Maine." She paused, remembering just how fraught that last summer had been in animosity between the two households over the stone wall. "But now you are here and that is all that counts." She put her arm around Jessica's shoulder and led her up the shallow steps to the great hall beyond. Huge portraits of long dead ancestors and faded tapestries graced the entrance way to the manor house. Grace led the way into a charming room off the hall, filled with light and flowers and graceful furniture upholstered in shades of green.

"This is the morning room," she explained. "I don't know if you are hungry. I'll be happy to ring for some breakfast, but I thought you'd prefer to have something in here rather than the dining room. Or maybe you'd prefer a tray in your room? I know you must be longing to get into bed."

"Bed, I think," said Jessica gratefully. No way was she going to be able to stay awake and make polite conversation after the overnight flight.

"Then bed it is," said Grace. "Let me show you up to your room, and please don't think about getting up until you feel like it. We'll expect to see you again whenever you are ready."

Jessica fell into the wide and slightly soft four-poster, hung all around with curtains of old brocade, and fell instantly asleep. She must have slept through most of the day, because when she awoke the shadows were just falling, sending shadow branches across her mullioned windows. She padded from bed across the room and gazed out to see the view.

Formal gardens stretched away from her, melting into rolling pastures, where she saw sheep in some, a few horses in another. An ornamental lake glistened, with a miniature temple standing above it. She remembered this would be called a folly. She turned back into the room and went into the bathroom which contained a huge tub but no shower. She remembered this as often a feature of English bathrooms, and turned on the taps full blast. A shelf held bath salts and fancy soaps and lotions, so Jessica poured in a generous amount and sank down into the bubbling water.

A half hour later she was dressed in a simple cotton dress and sandals, not sure what the proper attire for evening was in such a grand house. She descended the massive staircase to the entrance hall again, then paused, wondering where everyone was.

The manservant appeared as if by magic. "The family is on the terrace, Miss," he announced. "Let me show you the way." They proceeded through a massive room, which must have been the drawing room, with its graceful, 18th century English furniture and more large portraits on the wall, and out through double glass doors to a flagstone terrace which ran almost the full length of the house and had the same view as from Jessica's windows. Here she found Grace, George and a tall older man seated with drinks in hand.

The man approached her, hand outstretched. "Ah," he said, "the sleeping beauty has awoken. Welcome to High Gate. I'm Malcolm Bevington." His handshake turned into a gentle hug and Jessica warmed to the kindness of his greeting.

The next couple of days passed almost in a haze as Jessica became accustomed to the time change. She woke and slept at odd hours, which embarrassed her as she did not want to put the household to any trouble. They were accustomed, however, to American visitors and cheerfully produced trays of breakfast or tea at odd hours, and tiptoed past Jessica's room when the house was being cleaned so as not to disturb her.

Finally, on the third morning, Jessica awoke to early morning sunlight. Her watch told her it was 7:15 a.m. and she sprang from bed. Hoping she was now on English time, Jessica ran another deep, hot bath, and luxuriated in the tub for a quarter hour, dreaming of the day ahead.

She found her way easily downstairs, and into the huge dining room, where the sideboard was groaning under its load of silver dishes. The family was at the table, and George rose to greet her with a gentle kiss on the cheek, before leading her to her chair. "Let me help you," he said, moving over to the sideboard. "Eggs? Sausage? Bacon? A Kipper? Anything else you want."

She threw up her hands. "You choose for me," she said helplessly.

George complied, piling a plate high and placing it before her." Eat only what you want," he said.

Jessica gazed down at the beautiful bone china plate, in a design with which she was not familiar. It held a plethora of food from the sausage offered by George, to scrambled eggs, bacon, potatoes and a grilled tomato. Toast was passed in a silver rack, and butter and a selection of jam.

"Try the dark one," Grace urged. "Damson plums from our own garden. The cook makes it specially."

Jessica did so and found it delicious.

"What plans do you children have today?" Malcolm asked. "I think George can take a day off from the salt mines in honor of your visit, Jessica. Take two if you want." This got a hearty laugh all around the table and Jessica gazed with rapture on this family which had made her so welcome. Any doubts about coming evaporated and she dug into her huge breakfast with gusto, managing to finish at least a third of it."

Malcolm walked them out to the driveway, climbing into his own Range Rover while George held the door to his Jaguar for Jessica.

"Let's see Oxford this morning," he said. "And I'll take you for a punt on the Cherwell. Nothing like softening up a girl, I always say, like a tour of the quads of our celebrated university." He followed his stepfather down the long drive then onto the secondary road that would lead them out to the main road to Oxford. They parked in the courtyard of a very old half timbered building, a couple of streets off the main thoroughfare which ran past many of the colleges. "The office car park," announced George. "Parking anywhere in town is a huge pain, so we're lucky to have this."

"But you do such modern buildings," Jessica said. "Why the old world charm of your office?"

"Puts us in the continuum of architecture." George told her. "Gives overseas clients faith in us and our place in the field. Anyway, it's a great building and having its own parking is a big plus. I'll show you the offices later. Right now I want to walk you around some of the colleges."

Actually, I was here last when I was about twelve. We spent a summer in Europe then, but it didn't mean so much to me. Now I'm vastly impressed that students have been studying her for a thousand years. Imagine! When our country only had people dressed in skins and no buildings at all, some of this was here."

"Yes, I know what you mean," said George. "It's an inspiration to me, still, that I actually live and work here."

"I'd like to see the Shelley Memorial," Jessica told him. "I actually saw it in an Inspector Lewis program. I love seeing the scenes of Oxford and the mystery is always complicated. It takes tremendous concentration and even then there is usually a surprise ending.

George laughed. "Our most famous modern British cop. But yes, it's a good show. Okay, we'll do the Shelley tour. Over to the Bodleian Library we go." He took her hand and led her toward the high street. For an enchanted hour they strolled the side streets, from Cattle Street down to the High, where the Shelley Memorial was entombed in a part of University College. Jessica marveled at the oversize white marble statue of the drowned poet, resting on an ornate plinth and housed in its own building. Jessica paused, gazing at the gleaming marble, and a line from Shelley, unbidden, rose to her lips.

"Swift be thy flight," she recited softly. "It's almost as if he wrote it anticipating his own death. It would make a perfect epitaph."

George stared at her. "I didn't know you recited poetry."

"Oh, there's a lot you don't know about me," said Jessica archly.

"Smart alec." George struck a noble pose and recited:

"Swiftly walk over the westerns wave,
Spirit of Night!
Out of the misty eastern cave..."

Jessica chimed in and they continued together;

"Where all the long and lone daylight,
Thou wovest dreams of joy and fear,
Which make thee terrible and dear,
Swift be thy flight!"

They gazed at each other in admiration and George took her hand, leading her out of the sanctuary and on down the high street. They passed All Souls' College and continued down the High Street, crossing over the Cherwell via the Magdalen Bridge at the Water Meadow.

"I've reserved a punt, and I'm taking you out on the river. If we get hungry we can stop at the Boathouse for lunch. Does that suit m'lady?"

"Yes, please," said Jessica. "I've never been punting before."

"Well, I'm not all that experienced. I don't want to be left hanging over the river on the pole. But I'll do my best." They had gone under the bridge to the boathouse and been assigned their punt.

Jessica settled onto the seat in the flat bottomed craft, and George took up his position on the raised platform at the back, pole in hand. The boatman pushed them off and they glided out into the still, green water.

Willows trailed their lacy fronds over the water, and water lilies bloomed in the tiny eddies at the shore. Birds skimmed across the water under a sky of heavenly blue, dotted with puffed up cumulous clouds. Jessica trailed her hand in the water, realizing that poling down this small tributary to the mighty Thames was sheer bliss, one of the most romantic experiences of her life. She looked up at the length of George's body above her, pole in hand, eyes ahead, concentrating on propelling them down the river with sure swift strokes.

They stopped for lunch the Cherwell Boathouse, another center for renting all manner of craft for the river, with a charming pub on the bank, serving an amazing menu of modern and traditional dishes. Jessica chose goat cheese summer pudding and pan fried bass which tasted as though it had just been lifted out of the water. She couldn't manage dessert, but cadged a bite or two of George's goosebury compote.

"I should swim back, work off all this wonderful food," she said, stretching her arms overhead to the azure sky. "I am absolutely stuffed."

"You mean you have had a plentiful sufficiency?" George teased.

"Gosh my grandmother used to say that," said Jessica lightly.

"A formidable woman."

"Indeed." Jessica rose. "Let's get back on the water."

They poled upstream and tied up to an overhanging willow near the water meadow. George took the rug that had come with the boat and led Jessica off to a clump of trees on the bank, where they could not be seen either from the river or the land.

"A good place to while away an hour of the afternoon," he observed, flinging out the blanket on the damp grass.

Jessica sank down. This was probably it, the scene for which she had so arduously prepared for such a long time. Maybe, finally, she would find out what it was all about, with the man she now realized she had come to love.

George settled in beside her, laying his head in her lap, gazing up into her eyes.

"A little bit of heaven, eh?" he asked.

"Yes, a little bit of heaven."

The leaves rustled softly overhead and from the tree above a bird trilled to his mate. George lifted his head from Jessica's lap, then pulled her down beside him. He gathered her up into his arms, cradling her against his chest as if he would never let her go. She relaxed into his embrace, joyfully, knowing there was no place else she would rather be on earth at this moment.

Slowly, he lowered his face to hers, and gently he kissed her lips, only increasing the pressure slightly when she kissed him back. He stroked her back and neck, then lifted his lips from hers and nuzzled her ear. His tongue explored the shell like opening, then thrust softly into the ear itself, bringing a twinge of pleasure in Jessica's groin. She pressed up closer to him, awaiting what would come next.

George ceased any movement for a few moments, lying with Jessica wrapped tightly in his arms, content to stop for a while and not go further. Jessica reached up to caress George's neck, then ran her fingers down the front of his polo shirt, moving her fingers into the V at his neck. He reciprocated in kind, reaching up under her linen tunic, skirting the waistband of her slacks, bringing his hand to rest over the lacy bra Marcia had insisted she buy. Jessica wiggled in pleasure, and George cupped one of her breasts, lifting it out of its cup, stroking the nipple until it stood at attention. The tingling between her legs spread over her, causing her breath to come faster, wanting more.

As they whiled away the lazy afternoon, a dark cloud came up and blotted out the sun. So intent were the two on the bank in each other, neither noticed until the rain started falling, first gently through the willow boughs above, then in more earnest, pelting through the fronds and soaking them and their blanket.

"Crap," exclaimed George. "I didn't think to check the weather before we started out. Well, there's nothing for it; we'll just have to get wet. They returned to the punt and poled upriver back to the landing, passing other boats with equally wet occupants on the way. It was a warm summer rain, and not unpleasant until they slogged through Oxford, shoes squishing at every step. At the car George fished a single towel from his gym bag in the boot, giving it to Jessica to dry off as best she could, and they prepared to return to Wytton-Under-Lynchlely.

During the ride each waited for the other to speak, and, when finally they did, it was together.

He: "I hope I'm not taking everything too fast. You just have to tell me if I am."

She: "I really want you, I do, but I guess I'd better tell you some things about myself."

"I'm a captive audience," said George. "And I'm all ears."

So Jessica went through the litany of her sex life, from the savage beating at the hands of her grandmother and the admonitions she had been given about sex, through the drunken lout at the barn party from whom George had rescued her. She managed these two events fairly easily, but when she got to Trevor she paused.

"Is there more?" George asked. "You can tell me anything and I'll understand."

"Yes," said Jessica, and her voice broke. "There's much more." She willed herself to go on. "I was married to a homosexual," she said, her voice barely above a whisper. "And he made me do all sorts of sexual acts I didn't want to, but I did anyway. I thought he had the right to use me as he wanted."

"You poor, poor thing." George was all sympathy.

"And it ended when I found him in bed – our bed – with our best man. It was on our first anniversary. I've never really been able to trust a man again, after that.

"And you hope you can trust me?"

"Yes," she said with resolution. "I hope I can trust you. That's why I went to so much trouble to find you. That's why I'm here now."

"I want to earn your trust," he said with all seriousness. "Are you ready to try, or do you want to wait?"

"I'm ready now," said Jessica stoutly. "If you want me."

"I want you," he said steadily. "I think I want you forever."

"Do you really mean it? Forever."

"I do," he said slowly. "I realized it back on the river, how well we go together, how much we have to catch up on and make up for in the future."

Jessica said nothing, only put her hand on his knee. He took one hand from the wheel and, for an instant, covered hers. Nothing more need be said. He gunned the engine, sending the car flying down the motorway. When they reached High Gate and came to the turning, George shot down the right hand fork, pulling up a few minutes later in front of his wonderful Oast house.

"Oh," breathed Jessica. "So this is the Oast house. It's truly amazing." She ran her eyes over the rough wall, the lofty towers, the walls and walls of glass at every level. Flowerbeds flanked the large, oak door, filled with old fashioned flowers that reminded her of Maine: hollyhocks, delphiniums, roses climbing their trellises. It was if she had come home.

He took her hand and led her into the house. "First let's dry off, then come down to the kitchen and I'll make us a Pimm's," said George. "Time enough to take up where we left off at the river. He led her to the second floor and showed her into a large guestroom, with bath beyond. In the bathroom Jessica found a pile of fluffy towels and a dressing gown hanging behind the door. She toweled off and slipped into the overlarge silk robe, tying the sash securely around her waist. It was not the most flattering garment she had ever worn, but it was all that was available.

Padding barefoot over the beautiful plank floors, shined to a mirror finish, she went down the simple staircase which hugged one wall, then down into the gracious open space below and found the kitchen. George was slicing up a cucumber, and put it into large glasses already filled with some dark liquid. He topped them off with Ginger ale, and handed one to Jessica. She took an appreciative sip. A strange flavor, but not too bad. These could grow on her.

They took their drinks into the library, which contained a plethora of books, some neatly shelved, some thrown carelessly down into piles. A drafting table held scrolls of paper, and more was pinned up on the massive corkboard above it. Under the windows looking down at the manor house was a wide day bed upholstered in rich burgundy leather. An assortment of pillows was heaped at one end, and a plaid rug folded neatly at the other.

George and Jessica sat down side by side, sipping their drinks slowly. The soaking had not dampened either of their spirits and George took her free hand in his and brought it up to his lips.

"I'm going to do my very best to please you," he said to Jessica. "But if I do anything you don't like, just let me know and I'll stop. I don't want to hurt or frighten you in any way."

"I know you don't," Jessica replied. "I trust you implicitly."

George unfolded the plaid rug and spread it over the cold leather. "Try this on for size."

Jessica obediently stretched out on the warm blanket, holding up her arms for George to come to her.

He slid down next to her, putting her head on his shoulder, his other hand loosely across her thighs. He kissed her once, gently, then with mounting ardor, and she returned his caress with equal excitement building. He reached inside the loose robe and took out one of her breasts, bending over her and kissing and sucking at the nipple, tonguing down her tender belly toward the blonde bush at the crotch. She drew in her breath, arching her back in pleasure. Why had she fought this for so long? How much had she been missing? Even as she formed these questions, her mind told her: she needed someone to care, not someone who just wanted to shag her. And she perceived George wanted her, cared about her responses, promised to do only what pleased her. She responded to the sensations starting to vibrate through her very being, moaning in pleasure as George parted her labia with a gentle finger and commenced stroking up one side and down the other, lingering at each revolution on her rising clitoris.

She felt his erection, springing up from the front of his own robe, brush against her leg and, instinctively, she reached down for it, running her hand up and down its throbbing length, circling the head with an inquisitive finger. She heard George moan in pleasure and doubled her efforts. They seemed in perfect synch, playing with the other's sexual organs, bringing each other to a state of arousal. Everything he did to her pulsing body only brought more intense pleasure and Jessica's hips began to grind in the rhythm of intercourse, willing him to come to her, enter her and bring her to orgasm. The moans coming out of her throat seemed almost inhuman in her ears, matched only by George's own low moans which intensified in volume as he continued to stroke and caress, now thrusting two fingers into her hot, wet vagina, now covering a breast with his eager mouth. She realized there was much more George could try to give her pleasure, but also knew he was taking it easy this first time with her, sticking to basics. But basics were more than enough, as her desire rose higher and higher until she wanted to scream at him to enter her, pound her with his beautiful erect penis, bring her to shuddering, screaming ecstasy.

Finally, when she thought she could stand no more, George slipped on a condom, reared over her, positioned himself between her legs, and felt around between her twitching thighs with his magnificent erection. As if it were the most natural thing in the world, Jessica took his tool in her hand and guided him into her, hoping she would remember forever how this first strong thrust felt as he entered her slippery vagina and pushed the length of him up into her, deeper, ever deeper, causing her to writhe in something between agony and ecstasy. He thrust, she lifted against him; together they achieved the perfect rhythm of two people totally attuned sexually to each other. Something akin to music assailed her ears, and she rose with each swelling of the notes and fell back as it abated, each time achieving a higher and higher tone, until a whole orchestra seemed to be playing and, with a huge crash of cymbals, she achieved the exquisite, shuddering orgasm she had so long desired. At the same moment George shouted in her ear and they came together, crashing through barriers neither had ever thought to break, rising up into the stratosphere, then sinking slowly back to earth and the wide divan in the Oast house in Oxfordshire.

In later years Jessica would rekindle the scene in her mind, remembering the afternoon that would never grow old or stale, the perfect melding together of two bodies that were – always – meant to be one.